HOUSE
OF
DIAMONDS

HOUSE
OF
DIAMONDS

**Book One
in the
House of Jewels series**

Amber Jakeman

Lorikeet Press, 2021

This is a work of fiction. Similarities to real people, places, or events are entirely coincidental.

HOUSE OF DIAMONDS
First edition. February 10, 2021.

Copyright © Amber Jakeman.

ISBN: 978-0-6454625-7-9

Written by Amber Jakeman.

Also by Amber Jakeman
House of Jewels **series**
House of Diamonds
House of Hearts
House of Spades
House of Clubs

www.amberjakeman.com
www.lorikeetpress.com

For my husband, the inspiration for all my heroes!

It takes a community to raise a writer.
I warmly thank my family and friends, old and new,
who have supported my efforts by critiquing earlier versions and
simply believing in the potential, beauty, joy and power
of the words we share.

Chapter 1

Stella pushed the hair out of her eyes, stepped back and surveyed her stall, satisfaction surging through her. She'd done it. It was real!

Here beside a small street tree in the Oxford Street Mall in Sydney's Bondi Junction, her stall was ablaze with her unique jewelry, each piece a product of her imagination and hard working fingers, and each piece in its place. She glanced down at her soft cotton frock, dark blue with tiny red spots the exact red of her faux ruby drop earrings. Her simple summer outfit was such a welcome change from the office attire of dark skirts and jackets she'd worn for years. Yes. At last. *Stellar*, her own business, was ready to trade.

In the mild spring morning, the aroma of coffee wafted, mixing with the din of traffic and snippets of conversation in many languages. Stella pulled out her phone to record the moment, to send it to Jeannie to post on her new business's Facebook and Instagram. As she snapped, a tall man in a distinguished, pale grey suit sprinted out of the closest building towards her.

The cut of his suit was perfect, the lapels slightly open to show a shirt the same blue as his eyes. Striking.

Her first customer?

No. He surveyed the mall like he owned the place. Frowning, he fixed her with his gaze, making her heart jump.

"We need you to move about twenty metres, up that way, if you wouldn't mind," he said. Smooth.

What? Move? Why would she move? She'd only just finished setting up. It had taken her months to prepare, and so much time just that morning, arranging her earrings and bracelets. What on earth could he mean?

"... just for a short time, thank you," he said.

Her hackles rose. However handsome he might be, with that sun-kissed brown hair, and that way of smiling just on one side, as if life was a bit of joke as long as he was in control, he had no right to push her around.

"Actually, Mr ..."

"Huntley. James Huntley." He tipped his head back a little, indicating his connection with the three-storey building behind him, and she turned and read the ornate sign. Huntleys House of Diamonds.

Stella sighed. She didn't reconfigure her whole life, resigning and moving here from Perth on the other side of the country, only to fall into the trap of obeying the next handsome man. No. She'd been there and done that. For too long. She'd been totally, pathetically, at the mercy of her boss Damian's demands.

Obeying handsome men was a bad habit she'd finally kicked, hadn't she?

This new Stella was strong and independent, she reminded herself. Stella now worked for herself, trusted only herself and obeyed only herself. She would no longer be told what to do by men who assumed she'd comply. So, whatever this man wanted, and however attractive he might be - and he was, quite attractive, every bit as good-looking as Damian, his hair more fair, and with a bit of a wave at the front, and those eyes - intense - she knew she had every right to stand her ground. And she would.

He waited expectantly, but she was only just ready to trade. With customers gathering, she needed to sell, sell, sell - and not waste another moment. Her licence to trade wasn't a give away. It would take her months to pay back the loan she'd taken out to pay for it.

He lifted one hand up toward the side of her stack of display trays, as if to test his strength against its weight, to simply push her stall away. She could swear she saw his healthy bicep flex beneath that high quality pale grey woollen fabric.

How dare he! The flame of defiance inside her flashed fire. No. She would not be shoved away.

"Stella Rhys, Mr Huntley," she answered, keeping her voice low and controlled, and extending her own hand to be shaken. His was smooth, the hand of a businessman, as cool as her own. It was a fine handshake, pleasant even.

Her mother would have fun reading this palm, she thought, smiling. It was a mistake. He must have interpreted her smile as acquiescence. Nodding and smiling in return, he held her hand just a moment longer than necessary.

"Thanks, so much, Stella. These stalls… There was nothing here for months, and suddenly you appear! Today of all days. It's so good of you to move. Just for an hour or so." He gave her the full blue gaze again and smiled.

For a moment Stella weakened, but she remembered the advice of Fritz, the nearest stallholder, who'd welcomed her to the mall only that morning.

"I've been here nearly thirty years, young lady," Fritz had said. "Seen a thing or two in my time. Seen stalls come and seen them go. Can be tough out here on the mall. Don't you let anyone push you around."

Stella knew the terms of her licence. Thursday to Saturday, 11am to 7pm. Right here. So she lifted her sunglasses and fired back a dose of her own dark eyes - bright, quick and determined.

"Actually, James," she began, amiably enough, with a hint of steel. She gestured at the small crowd gathering to admire her unusual brooches, rings, earrings and pendants, all laid out so temptingly in the bright sunshine. Her excitement ratcheted up a notch. Behind James, two older women, sisters perhaps, were pulling out their purses. Her first customers! It was James who needed to move, so she could trade.

"Look. This is my business, James - '*Stellar*,'" she continued, polite yet firm, her voice steady. "And I'm not moving it. Not at all. I don't mean to be unreasonable; nothing personal; but as I see it, the Huntleys property boundary begins at the edge of your doorway. The mall here is public space, and this patch is mine."

His smile froze. What was this?

"That's right, isn't it? Look. Here's my permit. Nothing in it says I'm required to move. My licence is for six months, and my stall's position is right here, right now. And as you can see, I need to look after my customers."

"Come on, Ms Rhys, you wouldn't mind helping out just this once, for half an hour or so; help me out here."

The fire inside her ignited. She closed her eyes. Calmed herself. Opened them again.

"I thought I'd made myself clear, James. I do mind, and so I won't move." This time, her tone was pure ice, each word clearly articulated.

James conveyed his astonishment mildly, with raised eyebrows and a slight shrug.

She stared back, arms crossed. If it was a standoff, his stance wasn't entirely hostile. Amused? A flicker of interest? Frustrated? Was there a flash of challenge? Admiration, even? He wasn't like Damian - always controlling. James was sizing her up, those blue eyes drilling into her own.

Abruptly, he looked towards the street, where a cavalcade came into view, then answered his phone.

"Nicole? What's that? Running early?" He turned away, ignoring Stella. His sudden indifference to her felt like a dismissal, a loss even. At any other time, she would have found this man interesting. Had there been something else behind the arrogance? A kind of decency?

4

Her heart still raced. Defiance had never come easily for her. But there was work to do, and she served her first customers, delighted to wrap each purchase in her tissue paper covered with stars.

Beyond the women extracting their credit cards, the crowd grew. A radio reporter arrived, testing the microphones, then a TV crew or two.

Suddenly, at the curb, a grey Rolls Royce pulled up. James strode towards it, swinging open the rear passenger door. An elegant woman emerged, statuesque in a tight, green satin dress, and James offered her his arm. They made a striking pair, she so willowy and he so handsome. He escorted her right into the mall, through the throng, towards his House of Diamonds.

"Antoinette!" "*Heist!*" The crowd called, pressing towards them, posing for selfies. Now Stella remembered where she'd seen the woman's face. It was on billboards and buses all over town. This was Antoinette Lacy, star of the new film *Heist*, featuring the theft of a necklace of priceless diamonds.

Stella's stall was directly between the car and Huntleys.

Antoinette and James oozed glamour as they strode along the mall, her languid arm draped through his. James could be a movie star, too, Stella thought.

What a stunt! Fancy hooking a VIP like Antoinette Lacy for your celebrity endorsement. She'd just won a string of awards. James Huntley had a few connections alright. No wonder he'd wanted her to move. They were walking towards his store. But her stall was right in the way.

Her heart kicked up another notch. Exciting! Stella was as intrigued as the rest of the crowd, their mobile phones up like antennae, the young and the older, curious business people grabbing a coffee, retirees at the edges, and a few others with shopping bags, strollers and toddlers. Two big men in black suits hovered, speaking into their ear pieces.

More reporters and media cameras appeared from nowhere and surged into action, all bent on capturing the smiles and actions of the rich and famous.

Directly before her stall, at the centre of the commotion, James and Antoinette paused. James extracted his arm and reached inside his suit coat. He pulled from his breast pocket something glittering like fire in the bright sunshine - it was the delectable diamond necklace featured in the film. All eyes upon them, James held it high for the cameras, then dribbled it, diamond by diamond, into Antoinette's elegant hand as cameras whirred, clicked and binged.

It was PR genius, but there was a problem.

"No. No, James. Not there. Here." A frazzled woman in a tight, mustard yellow suit arrived and tried to encourage the photographers and videographers to take the shot again. This must be Nicole. She saw at once the skirt was awry, Nicole's mascara was smudged and the asymmetric streaked bob was not sitting quite right. Stella felt for her, remembering a few of her own wardrobe malfunctions from her old corporate life. Antoinette's earlier than expected arrival must have caught Nicole out. Stella had often been responsible for events in her old job. She could tell this one was kicking off too soon.

Nicole obviously wanted a better angle, with the Huntley's facade more clearly in the background. In that glaring mustard suit, Nicole pointed and pushed and pulled spectators and camera crews alike, clearing the way and directing them, trying to nuance the shot.

A camera operator backed into Stella's stall, rocking her trays of necklaces and pendant earrings, which danced like miniature disco balls, dazzling the crowd.

Nicole tried to intervene. Too late.

Antoinette Lacy halted her leggy stride right there at Stella's stall and was suddenly showing a deep interest, fingering her display of huge faux emerald drop earrings. They were eye catching, suspended within shiny wire secured with one of Stella's characteristic Celtic knots. As they tumbled inside their tiny silvery cage, they shot out flashes of reflected sunlight, and the camera shutters clamoured in staccato.

"Please, take these," Stella jerked into action herself. It was PR gold, right here at her humble stall. In a dream, she unpinned the dazzling pair that perfectly matched the green of Antoinette's satin sheath dress.

As Stella handed them across, the star held them up for the cameras, which clicked again as Antoinette unleashed that famous, winning, movie star smile.

James froze, the priceless diamond necklace dangling from his outstretched hand, ignored.

"This way, Ms Lacy," a furious Nicole hissed, firmly pulling Antoinette around Stella's little stall towards Huntleys. "Our other VIPs are dying to meet you, Ms Lacy. Inside, please. Media, this way!" Nicole's call was as strained as her voice as she tried to usher reporters inside with the star. "Champagne's on the third floor. Invitation only."

The media and best-dressed members of the crowd followed them, but more and more people stopped at Stella's stall, buying the same earrings Antoinette had admired.

Stella couldn't trade quickly enough, cash, credit and sparkle trading hands faster than she ever could have imagined. She was elated. Her dream was coming true. Here she was, her own boss, making her living from creating beauty; and the customers just kept coming, spurred on by Antoinette's star power, clustering, clamouring, all wanting *Stellar* jewelry.

Only one person seemed unimpressed. Stella glanced up from her customers to meet James's icy stare. His eyes flashed fury right into hers. He turned on one heel and followed Antoinette and Nicole into his building.

The sun went behind a cloud.

Stella's phone rang. She tried to ignore it, still trading fast, but there it went again. Jeannie? It was only as a woman with purple hair hesitated, trying to decide between the green earrings and some red ones, that Stella took a moment to answer it.

"OMG, Stella!"

"What is it, Jeannie?"

"OMG!" Her sister, Jeannie, sounded pleased, and Stella relaxed a little.

"Jeannie, I'm flat out here. What is it?"

"Antoinette Lacy! Stella!"

"What?"

"What do you mean, 'what?' You've done it. You've got it. You've already got 115 'likes.' No, that's just gone up. 143. 181. 221. Stella. OMG."

"Look, I'm super busy here, Jeannie. I've got more customers than I can deal with right now. Can we talk later? Would you mind?"

With two children under three and a travelling husband, Jeannie was fond of a chat.

"311. No. Look. Incredible. It's almost 400 now. This is *insane*, Stell. We've got to get your online purchasing up and running."

"Thanks, Jeannie. Can you please just go ahead? I trust you. You know that. Go on. Go ahead."

"Thanks, Stell! Can't wait."

Stella closed her eyes in gratitude for her sister, two years older and so generous. Without Jeannie, she simply wouldn't be here, finally taking this chance on her dream future - to make real money creating her own jewelry. She couldn't begin to count the ways Jeannie had helped her throughout childhood, and especially now. How many other sole traders had a sister with marketing skills, happy to run their social media and create their website? Stella beamed and held up a finger to two customers waiting to pay. "One moment, please," she mimed.

"Great. Thanks. Stellar web sales coming up. *Sensational*, Stell. I knew you could do this!"

"Thanks, thanks. Thanks so much. Bye, Jeannie. Talk later." Now was no time for a lengthy discussion. Customers were thrusting $50 notes and credit cards at her.

"Got any more of those green ones, the dangly ones?"

"Hey, that's my pair!"

There was a minor tussle as customers fought over the last pair of green earrings on display. From now on, Stella would call them the "Antoinette earrings."

She made seven instant friends by pulling out another tray of them. The customers, including the woman with purple hair, bought three pairs each.

"For my nieces. They *love* Antoinette. I love your stall!"

"Thank you, thank you."

Stock was flying off the velvet trays. It was a frenzy. Never in her wildest dreams had Stella imagined her new venture would succeed so well. She'd taken a huge risk in setting up her own business, but as Jeannie had convinced her, there'd been a danger in not doing it, too.

She'd needed this fresh start. As the sales kept coming, Stella's old life in Perth seemed a world away.

Chapter 2

The lunchtime rush on her brand new Bondi Junction stall was over. In the sudden lull, Stella watched a trio of birds on a lamp post. Two took flight, and one stayed put.

That had been her, that lone bird, more than a decade ago, when Jeannie and their mother had packed up again and left for Sydney. At 16, emboldened by a well-meaning teacher, Stella put her foot down and stayed on in Perth by herself - to her recent regret.

She'd accomplished some things she'd wanted, like enjoying a stable income and putting a halt to a life of constant change with their nomadic mother, but every gain had come at a cost.

Denying her natural creative talent, Stella ended up working in offices for more than a decade, her fingers busy on keyboards and telephones, far from her beloved needle-nose pliers. Worse, she'd fallen for Damian.

Jeannie knew her best. She saw it coming. Tried to warn her.

Awed by the realisation she could make her own decisions about where to live, Stella applied at a temp agency to become an office assistant, a job which freed her to continue creating her jewelry at night.

Yes, she'd wondered if she'd made a mistake the day Jeannie and Stella had packed yet again and actually moved out, but she'd been starting work in the city next day - paid work - and the exhilaration of running her own life, managing her own expenses and making her own decisions thrilled her.

Stella barely noticed she spent less and less time creating jewelry. Every few months, the agency found a new work placement for her, and then she'd scored a permanent position at WestMine with a spectacular salary. They'd even trained her, giving her time and funds to finish high school and gain tertiary qualifications in office management. Busy with evening classes, Stella left her creativity on the back burner.

Learning new skills, she gained more responsibility. It was only a matter of time before one of her bosses who'd left WestMine to run his own show headhunted her away to work with him at Exos, his new mining investment consultancy.

He'd been smooth alright. Damian Beaumont. She'd never forget the day he pulled up beside the curb when she was out at lunch.

"You," he'd said, with those dark glasses and a perfect smile that reached right out through the open passenger side window, transfixed her and reeled her right in.

She should have known Damian's world was too smooth to be real. She'd grown up being driven around in cars that blew head gaskets or with banged-up doors that wouldn't open. Or if they did, they wouldn't close. Once, when her mother Flame's old car broke down on the way back from school, their mother simply bundled up the girls, collected the shopping bags from the trunk, and calmly told her daughters to grab their library books and school bags. They'd all just abandoned the car and walked away.

So, when Damian's vehicle glided to the kerb in front of Stella showing not one speck of dirt, and that tinted window slid down without a sound, and there he was, suave, with a slight smile, in his designer sunglasses, Stella was swept off her feet and into the passenger seat without a backward glance. The door closed quietly on the city bustle. Stella was enveloped in a little capsule of Damian's world that smelled of leather and money and expensive aftershave.

It took her a long time to question the source of Damian's wealth and the way she was spending her life. Four long years.

First into the Exos office to ensure the water cooler was full, the air conditioning on and Damian's appointment files in order, Stella always greeted her colleagues and his clients with efficient smiles. She would ask about their families and pets. Exos was growing quickly. Always sympathetic to newcomers from a childhood as the perpetual outsider, she went out of her way to ensure new staff felt welcome and knew where to find everything they needed, even the shoe repairers, dry cleaners and specialist shops. Stella was the one who fixed people's staplers, sorted their printing and made sure the office ran as perfectly as Damian's orthodontically corrected smile. Over time, she took on the brand management, admin and human resources, hiring more staff as Exos grew.

When Damian's PA, Jacqui, left in a huff one day, it became Stella's job to work more closely with him. He came to rely on her efficiency, showing his appreciation with his eyes and praise. Damian valued her. Respected her.

She loved his glances and smiles, striving to please him, needing that injection of joy only he could provide.

That year, Stella took charge of the office Christmas party, with the theme of winter wonderland. With almost forty staff, it would be their biggest ever.

"Watch out, Stell," Jeannie counselled as Stella rang her for a chat one lunch time.

"What do you mean?"

"You realise you can't start a sentence without saying 'Damian' first? It's all 'Damian this' and 'Damian that.'"

"What's wrong with that?"

"Is he some kind of father figure to you, Stell? Or have you got a crush on him? Just be careful, okay."

The festive white tinsel and helium balloons bumped along the ceiling, pearly ones, trailing silver ribbons. The boardroom was pumping to schmaltzy Christmas music - *Six White Boomers*, *I'm Dreaming of a White Christmas*. Stella's colleagues gasped as they entered the room and were handed their salt-encrusted glasses with dry martinis, gin and tonics, champagne flutes or sparkling mineral water.

Damian loved her idea of the ice sculpture, a huge EXOS for the centre of the table. A sea of dry ice fog swirled around the platters of almost all-white foods. Oysters, salty white sweet potato wedges, onigiri, sushi, Japanese white rice treats, tofu selections and towers of sweets - meringues, marshmallows, and an enormous, creamy pavlova.

When Stella turned on the blue light, Damian, immaculate in his white suit, stepped forward into the hush to toast the company's successful year.

Stella blushed as he lavished praise on the celebration. He didn't name her. Instead, he stared at her, all of her, starting with her necklace, one she'd just finished, each pearl strung on its own silver wire, radiating from a silver choker.

Damian's eyes were on her the whole night, and when she stayed back to clean up and he emerged from his office, they were alone together. Several martinis down, there was a kind of inevitability about him stepping in closer and grabbing her wrist.

Finally he was going to notice her matching bracelet, she thought, before he twisted her even closer and kissed her, hard.

She surrendered to the moment. Hadn't she been half expecting this, half hoping for it? Jeannie was right. Stella was in love with the boss. Half the staff were. Damian had chosen her.

"What's up, little sister?" When they hadn't spoken throughout the week as usual, Jeannie phoned her.

"What do you mean?"

"Don't hold out on me, Stell. Something's up. You're in love, aren't you? So, who's the lucky guy? How was the Christmas party by the way?"

"Went well, thanks. The blue light was a great idea. Thank Matt, would you?"

"Sure will. So come on. Who's the guy?"

"How's your own Christmas prep, Jeannie? Tree?"

"Had to go for a tiny one, for the centre of the table. It's just too risky with Lucy. Everything goes in her mouth. Can you imagine? Christmas is a nightmare! Everything's new and different and shiny and it's all either tin foil or plastic and breakable. When are we going to see you?"

"Not sure, really. Damian needs me."

"That boss of yours. No. Stella. Don't tell me it's the boss. Are you sure about this guy?"

Her sister knew her too well.

"Gotta go, Jeannie."

"Hey, don't freeze me out here, Stell. Am I right?"

"It's easy for you. You have Matt. Not all of us can find Mr Perfect. Besides, it's not serious."

"Not serious? Sex is serious, Stell."

"Please. When did you get so pious, Jeannie? After our upbringing, I would have thought you'd have an open mind."

"I just don't want you to get hurt, Stell. Guys like that. They're into power. Do you want a fling, or do want a future? And the moment it's over, your job will be, too. I hope you know what you're doing."

She did, at the time, anyway. But in the longer term, Jeannie was right. Damian Beaumont had it made. His efficient young PA accompanied on business trips out of town. Adjoining rooms.

A year passed and then another, and he was no closer to committing to any kind of formal future with her, beyond his vague allusions to "one day." They'd worked together so easily and for so long that she rarely had a thought of her own. It was "Damian would like this" and "Damian will need that." When visitors from the UK were expected, she'd book the restaurant for them without being asked. She even knew what table he'd want reserved.

Maybe it was another phone call from Jeannie that forced her to question what she was doing with her life.

"Coming over for your birthday, sis?"

"Oh."

"Yep. Your big one. Big three oh. The hill. We always said we'd celebrate it together… What's wrong?"

"I don't know, Jeannie. There's another meeting. In London."

"Surely you don't have to go this time. You can get leave can't you? You do enough overtime."

"I just don't know, alright?" She hadn't meant to snap at Jeannie. The truth was she knew exactly what she wanted. She wanted Damian to take her with him to London as he often did. And she wanted him to take her to dinner for her big birthday. Anywhere. Just the two of them. She could see it. He'd hold her hand in the candlelight and ask her to marry him. It wasn't an unreasonable expectation. Hadn't she spent every waking minute for the past few years working for his every benefit?

Birthdays! Stella remembered every colleague's birthday. She was a specialist in finding the right kind of big card for each person, furtively taking it around for everyone to sign. She'd buy their favourite cakes, even remembering who was "gluten free." She was the one who washed up all those matching plates and forks when everyone else returned to their desks and meetings. If Exos staff felt appreciated, it was because of Stella's efforts.

She could see what she was doing, and began to hate herself. She'd wait back every evening until she was the last to leave, waiting for Damian to give her that special smile of appreciation, or a touch on the arm, or sex in his office the way he liked it, in the dark, fast and thrilling.

15

Yes. Stella had every reason to think her thirtieth birthday with Damian in London might be special. She'd booked their flights and a suite in the Knightsbridge hotel near the head office, with another adjoining room for herself.

"Shall I book a restaurant as well, for the 16th?" she'd asked.

"Why's that? Miles doesn't fly in till the following evening. You know that."

She shouldn't have been surprised. Damian didn't have access to her calendar, with its big thirtieth looming, and nothing much else. But she'd swallowed and dared to dream.

"I was wondering whether you might want to take me to dinner."

"Hmmm?" He'd been checking his phone. Not that there was much need. Stella was right on top of his schedule.

"No. No time."

So that was that. She stood in a London bookshop and stared at birthday cards, quietly crying, furious at herself for not telling him about her special day, for not insisting he acknowledge her as a human being, with her own needs beyond a pay packet and the calculated flash of his smile.

"You okay?" he asked her over the coffee she'd brought him at Heathrow Airport while they waited for their flight back to Australia. It wasn't exactly a caring tone. More critical. He liked her best when she was smiling and agreeable, much as he liked a pristine bathroom. He was far too busy to enquire into the real state of her wellbeing.

Normally she would have smiled reassuringly. But something inside her had changed, had woken up, and refused to back down.

"I just turned thirty, Damian."

"Commiserations. Welcome to the other side of the hill." Then he asked whether she'd arranged a hire car for him back in Perth.

She should have known Damian wouldn't rescue her, that the whole fantasy she'd built up about him caring for her, actually loving her, was just her own elaborate wishful thinking. All these years he'd let her think they might have a future together, he'd reaped all the benefits of her hopes.

"Ever thought of, you know..." Stella said, reaching for his hand. Their plane was delayed. It seemed as good a time as any to see where he thought their relationship might be going. But she hated the way her question made her sound. Needy. Pathetic. But she wanted some certainty, dammit. Friends were starting to settle down. She wanted his babies. What was so wrong with that?

Damian's expression turned stony. He looked away from her, withdrew his hand.

He always did this. All those times she'd suggested she stay over, or invited him for dinner at her place. He always backed away. Always kept his options open. Refused to pin "one day" to an actual timeframe.

When her friend Bonnie from night school invited her to her housewarming when she and her boyfriend moved in together, Stella asked Damian along.

"No. You go," he'd said. "I've got a dinner. Potential investor."

Or that time she'd left some of her things in his spare bathroom for those rare nights she stayed over. He packaged them in a sealable plastic bag and dropped them on her desk.

"No need to leave your stuff lying around," he'd said. "I'm sure you want these back."

"Oh no ..."

"You know me. I like things clean and tidy."

"Shampoo is clean, Damian. It takes up hardly any space."

He stormed off, telling her to get his tax advisor on the line, as if she and her feelings were an irritation.

Jeannie was scathing.

"Can't you see what he's doing, Stell? My heart aches for you."

"What, Jeannie? He's a clean freak. What's wrong with that?"

17

"Oh, Stell. If he has that rule for all his girlfriends, you'll never find out about each other."

Was it true? Stella had Damian's calendar. She checked it. He didn't have time for any other girlfriends, did he? Unless "Alex" wasn't really his personal fitness coach. And he did seem to have a number of inexplicable appointments at odd hours. She'd always thought he was at tanning clinics, or entertaining potential clients.

She decided to test him.

"Let's move in together, Damian. It would make things so much simpler for us both, don't you think?"

"Hmmm. I'll give it some thought. Look, I need to get some statements out to our biggest investors today. How are you placed? Can you package them up for me?"

Later that week, she noticed Damian beam at the youngest office assistant, then wink at her when she'd brought him his coffee. She didn't fawn. But she didn't look unhappy with the attention. Damian did that to people. Charmed them. She remembered how eager she'd been to please him. Still was. Desperate for the fix of his approval.

Surely there was more in her life than this obsession with Damian. Jeannie was right. Stell's every waking minute was consumed by ensuring his happiness, making his business successful, full of hopes for their future together.

That lunch time, she forced herself to go to a craft shop. She bought a sketch pad and began to sketch jewelry designs right there on her desk, an old passion from her school days that never failed to bring her joy - neglected for far too long.

Collecting the spare agendas after a board meeting, she absentmindedly squashed one of the empty coffee pods and noticed its potential for making jewelry. There and then she retrieved all of them she could find, took them home and began experimenting, excited by what she could make.

When she wore her new earrings to work the next day, Shamira, the accountant, admired them.

"Get another pay rise, Stella?" Shamira stared at her ears.

Stella laughed. "You like them? They're yours!" She took them off and handed them over, explaining how they'd been destined for the boardroom bin the day before. She liked Shamira, one of her hires. She worked hard and was always ready to share her interesting herbal teas.

"No way. They're beautiful. I'll pay you for them."

"No you won't Shamira. You have no idea how thrilled I am that you like them."

Stella left work at 5pm from then on, rushing home to create more jewelry. No longer would she wait around for Damian.

Before long, Damian's kindnesses to the new assistant, Lexie, were ramping up. "Get yourself a pot plant," she overheard him saying to Lexie one morning when she'd greeted him. He'd thrust a $50 note at her and waved away her attempt to return it.

Another time he sent Lexie down to Switzers to buy mints, insisting she keep the change. All these things, he'd done with Stella when she'd been new. Would Lexie fall for it, too?

Suddenly the contempt his old PA had shown Stella the day she'd replaced her began to make sense. She saw her relationship with Damian in a new and shocking light. How naive she'd been! He'd been grooming her, totally taking advantage. #MeToo, alright. It sickened her to think she'd always believed he genuinely cared for her. She must catch Lexie and warn her; let her know she didn't have to put up with that way of behaving from anyone. Tell her she could keep a professional distance without appearing rude, and still keep her job.

Or was she just jealous? But what was "just" about jealousy? Could he replace her so easily? How dare he!

Her gut jacked up. It waged war with her. She rose from her ergonomically perfect chair and knocked on Damian's door, entering and closing it behind her. Immersed in his computer screen, he ignored her.

"Damian."

"Mmm?"

"We need to talk."

"Can it wait? This is important."

"This is important, too."

He sighed. Like a child interrupted from play. He gave her his exaggerated attention, as if she were an annoyance. Why had she never noticed that about him before? A petulance.

"Why did Jacqui leave? She was good at her job. You two seemed like a real team."

Silence.

"How many PAs have you had, Damian?"

"Three? Four? Why?"

"Did you sleep with all of us?"

"Stella!"

"And when exactly did you move on from each of them? Was it when they started asking about their future?"

"Stella!" He pushed back his chair and stood, his full height a threat to her, but she stood her ground.

"You made me feel like you loved me, like the care and attention I've lavished on you all these years might be reciprocated. I'm feeling used, Damian. As if I'm as replaceable as your office chair."

Damian was no fool. Stella had watched him in countless meetings, reading the room, hedging his bets, ensuring his survival no matter the issue. He was reading her now, flicking through his options, evaluating her worth to him, her expendability. It occurred to her she was behaving exactly like his previous PA. Why had she been so blind?

"So. After all I've done for you, Damian. What do you say?"

"Stella. What's this about? We've been good for each other, haven't we? You've had pay rises. You've travelled the world. "

"A few airports. A few hotel rooms, Damian."

"You've never complained before now. What is this? Do you need a holiday? Is that it?" Conciliatory.

Her face felt like stone. Maybe she did need a holiday. No. She simply wanted more than this, this fear she was temporary, that she'd be thrown over for the next pretty office assistant.

"How about marriage. It's a normal progression, you know. It's not unthinkable."

"Look, let's talk about this later. Not now. These things take time, Stella. You should know that."

"One year, maybe. It's been four."

"We'll discuss it later."

Her heart pumped so hard it threatened to explode. Was this really happening? She could stay and be placated and they'd be having this conversation for the rest of her life. Or she could go.

"No. I don't think so. I'm resigning, Damian. I'll leave the keys in my top drawer."

Chapter 3

She'd kept walking, past all the coffee shops, through all the streets of the CBD, down to Kings Park and down to the Swan River where a couple of black swans glided, serene. What had she done? She checked her watch without registering the time, felt the sun move overhead and then begin to set.

She sat as the rush hour traffic built and crawled and dissipated, as the chill of dusk descended.

Fury at Damian rose like poison. She replayed their every exchange; his special smiles and comments, the way he'd made her feel so needed.

She'd had her eye on him since she'd first won the job, always tried to please him. Had he really just used her, without returning her love, year after year after year? What kind of a fool had she been?

After that Christmas kiss, there'd been their first business trip to Paris, the first time he'd suggested adjoining rooms. He'd taken her to a beautiful old restaurant in the Latin quarter. He'd let his fingers brush hers as they explored the menu, and then encouraged her to drink from his glass as well as her own as he discussed French wines with such authority, and they'd laughed like school children as they headed back out into the cold, onto those famous streets on a wet night, with the lights reflecting back at them from the slick pavement and the Seine diaphanous and magical as they walked together. She'd been unsteady on her feet and his strength beside her comforting, then exhilarating as he'd offered her his arm, then nestled her up against his warmth beneath his big coat, and she'd become aware of him in a new way.

There was no denying it. It was pure exhilaration to be needed by someone so powerful. But when did all Damian's desires merge into her own? When had she lost herself? No more. Selfish Damian? He was the past. Her investment in him had not been repaid. Never would be. There was no future for them. She no longer had the heart for it.

Well after dark, she let herself back into her apartment and saw her weary, miserable self in the mirror. Who was Stella Rhys anyway, if she wasn't Damian Beaumont's support system?

She'd gone to bed then, for days. When Rita from Human Resources contacted her, she told her she was unwell and had resigned.

"You should know Damian wants you back. He's intimating there's a payrise in it for you."

"Damian's good at intimating." Stella liked Rita. Sensible Rita, in her forties. She'd been the first person she'd hired to build up human resources when she'd moved on to become Damain's PA. Rita had been around the block.

"What would you like me to tell him?" She could tell Rita, couldn't she? But what was the point? The whole office was probably talking about her anyway. What a fool she'd been, and the worst thing was that part of her was missing him, missing Damian.

"Tell him I'll consider it," she repeated, though she had no intention of doing so.

Why did the idea of returning to Exos not excite her? Hadn't she been wanting an acknowledgement of her value to Damian for years? She just felt flat.

"Look. No. Tell him 'no.' Nothing personal towards you and the others, Rita. I'm going to miss you."

"We'll miss you, too. Big time. Get well soon."

No sooner had she and Rita hung up than her mother rang. Christened Fiona, her red-headed mother renamed herself Flame as a teenager. Wild and free, she'd run off with a Swedish backpacker named Sven, had Jeannie, then moved in with a miner in Darwin when Sven returned to Sweden without her.

Flame was still running, to and from one new man after another. This call was about her latest love, Grady, up on the NSW north coast, a musician she'd met at a bar.

"Beautiful up here, Stella. Really. Come and see it."

"I've resigned mum."

"Have you, dear? Good. You can come up then. Any time. Come up now."

"Damian. The boss. It's over."

"Yes, dear? Yes. Well. Damian. Never liked the sound of that one, to be honest, dear, though I never wanted to tell you so. That mining company? Raping the earth. So what do I say? Good. Move on, dear. That's what I always say. Plenty of good men around, though you're probably not ready to hear it yet. He was your first real love, wasn't he?"

"Maybe." Had she loved Damian? Stella had done everything in her power to make him love her back. She had wanted him to be her first and only love. She'd been seeking a different path to her mother, who was always on to another relationship.

"But now I want to do something with my life, mum."

"Of course you do. Do what you love, dear. Be happy. Look. Can't talk now. Grady's back. But don't you worry. Everything'll work out just fine. Always does. Take it from me. Talk to you later."

Jeannie had been more understanding. She didn't even say she'd tried to tell her that Damian never sounded like marriage material.

"There are plenty of men like that out there, Stella. It's all about their egos. And their dicks, I'm sorry to say. So, are you alright? Will you get another job?"

"What do you think Damian's going to say on my reference, Jeannie? Besides. I'm done with office jobs. It's never been what I wanted to do with my life."

"Well, I did wonder. Someone creative like you, Stell. Not everyone's got real talent like you."

Had Stella underestimated Damian? Flowers arrived the next day, all white, as Damian preferred them, in keeping with the company branding. "Please phone Damian at your earliest convenience."

No. She would not phone him. She had no interest in any of that. Not any more. Not with Damian.

Instead, she'd skyped Jeannie.

"I just don't know how I could have been so blind, Jeannie! Somehow I just convinced myself that after the boardroom led to the bedroom he'd want to marry me. He never said as much. But he let me think it. I know he did."

"Don't beat yourself up, Stell. I'm so relieved you've finally seen what I've been trying to tell you. Love's blind, they say. So. You've fallen out of love. What matters now is you think about the future."

Thank goodness Jeannie understood; busy, faithful Jeannie, always there for her, and for her own girls, Stella's lovable nieces with their chubby cheeks and non-stop curiosity. Jeannie was jollying a grumbly Sienna on her lap while stopping Lucy from careering into the keyboard.

"So good to see you, Jeannie. Yes. Hello Lucy. Hello! How are you?"

"Howaa ooo?"

"Where's your teddy, Lucy?" Lucy lurched away to search for it, giving the sisters a chance to chat.

Lucy came back into view, teddy aloft, chattering away in her own language.

"Hello, teddy. Yes. Hello! Lovely to see you." Alarming brown fuzz took up half the screen, but Jeannie's voice cut through.

"Ring me after seven, Stell. The girls will be in bed. Matt's away again. He loves his new job. Such a great promotion. Australasia. But there's so much travel!"

"Okay. Thanks, Jeannie. Bye bye, Lucy! Bye Sienna. She's adorable, Jeannie. They both are. Speak tonight."

Jeannie picked up the phone the moment Stella rang, on the dot of seven.

"Tell me, Stell. This crazy idea. What's up?"

"My jewelry."

"What about it? I love it. Always have. All of it. You've always had real talent. I used to be jealous of you, but now I'm just plain proud."

"Do you think I could make a go of it? Sell it?"

"Of course you could! It's unique. It's quality."

"But a lot of it's so easy."

"That's just not true. People love your jewelry. It's stylish. It's affordable. It's fun. I've always loved your stuff. You were upcycling before anyone even invented the word. I still wear those spoon bangles you made me in primary school! And the girls play with the old toothbrush ones now. Remember the old orange one? Sienna's been using it as a teether! Didn't you say you'd been experimenting with coffee pods? Got anything new there? I love to see what you're up to. Of course you could make a go of it."

"But I'm scared."

"Scared?"

"You know, Jeannie. I never wanted to be like Flame, never quite making a go of it, drifting here and there with the scarves and tarot cards, jumping into one failing scheme after another with the next man. I'd hate that. I need certainty. I loved my regular wage, dammit. Damn Damian."

"Listen to me, Stell. You're not remotely like Flame. Unlike me, you don't even look like her. Whatever you do, it will be done completely differently to the way mum does things. Come on. What's your plan?"

"I've been working since I was sixteen, Jeannie. All those temp jobs, and then WestMine took me on and trained me up, and now four years with Exos, most of it starstruck by Mr Powerful, and I've done nothing else. Not really. No proper holidays. I ended up with no time to even make jewelry. I'm thirty and I backed the wrong horse. I feel futureless."

"If anyone has a future, it's you, Stell. You're brilliant. Not only can you make jewelry, but you've got all those business skills as well. And you must have some savings by now."

"Yeah, but they can't last forever. I don't want to be irresponsible."

"What's irresponsible about having a change, giving it a go? I'm excited for you! I know you don't want to drift. Neither of us liked that way of life much. Flame's way. That's why I got my marketing degree, and I'm so lucky I met Matt, a steadier man than any of our step dads. But you don't have to do markets. You could leave your stuff on consignment with other outlets or galleries, or …"

"You actually think I can do this?" Hope surged through Stella like wildfire. So many ideas crowded into her head, for new designs, ideas she'd been suppressing for years.

"I do. Totally. Make your plan, little sister."

"A business plan. I can do that."

Back came that buzz, that joy of anticipation, and the thrill of creation.

Stella's sense of meaning returned as she filled her mind and hands with materials and tools, creating beauty. Days flew by.

Jeannie began ordering gifts for her friends, insisting Stella was doing her a favour. Soon Stella was busy dreaming up new designs and sourcing beads and wire and fastenings, and expanding her set of files and drills and other tools. Only the work in her hands mattered now, along with the vision in her mind and her will to transform the materials between her fingers into items of beauty.

Stella loved working with the coffee pods. They were light and came in all kinds of burnished, earthy hues with an attractive sheen. Squashed flat, they became small flowers. They practically made themselves into earrings, necklaces and bracelets.

She spent a whole day visiting businesses in the CBD office towers, collecting them. Being back in those elevators made her feel trapped. Not for one moment did she regret her decision to leave Exos. She barely thought of the place any more.

Instead, she visited craft stores and bought up the spools of silver in all gauges she'd once coveted, and three more sets of pliers with different noses, wondrous things that transformed the wire into something new - intricate rings featuring celtic knots, cages for pearls and other objects, coiled and twisted earrings, many with one special bead or rhinestone to catch the light.

Working till her fingers became calloused, she created shining objects of beauty, one after another, multiple rings of all sizes, and variations of all of her favourite motifs.

The joy of creation was so intense she didn't want to think beyond the next item, but one day soon, she knew, she must.

The phone snapped her out of her reverie one evening.

"I hope you've enjoyed your little holiday, but it's time you came back, Stella. We need you."

Damian. Her heart leapt. Yes! No! She nearly hung up on him. He hadn't even asked how she was.

She was speechless.

"So you can stop playing games. Did Rita tell you I'm offering a pay rise? Your pay was already generous, and I'm prepared to up it by $10k."

She still had no idea what to say. If she'd been worth that much more money, why hadn't he offered it sooner?

"We have nothing to say to each other, Damian Beaumont," she said, keeping her voice steady. He'd always hated rejection. It was why he worked so hard at finding and keeping investors. She'd dented his pride by leaving. Tough. He'd get over it.

"Oh. But we do, though." He'd dropped his voice into that seductive tone that used to set her blood racing. She'd never said no to him. Not until that day she'd walked out. She could picture him, suit coat off, sleeves rolled up at the end of the day, tie hanging loose each side of his neck, top button undone.

"No."

"Think about it." He hung up before she could repeat her refusal.

It was upsetting. It was bullying. It was the Damian she'd refused to see. The MD who drove hard bargains. Well, she wasn't for sale. Not any more.

As she worked at her kitchen bench, cutting and twisting and welding and threading, realisation dawned on her. She put her phone on speaker and worked it through with Jeannie who was cooking a huge batch of baby food to freeze for Sienna.

"He was so bloody confident. Arrogant. What is it about people like that, Jeannie? We watched them, you and me. At every school we ever went to. Remember them? The ones who were born to rule? They even had the teachers conned. I don't know what gave them the right to walk all over everyone else and tell us what to do, but they got away with it, again and again. You tried to tell me, Damian was kind of absorbing me, using me only for his own ends. But I have to tell you this, what I know now. So much of his success was because of my work. Even the staff I hired for him. Good people. They joined because they liked me."

"Exactly what I've been saying, Stell."

"Well of course they were really there for the pay. And to be fair, Damian took the risks, investing in the right companies, and convinced more investors to back his decisions. But they liked me, too. I was the one who was nice to them on the phone, who asked them about their families and pets and illnesses, who remembered their dietary requirements. God,

Jeannie. I was a total expert on all of them. And while I was at it, I forgot who I was."

"So all you need is the confidence to support your own business. I know you can do this."

"And I've stopped straightening my hair, the way Damian wanted it. Neat and tidy. Total waste of time, that, straightening it every morning. You should see it, Jeannie. Pretty wild. Back how it always was when we were kids."

"Can't wait to see you!"

Stella's new plans made her feel more alive than ever, as if Exos was a life lived in limbo, and her real life only just beginning.

What would life be like without that injection of money into her account every two weeks without fail? Did she even have the guts to do this? Too bad. Too late. That's what happened when you walked out.

Everything would change. Back to powdered milk and oatmeal for breakfast. No more restaurant meals. Not even fast food. Mince meat and spaghetti; a huge pot of it, to last all week. But no more fish fingers. Ever. Stella laughed. They were Flame's "go to" meal. Cooked in the microwave. All lined up like yellow fence posts. Never again.

Stella seized the nail clippers. She studied them before she consigned them to history - those long painted nails Damian loved - so sophisticated, and so constricting. She needed full use of her fingers. Goodbye expensive nail salon.

Excitement became ambition. Hope became stock. Boxes of her creations became heavier.

Fear still gnawed at her. Childhood with Flame had taught Stella how to survive without much money - but it also taught her she never wanted to go back there. Poverty scarred her and scared her. How could she ever find enough faith in her skills to trust in a future solely of her own making?

In her years as an admin assistant and PA, perfecting business plans for the boss, she'd learned a lot about budgets and strategic planning, if not about matters of the heart. The affair with the big boss, Damian? Total fail. But at least she'd learned enough about profit and loss to create a plan for this new venture - her own business. She even had a name for it - *Stellar*.

Elation dipped to despair. Without an income, how could she hope to pay her rent, her phone bill, or a grocery bill? She'd be no different from Flame, eking it out all her life, living from one meal to the next, always shifting house, half a step ahead of eviction.

She burned through her savings, Damian's offer circling her consciousness like a shark.

"Am I being irresponsible, Jeannie? Part of me thinks I should swallow my pride and go back to Damian and save up more money first, but ..."

"Do not go back there!" Jeannie insisted. "Think of all the reasons you left. No. We can do this. Just take out your living costs. Come east! Come and live with Matt and me. I'm going insane home alone with the little ones, what with Matt travelling all the time. Power saving software. Everyone wants it! 'Australasian manager' sounds so fabulous and the money's good. And it's good for the planet. He loves it and I know he's the right person for the job, but he's almost always away! Do it. Come east. Go on. Please. Just give it a go. You've got nothing to lose. You keep telling me you'll never sell enough to make a living. Well, how do you know? You keep wondering if people will actually buy your things. Well, find out! Get a stall like mum's. Just run it while you work out what people want to buy. Call it the first step of your own business venture. You can hire stalls right near our place. Take a space in the Oxford Street mall. Think how much you'll learn! Find out which designs sell best. Experiment with your pricing. See what happens, Stell. If you can make a go of it for six months, I'm sure you'll be able to make a case at a bank to get funding to mass produce your designs or something. And if nothing else, you'll enjoy a well-earned holiday and a bit of an adventure out east. And you'll be keeping me company. Come on."

It didn't take much to convince her.

Bing! Here came a selfie of Jeannie and the girls at Bondi Beach.

Bing! Another of them heading across the Sydney Harbour Bridge in the double stroller - glimpses of the city skyline, the parks and bays and beaches, and that great, big blue horizon out to sea. Why not?

How she wanted to hug those adorable nieces who were growing up so fast!

Yes. She would sell her jewels in Sydney, at least for the first six months. After that, the world! She'd progress from the stall, unlike Flame. She would show the world the beauty of her designs, sell them to other jewelers, and go on to design even more dazzling possibilities. Stella had big plans. She could do this.

Whole days disappeared as she refined her designs. She stockpiled creations and dreamt up new ones, bringing long-imagined designs into reality.

If ever she thought of Damian, another stab of fury propelled her to work faster. He'd taken Stella's innocence and wasted years of her life, but he would no longer take her future. She'd finally broken free, and she would never, ever allow herself to fall in love with someone like him again. Bosses? Forget them. Stella was her own boss now.

Chapter 4

And now, here she was, selling it all, not just surviving, but thriving, her dream a reality.

Strangely, here in the mall on her first day of trade, Stella had another problem. She'd worried about failure, but nothing had prepared her for this kind of success. A good part of her day's supplies sold out, and if she didn't work for hours tonight, sorting, polishing and arranging more stock, there'd be nothing to sell tomorrow. She was glad she could only trade Thursday to Saturday, 11am to 7pm. At least that left her with Sunday to Wednesday to make more pieces.

At that moment, a glint of sunlight reflected off the polished brass handles of Huntleys doors as they swung open. Stella noticed the strikingly ornate H shape they made. Clever. Classy. A bit Art Nouveau, they oozed distinction. How she'd love to go in there and explore some time.

A short man with a large microphone emerged. He bustled right up to her, his microphone and small camcorder aimed right at her mouth, and his own smooth voice already recording.

"I'm in Oxford Street Mall right outside Huntleys, at the new stall, Stellar, that's caused all the commotion. New jewelry stall owner Stella Rhys achieved a major publicity coup earlier today, hijacking *Heist* movie star Antoinette Lacy's attention as she was on her way to promote the famous Huntleys House of Diamonds.

"Refusing to move her tiny stall at the request of third generation Huntley's heir James Huntley, Stella created a social media storm by giving Antoinette a pair of Stellar earrings. Stella, how does it feel to have attracted the endorsement of a star like Antoinette?"

There was something a bit wild about the reporter's eyes. They were shiny, and she could smell the alcohol on his breath - no doubt Huntleys' French champagne. Who was this guy? Stocky, insistent...

"Um. Hi. Thank you. I'm quite busy …" She quickly reconsidered. This was a golden opportunity to raise her profile. Any publicity was good publicity, wasn't it? That's what Jeannie had told her, and she knew a lot about marketing.

"Busy indeed. Just look at the custom Antoinette's endorsement has created. Stella's stock of faux jewels is flying off her stall as passers by capture the magic of the moment. Stella is practically out of product. Yes, it's pure PR genius. What gave you the idea, Stella?"

"Pure accident, more like. I'm thrilled Antoinette likes my earrings..."

"Likes them? Antoinette loves them. She was still wearing them when she left Huntleys. Stellar earrings are the hottest product in Australia right now. Before we know it there'll be a retrade racket."

"Really? Look, I had no idea Antoinette was going to be here. It's my first day of trade. It's sheer good luck, I guess."

"Sheer talent, I'd say, and all these customers seem to agree." He switched off the recorder.

Stella rapidly handed over some of her stock.

"That was so nice of you. I wasn't expecting an interview."

"Wow. These are really beautiful. Got any more brooches? Anything purple? My girlfriend's crazy about purple."

"Uh, yeah. Purple's over there. Please, take the brooch, earrings and choker for free. Tell her it's the very first Stellar 'Antoinette set.' I didn't expect this free publicity."

"Brilliant." He's videoing again. "So, give us a few facts, would you? How much trade have you done?"

"I haven't actually done a stocktake, but you can see for yourself these trays are nearly empty. It's been amazing." She forced herself to make the most of the unexpected opportunity. "Hello, Sydney. You are amazing." To her own ears, it sounded awkward, but at least she could tell Jeannie she tried.

"Do you make these yourself? Where did you get the inspiration for these things?"

"I've always loved jewelry. Doesn't everyone? It's just a bit of fun, to brighten up your day or spice up the night. A bit of a novelty, you know. So we're not always 'same old, same old.' jewelry makes us feel fresh. A bit of sparkle never goes astray. jewelry makes people happy."

"Well, it's certainly made Antoinette happy, and these customers are ecstatic. This is Ruben Slavonicus, multimedia influencer."

Pigeons and seagulls competed for scraps as more workers emerged from the office towers. It smelled like fast food – like franchized hamburgers and pizza and coffee.

Ruben Slavonicus, huh? Stella would have to remember to ask Jeannie about him. There was so much to learn.

Ruben had switched off his mic and was over at Fritz's stall, buying a cold soft drink. Stella eyed it thirstily, reminding herself she must bring water tomorrow.

Ruben was back. He thrust a cold lemonade into her left hand.

"Complements of Fritz. Great guy. He'll help you out. Heart of gold." Ruben settled himself on the concrete edge of the planter beside her stall, as if he'd sat there a thousand times. Maybe he had. He started up a commentary. Couldn't seem to help himself.

"Yeah. Huntley's, eh," he said conversationally, between swigs, gesturing with the bottle at the fancy old building. Always a reporter, even when off duty. "Had the chance to sell up and get a prime space in the biggest new mall, but Jimmy wouldn't do it. He was the second Huntley..."

Stella listened to him as she smiled and handed over change and tiny parcels of her unique jewelry to her customers.

"Jim's the original Huntley. Must be in his 80s now, all stooped over, but still on it. Bright as can be. Not one to underestimate. No. He did alright. Married Eleanor Montgomery after the Korean war, after her sweetheart was killed. Quite a story. Her family already owned the building. Jim was the one who turned it into a jewelry business. Saw the potential. Everyone got married back then, not just him and Eleanor. Engagement rings were big business."

Ruben took another long swig then wiped his mouth with the back of his hand.

"Those must have been the days. Everyone who was anyone went to Huntleys. Engagement rings, wedding rings, then eternity rings, Christening spoons, pearls, cufflinks, shirt studs, tie pins... All that stuff's still in there, you know." He gestured at Huntleys again with his half empty bottle. "Council got me to do a series on Waverley landmarks, you know. Noticed all the old businesses literally shutting up shop. A lot of 'em went bust when the new malls went up. Chain stores have taken away loads of custom here over the years. I reckon even this lot are still struggling."

He gestured at the strip shops lining the mall on both sides, some a hundred years old and showing their age, while others were constructed in the sixties and seventies, replacing the originals. Huntleys stood out. Grand. Still in good shape, at least on the outside.

"Interesting family, the Huntleys. Jim's got a memory as big as their safe. Told me all sorts of stuff about those days, 1950s, '60s, when he transformed his wife's family's old department store into the jewelry store. He and Eleanor had their boy by then, Jimmy Huntley the second, and he took it all on in the 1980s when he turned 21. Jim and Eleanor were going to retire, go around the world, but by then Jimmy and his wife, Cynthia, got a bit busy with their own family, and then Jimmy got this cancer."

Stella hadn't said a word to encourage the commentary. She kept serving, swiping cards and accepting money, wrapping the purchases, whipping out new stock at every available moment to replace what was sold. Ruben could be talking to himself for all she'd shown any interest. Still, it was great to get some background, especially James Huntley. James's blue eyes had been distractingly attractive, even though she'd clearly annoyed him by refusing to move her stall ahead of their publicity stunt.

"They got the chance again when the other new mall was being planned, but by then Jimmy the Second was dying and James was in charge. Bet he wishes he'd made the big move after all. James, eh. And Will. Younger brother. What a playboy! James wanted to do it, sell up and move in with Eastleighs, the newest mega mall, but his mum got a heritage order slapped on the place when Jimmy died, just before she went overseas. Maybe she wanted to keep it as a memorial to Jimmy, you know. She loves heritage stuff. Showed me all around the place before she went off to France. Beautiful wooden cabinets with bevelled glass. They've even got one of those old gold cash registers you see in the movies. Council's right to make a fuss of these places. Bondi Junction'd be dead boring without it. Character. That's Huntleys. Class."

Ruben's drink was all gone. Stella hadn't asked for a history lesson. Still, she'd found herself increasingly intrigued. Ruben could certainly tell a good story.

"Can't imagine Jim would have wanted to pull it down. Eleanor died about 10 years ago. It's his home now, as well as his work. Top floor. Top guy, too. Always welcomes me. Real gentleman. Where're you from, anyway? Haven't seen you around."

He burped and tossed his bottle in the recycling bin, then checked his phone.

"Perth."

"That where you learned to make this stuff?"

"No, I've always made things. Ever since I can remember."

"Yeah?"

Stella remembered all those markets of her childhood. She'd linger by white elephant stalls, riffle through the costume jewelry from every era, hoping for scraps of beads or chain, and seek out spare coils of wire in the stalls that sold hardware.

Creating things was her consolation. Sometimes Stella thought of her childhood as a long silver chain, each link just one of the many places she, her mother and Jeannie had unpacked their precious possessions before bundling them up again, bound for the next adventure.

"Wire shapes - coils, circles, triangles and, once I learned to read and write, I'd make letters and people's names.

"I sold them from a coat hanger on my mother's stall of scarves - earrings from buttons, beading."

It was the elegance of her shapes that caught people's eyes. They were almost organic.

When she ended up at Mandurah High School in Perth, and Mr Finnigan taught her how to use a jigsaw, her designs really took shape - teardrops, moons, stars and flowers. When he taught her how to solder, she spent every spare minute in the art room creating jewelry. Her pieces were so professional she could start to charge real money. She was well on the way to a career of making jewelry, selling it with her mother at markets, all around Australia. Except she'd stayed in Perth. And fallen for Damian.

"Fantastic!"

Not really, but she wouldn't tell Ruben all of that - how she'd hated her nomadic upbringing, always having to move just as she was starting to make friends.

As an adult, Stella came to realise that most people stayed put. It was her mother, Flame, who grew no roots. Flame loved to tell the story of baby

Jeannie, and pull out the old photo, now burnt in Stella's memory - of her grandparents, a kindly couple with strained smiles, Stella a tight-wrapped cocoon in a soft bunny rug with a dark fuzz of hair, nestled in the crook of Pop's huge arm and Jeannie a red-haired toddler with an open smile, one chubby hand held high to almost touch the wonder of her baby sister. The trio moved to Wollongong soon after, then Newcastle, Woy Woy, Ulladulla, Orange, Armidale and Albury.

How Stella hated all those moves!

"No, not again!" Stella's heart would drop every time Flame started stacking the saucepans and throwing their clothes into bags. With barely enough time to farewell new friends, she dreaded walking into the next school, "new girl" again in a sea of strangers.

"You're okay, Stell," Jeannie would say, arranging their favourite dolls and teddies. Jeannie, two years older, never minded all the moves. She found friends easily, but Stella was quieter, shy. She learned to laugh about the things they left behind, especially one shoe. It was easier to run barefoot. They'd left the other half of multiple pairs all over the country. In years to come, Stella would point at the map with a straight face and rename their old home towns. "Gumboot." Or "Flipper." And in reverse. She was particularly fond of her riding boots, picked up second hand in Ulladulla. When one was left behind she wandered around for days making Jeannie laugh. "Is this one 'Ulla'? Or 'dulla'?"

Constant disruption forced Stella to discover her salvation. The space between her hands was the only thing over which she had total control. With her gift for drawing and imagining and making things, she always had something to do, no matter where they were living and which stepfather was in the background. Time disappeared as she crafted one beautiful thing after another, the joy of creation feeding her soul.

Markets were a high point of her week, when she and Jeannie wandered together in relative safety under the watchful eyes of the other stall holders, enjoying unsold baked goodies and over ripe seasonal fruit, and helping themselves to anything they found lying around, particularly a new pair of shoes that actually fitted.

The girls would mind Flame's stall while she told fortunes, the scarves wafting softly about them, whatever the weather.

She knew the market life alright. No surprises there. Yet she shrank from the idea of repeating her mother's life, particularly the drifting. In the longer term, Stella wanted some certainty. Security. But not Damian's kind of security. All about him.

Ruben's voice brought Stella back to the present, the bustle of the mall, the sparkle of her jewels, another few customers inspecting her glittering wares.

"You can ask me anything, Stella Rhys of Stellar," Ruben said, adding her to his contacts, scrolling through his phone and clicking on things. "You need to follow me. Facebook, Twitter, Insta. Whoa! Just topped 26k followers on Insta! They're gonna love Stellar. Insta's really starting to pay. I'm loving this social gig. Started off in print, but print's shrinking, you know. Didn't take much to expand to podcasts and vodcasts. Like my tagline? 'Ruben Slavonicus, multimedia influencer.' You might even want to pay me for a post some time. Doesn't actually cost that much. I've got clients. Clothing, mainly. Fitness industry. Bit of food and beverage. I'm still a reporter at heart. I only post stuff I would have posted anyway. No fake news for me. That would be shooting myself in the foot. My followers trust me."

"Sure I'll keep it in mind," said Stella. "So good to meet you! Thanks again for the free plug. Amazing! And you really do know a lot."

"That's my job. Righto. I'm off. Better file this 'jewelry wars' story. Great move, by the way, snaffling that Antoinette's attention like that. Worth PR thousands. Huntleys won't be happy, but what can you do? It's a free country, right? Better get going. Got a couple more stories on my plate. New principal at one of the schools and a big council meeting tonight. See you."

"'Jewelry wars'?" Stella snapped her head around, finally giving him her full attention.

"Yeah. Good one, eh? Bit of an exaggeration, maybe, but that's why they pay me. I keep things interesting. See you."

And he was gone, working his way back down the plaza on the hunt for more stories.

Neither Stella nor Ruben noticed they were being watched. From the third floor of Huntleys, James glanced down. He'd been helping clear away some of the empty champagne bottles and glasses, stacking them in the little staff kitchen on the side. There'd been a few old customers and some of the younger ones, Ruben and a fraction of the other media they'd invited. The turnout wasn't as large as they'd hoped, even with Antoinette as the drawcard. Still. Events were like that. You never knew what would happen.

He'd often looked out this window at the weather, at a passing seagull or a lost balloon drifting into the sky past the towering new apartments, but rarely did he peer straight down like this, right into the mall.

He rested his hand on the window sill, tension tightening his grip. From here he could see exactly how their PR stunt went wrong. That new stall was in exactly the wrong place, smack bang in the path of the movie star. No wonder Antoinette stopped and took a look. She could barely have avoided it.

Even from here, the bright new stall was attractive, sparkling in the spring sunshine. *What did she call herself?* Stella? She was still busy.

And there was Ruben, James noticed, moving closer to the window. That man's whole life was a newsreel. He was glad he'd turned up to interview Antoinette, like he'd said he would. That was something. Nicole would be pleased.

A bright bird flashed across the window, shrieking, then clung to the edge of the gutter, green tail feathers teetering. It squeezed itself into a

41

hole in the eaves. *Must remember to mention it to Jim*. The building was falling apart.

Chapter 5

Sunlight flashed off Huntleys' ornate door handles as they swung open. Out came Nicole in her mustard suit. She stared straight across at Stella, displeased, openly hostile. Stella recognized fury when she saw it. Nicole practically snarled.

Stella caught her breath as James emerged from behind Nicole, immaculately dressed in that perfect suit, carrying a big, black briefcase. Inscrutable. Those blue eyes. No smile for her this time. Not at all. They locked gazes, both lifting their chins, defiant. Well, if there was to be a challenge, she'd be up for it. This was the new Stella. She was immune to handsome men, men like James. Men like Damian. Besides, she'd done nothing wrong.

The couple disappeared around the corner, Nicole holding James's arm tightly with one hand as she minced along in those high heels; and pointing her phone at Stella with the other, turning her head back to nod at Stella's stall. Stella had the distinct impression Nicole was talking about her, and that the comment wasn't pleasant. Who was Nicole, anyway? A supplier? An employee? Maybe James's partner. They seemed pretty familiar with one another, unusually close for a boss and an employee, not that Stella had any great interest in James and his relationships. Why should she?

Surely they couldn't think she'd deliberately snaffled Antoinette's attention. And what could they possibly have against her? She wasn't even competition. Her jewelry cost a fraction of the prices they'd be charging. They wouldn't even attract the same customers, would they?

Huntleys was old money, old world, so Ruben said. Top line. They'd done very little to make their store welcoming for everyone - well, apart from their expensive publicity stunt - so why should they give her a hard time?

They could do with making their wares more obvious for window shoppers. Why didn't they even have windows on the mall level? Were they worried that they'd be smashed and their jewels stolen? Or were they just marketing to the rich and famous? Was this a Sydney snob value thing? Did only certain people with a lot to spend venture inside?

The mall dragged her attention away from the mysterious Huntleys. There was the constant sound of traffic trundling along the cross street, and the passing parade of potential and actual customers. It was a fantastic meeting place, a brilliant location for her stall. Here were people of all ages and backgrounds. Some in a hurry, and others with all day to wander and browse, with or without a coffee, some with strollers and shopping bags of every kind.

It was thirsty work, selling jewelry. Stella couldn't believe her early good fortune.

In the wake of the excitement of Antoinette's appearance, the crowd was still primed to buy, and her stall was perfectly placed, all her goods celebrity endorsed. The new earrings almost sold out, along with everything else emerald green - the rosette chokers, brooches and rings. Everyone wanted a memento of the moment, their own *Heist* souvenir. She couldn't have planned it better if she'd tried.

Flat out trading, she'd had no time to glance across to Huntleys again, nor even to wonder where the celebrity who'd blessed her stall with a touch of magic had gone.

Once school was out she even attracted a few browsers in their uniforms as they headed for the buses and trains. Two were meeting behind the little trees, having a flirt and trying out cigarettes, thinking they were invisible.

It was 4pm before the crowd thinned. By the time she looked up again, the red carpet had disappeared. Her stomach rumbled, her throat was parched - Fritz's gift of a drink long gone - and her fingers fumbled with exhaustion.

So many sales! Elation and adrenaline kept her on her toes, trading faster than she ever dreamed possible, but now, she was tired. Worse, she needed to find a toilet.

Glancing up and down the mall to ensure no other customers were heading her way, Stella stacked her trays into her wheelie bag. Matt had been so helpful. His clever solar panel and ritzy LED-lined letters proclaimed her business name on both sides, *Stellar*, winking and blinking even in daylight.

She slipped her smart card reader into the bag with her cash takings, looped it over her shoulder and waved across at Fritz at the next stall, who gestured at his lineup of refrigerated bottles. When she nodded at the lemonade, Fritz had the top off and hissing before she got there.

A man of few words, Fritz was a stalwart of the mall, who knew its crowds and moods in every season. She'd met him the day she'd arrived, when she'd applied for the permit. Stella felt lucky to be stationed next to him. She held her hand to the wiggling nose of his old dog, Rex, who allowed her to pat his head, then dropped his greying snout back on his paws to snooze again.

"*Heist*, yah?" He winked at her and gave her a thumbs up, then stood and offered her his stool. She couldn't be more grateful, sinking onto it like a deflated balloon.

"It wasn't deliberate, Fritz. It all just happened. I'm practically out of stock. I'll be busy all night bringing out replacements and giving them a good polish, ready to sell."

"This is good, yah. First day." Fritz also benefited from the media moments, drawing in five times his usual custom, he said.

"Couldn't be better. Honestly, I had no idea. None at all." Fritz's cold drink was delicious. The problem was, she needed a toilet. Quickly. When she asked Fritz, he pointed at Huntleys.

She raised her eyebrows. Surely not. Maybe Fritz hadn't seen the altercation with James, that withering stare he'd given her after she'd stolen his media moment, and Nicole's hostile gestures. Stella hadn't planned to steal their show, but that's what had happened. Yes. "Jewelry wars." Ruben Slavonicus had summed it up perfectly, unfortunately.

"Third floor," he nodded.

Recalling James's icy glare, she frowned.

"Really?"

"Closest restroom," he nodded again.

Stella knew her other option was two blocks away, at the railway station. It was one of the reasons she could afford her location, at this end of the mall, far from such services.

Could she bear to face James's hostility? *Of course. This new Stella was strong*, she told herself. She was perfectly innocent, after all. She had every right to visit the famous jewelers, didn't she? Didn't all retailers want potential customers? "Footfall?" In fact, hadn't James just gone to great lengths to attract customers? He must have paid a small fortune for Antoinette's appearance.

But her resolve wavered. Who was she kidding, thinking she could afford the kind of jewelry sold in Huntleys? The place reeked of wealth and power. Then again, her bag was bulging with cash and the card purchases had been even more lucrative. Maybe she was in the market for a diamond necklace after all, she realized with a burst of excitement. Sure, it wasn't her real motive for entering those "you wish" doors, but it wasn't a bad cover.

Stella stood and pushed back her shoulders, resolved. Fritz had already offered to keep an eye on her stall and takings, and she told him she'd gladly do the same for him in return. Anticipating the rush of energy from the drink to replenish her strength, she ran her tired fingers through her hair, then headed towards the Huntleys' grand doors, adding her empty bottle to the recycling bin with a clunk on the way.

The heavy doors were intimidating. She placed her hand on one ornate brass handle, then hesitated. Turned. From here, her stall was so much smaller. Yes, the lit sign was bright and bold, but it was such a tiny venture, whimsical, more of a hope than an establishment. Too bad. This was what she was doing now. *Damian, be damned!* Making jewelry was her real passion, and she'd finally unleashed it.

Her sign flashed out in the sunshine, up in lights, solar powered and powerful.

Stellar. Dazzling. Excellent.

From here, though, she couldn't help reconsidering her extraordinary morning. Hers was a standard stall, metal framed with canvas skirting, easily moved. Together, she and James could have pushed it along a bit, then brought it back, after Huntley's stunt. Stella bit the side of her bottom lip. She had to admit she felt a tiny speck of shame at her reluctance to cooperate. Then again, what did she owe James?

I'm tired of simply complying with men and trying to please them just because they always expect it. Damian spoilt all of that. For good. I'm never going there again, demeaning myself for nothing, for years. Forget it.

Now, sheer urgency forced her to find that toilet.

When she pulled open the grand Huntleys door with its big, cold brass handle, she entered another world, a world of glowing wood, glass and gleaming brass. It was cool in there and dark, despite the shiny white marble floors. Behind more glass doors there was a gleam of old wooden and glass cabinets where she glimpsed jewels nestled in plush velvet.

With her stall waiting outside, browsing through the Huntley jewels would have to wait for another day. For all the pomp and hefty prices, the

Huntleys offerings were probably not so different to her own, she reasoned - enticing trays of baubles to embellish people's bodies.

She inhaled the faint smell of brasso and timber polish. Just being in this building, her hope for her own venture soared. If the Huntleys could trade for three generations, surely she could make it through the summer. Six months. That was the plan. Learn all she could about customers and trade, and build her online business, doing what she loved. What a start she was already making!

She headed straight for the grand old elevator, pressing the polished brass button with anticipation. It was so quiet in Huntleys, away from the bustle of the traffic and busy mall. A hush of air conditioning added to the atmosphere of comfort, subtle and expensive.

As she waited for the ancient elevator to rumble its way up from the basement, she smoothed her hands on her simple dress, anticipating the joy of washing them in a proper sink after handling all that cash. She was sticky from her hours of trade - couldn't wait to freshen up to see how evening trade might turn out. She would stay till 7pm and catch the office crowd as they set off home, maybe even make some sales to people going out for dinner. She let her face relax. She'd been smiling with customers, helping them with their choices, enjoying their delight in her products, thrilled there'd been so much interest.

But now, no longer flat out dealing with the public, she noticed her muscles were aching. Elation had pulled her through, hour after busy hour, but now she was plain tired.

When the elevator doors finally opened, there was already someone inside - tall. It was that pale grey suit again, right there in front of her. James. He must have come back in again through a back door, or when she'd been busy with her customers. *Awkward.* Worse, the interior of the thing was fitted on all sides with bevelled mirrors. There were dozens of grey-suited men. Everywhere she looked, James stared back, scrutinizing her.

Well, so what? She lifted her chin and pulled back her shoulders, defiant. She had every right to be here, and nothing to hide.

He was studying her every detail, from her windswept hair to her flat leather sandals. With all those mirrors, her skin prickled as he took in her ankles, the compact shape of her, her hips and waist, the soft pull of the bodice of her cotton dress, the set of her neck and shoulders, straight, unyielding, even the beat of her pulse at her throat.

Two can play this game, she thought, as the elevator rose, oh so slowly. They were trapped inside. Together. Butterflies surged in her stomach.

She studied his hands, the long fingers, wondered whether he too made jewelry, or whether he only sold it. She remembered the lovely warmth of his hand from their handshake this morning. Her eyes sprang to his. Stella couldn't believe their depths of blue. She wanted to decipher all those shifting thoughts.

"Stella," he said. It wasn't a friendly tone. More of an accusation. Possibly even a hiss.

"James," she responded in the same tone, lifting her chin.

"To what do we owe this pleasure?" His voice was deep, mellifluous. In other circumstances she would have enjoyed sparking a longer conversation, just to hear him speak. It was a cultured voice. Well educated. That same half smile.

"Getting to know the neighbors?" she ventured. She didn't want to confess the real reason.

"Really?"

This was way too close to be standing. James was far too attractive. *Dangerous.* She never, ever wanted to make that mistake again, of falling for someone so powerful, however gorgeous he might be.

Not. Going. There. Not noticing at all the slight wave in his hair, and the crinkles at the edges of his eyes, as if he smiled a lot. Nor the way he looked at her. Even so. She hadn't crossed the country to fall right back into some kind of silly love trap again. It wasn't what she needed right

49

now. Far too distracting. She had a business to build, and it was off to a flying start. Why take her eye off the ball, even for an instant?

It was a slow old contraption. It stopped and opened at the next floor though no one was waiting. Here were more rows of glass cabinets, one or two black-clad salespeople, and a section in the corner where an old jeweler with a magnifying glass might be changing a watch battery or making a repair.

Otherwise, it was alarmingly quiet, given there'd been a function there earlier in the day. There was a whiff of ancient carpet and Stella glanced down. Royal blue, but it had clearly seen better days. Near the elevator, it had worn so thin the underlay showed.

As the doors took forever to close, she chanced a glance at James's face in mirrored walls again. It was troubled, as if his thoughts reflect her own observations. Where were his customers?

Traces of worry etched the handsome face, and she felt a pang of empathy for him. Maybe inheriting a business wasn't all it was cracked up to be, as Ruben Slavonicus had been saying. She could hardly bear the worry of employing herself, let alone take responsibility for employing others, week after week, year after year. And what must the upkeep on this place cost? Was James as invincible as he looked, she wondered.

The silence was excruciating. When the elevator doors finally closed again, she was more aware of him than ever, could feel him there, all six feet of him, could smell that expensive cologne. More worrying, he returned her scrutiny in the reflection, taking in her own face, shiny from the heat of the day, her too-bright eyes, intense with lack of sleep from working most of the night polishing and packing stock.

She was exhausted from selling, selling and selling all day. She placed them in her pockets, fingering her phone, wishing she'd taken the stairs, wishing to be anywhere but here.

It was the intensity of his attention, unstinting, yet giving nothing away. Hostile, not at all warm like the charm he'd tried on her this morning. So.

What should she have expected? She'd refused to move her stall for him. Would it have hurt her to be more gracious? Why had she been so stubborn? This was just plain awkward.

When the doors opened on the next floor, he waited like a gentleman for her to step out first. Dignified, she headed straight for the privacy of the Ladies with a sigh of relief.

She entered the quaintly named Ladies Parlour immediately, grateful to Huntleys for providing it. Too bad James now knew her true reason for visiting his establishment. So be it.

Here, too, the age of the place was evident. There was one small sink and an ancient tap and the mirror was mottled with age. She'd imagined something grander. Did James ever notice how shabby it looked? Even the old chaise lounge was worn, long due for a re-cover. Not quite "shabby chic"- more forlorn. Despite the former grandeur of this original powder room, it could definitely do with an overhaul.

So could she. She frowned at her reflection, pushing her dark waves into place again, and splashing water onto her tired face. The water was refreshing. She ran it over her wrists and then held it in her palms, pressing her eyes again for a few moments with her fingertips, then drying her hands on her dress.

Relieved and reinvigorated, she stepped out, peering around at the third floor offerings, the VIP room, smaller than she would have imagined, but still with the grace and style of a respected establishment, if a little faded. Behind an old ornate screen there were some smaller rooms, perhaps an office and storerooms.

Inside the VIP room, large windows on two sides were flanked by velvet curtains, and there was gilded fretwork and a large chandelier reflected in the other two walls, hung with two enormous, gold-framed mirrors. Two pull-up banners featured the Huntley's brand in gold copperplate, showcasing exquisite rings against a ruffled purple velvet backdrop. There was still the faint scent of expensive perfume and champagne.

Not keen for another episode in the lift, she headed for a staircase in the far corner, hesitating as she passed some black and white photographs. In one, a man in a hat with round framed glasses and a big coat had been captured stepping out of the Huntleys doors, head high. The picture must have been taken in the 1950s, from the woman beside him, with her cinched waist, wide skirts, hat and white gloves. One hand was tucked into his arm like it belonged. There was the edge of a tram in the foreground, not far from her stall's position.

In the next photo, the women wore suits with big lapels and shoulder pads. The cars were boxy. 1980s? A tall man, also with glasses, was waving out of the brass-framed doorway. He looked confident, happy, a man on a mission. How many people had passed Huntleys threshold since then? What dreams had this man had? Was success easy back then? It was another world. She had to get back to her own - to make her own dreams come true.

Fritz saw Stella coming and handed over her bag of takings. She was grateful. He'd made her feel welcome since the moment she'd arrived; exclaimed over the quality of her work and wished her luck. He'd been glad to share his knowledge of the mall and its people with her.

"Thank you, Fritz! Nearly 5 o'clock already!"

She headed back to her stall to try the evening rush.

As she refilled the trays of goods from her spare supplies, the doors of Huntleys opened again. There they stood, James, so handsome and Nicole a bit awkward, her lips pursed, staring at her with clear, cold contempt.

Stella straightened and met their gaze, rapidly running through some options in her head. How would she handle this? She was ready to apologize, now that she understood why James had needed her to move.

She gave them both her widest smile.

"Good evening," she called out, waving to them both. She hadn't deliberately planned to sabotage their event. She had nothing to hide from them and nothing to fear, not really. She had her licence, and a great product. Antoinette's endorsement had proved it.

Nicole merely sneered. James nodded back at her, catching her eye. He really was good looking, damn him. Well, she knew all about good looking men, and she was perfectly immune. Damian had seen to that.

Thank goodness she'd woken up to all of Damian's deceptions in time to salvage something brilliant - her own business, Stellar.

Nicole, far too haughty to smile back, turned to James. For a moment, he'd looked like he might have even been about to come across and talk to her, but Nicole had taken hold of his arm, possessively. She was clearly asking him something, keeping his attention.

James frowned as if Nicole were an irritation. Stella looked away. Their relationship was no business of hers, though she hated friction. There'd been enough of it in her childhood, slowly mounting before their little family would move on once more, minus the latest man.

Stella closed her eyes and clenched her fists, a habit from childhood. It reminded her she had control over the space between her hands, if nothing else.

Opening her eyes again, she took in the work in hand, her need to refill the velvet tray in front of her, now that more than half of her pendants were gone. Spinning on one heel, she turned her back on both of them, stooped and grabbed a handful of brooches to replenish her display tray. Let them think what they liked. She had work to do.

Chapter 6

Stella was checking her supplies, mentally calculating which additional goods she must polish that night to restock, when she heard a voice behind her - her first customer of the evening.

"One moment, please. Can I help you?" She straightened, smiled and turned; straight into the interested gaze of James, who was fingering some drop earrings. His was a fine hand, a cultured one, a hand accustomed to dealing in precious jewels. He turned one of her Antoinette earrings in those practised fingers, examining it carefully, assessing its construction and proportions as professionally as if it were one of his own. He seemed to like what he saw. Very much. Why did his gesture suddenly feel so personal?

Without thinking, Stella reached up to her own earlobe, to touch the faux jewels she'd placed there this morning, wanting to showcase her wares.

His eyes snapped to her fingers and wrist, curiously intimate. *Exciting.*

The slight smile on his lips was deeply interested, discerning. Appreciative, not just of her jewelry, but of her. She drew in a breath and bit her lower lip. His gaze was way too intense, far more than the detached interest of a customer or competitor. Why did it feel as if he were touching her?

"These are good, very good," he said, igniting her with his blue eyes, scrutinizing those ruby red droplets as they swung at the edge of her jaw. She swallowed.

In the darkening evening, her solar-powered sign blazed. When she glanced in one of her customer mirrors, she saw her earrings catching the lights from her sign and reflecting, red, at her throat.

At this proximity, Stella could see James's own jaw, the faintest shadow of beard. She chanced a glance at his lips, imagining, despite herself, how it might be... It was undeniable. There was a warmth about him despite his formality, despite everything. She wanted to step even closer. He was...

"Beautiful. Truly beautiful," he announced. "I see a lot of jewelry, you understand." Authoritative. Not patronising. It was a true compliment. Astounding. Flattering.

"Yes, well..." Shouldn't she have been on her guard? Flattery from handsome men made her wary.

"I'm not just saying it. Did you design these?"

"I make everything myself."

"$50 a pair, you say? No wonder these're selling. You're giving them away at that price. You'll go broke."

"I don't intend to." She took a step back. Was he insulting her? She lifted her chin and stared at him.

"None of us do," he said, shaking his head, contemplating her. Was he bitter?

"Here." He pulled out a wad of notes from his suit pocket. "I'll have one of everything, please."

"You don't owe me anything, James. I'm not a charity."

"Nor am I. In fact, I rather think you owe me something, don't you?"

She turned away from him, busying herself with change. A purchase was a formal transaction after all.

Turning to him again, she stood tall.

"If you mean I planned the whole Antoinette Lacy thing, I'm pleased to tell you I had absolutely no idea Antoinette would come here today. None at all. And, can I help it that she happened to like my earrings, James?"

At the sound of his name, he pinned her again with his eyes. She stared right back, innocent. Why should he be so astonished that a jewelry business so close to his own should be trading so successfully? His own customers might operate in the stratosphere, with spending power many multiples higher than that of her own, but everyone was entitled to buy jewelry if they wished, whatever their budget.

What was it about his eyes that so fascinated her? Was everyone so mesmerized by their intensity? Deep water. Shifting thoughts.

Despite her determination to avoid this man, she found herself smiling. That did it. It snapped the spell. He gave her a tight little smile back. Was James shy?

"No, don't worry about wrapping them, thank you," he said, looking away from her. "I have to get along."

She handed over his purchases. The joy in his expression was astonishing, light years away from the ponderous mood she'd seen earlier in the day as he'd readied himself for Antoinette's arrival, so concerned about her stall being in the way, and the heavy way he'd carried himself as the famous star broke the script and helped herself to Stella's earrings; not to mention the sombre atmosphere in the elevator.

She studied his tall frame as he departed, a spring in his step. She could swear he was almost whistling as he sauntered away around the corner where Nicole had disappeared 10 minutes earlier.

"Get along." Such an old fashioned expression. Stella shook her head, puzzled. Her smile widened as five more people approached her stall, reaching for their wallets and purses. The Antoinette magic continued!

It was 8pm before Stella reached her sister's townhouse, a barbequed chicken in one hand and her bag full of cash and the EFTPOS reader nestled in her other arm. Her stomach growled, and she couldn't wait to sit down.

"Champagne?" Matt offered. "Your first day of trade was a triumph from what I hear."

That was Matt. Totally supportive. How he could let her move in and take over his workbench in the garage as well as the spare room without one word of protest still amazed her.

"You guys have some, please. Have my helping. I'll fall asleep. And I absolutely need to work tonight. Maybe all night. You can't believe how much I've sold."

"I can," he said, pouring one for Jeannie and one for himself and grabbing Stella a sparkling mineral water. "It's all over social media. She's got me following you, too. Everyone's wearing the Antoinette earrings, Stella. You're a genius!"

"Total first day luck for me. Not for Huntleys, though. Matt, Jeannie - I've made an enemy."

Stella flopped down on the couch next to Jeannie, exhausted. "You wouldn't believe it. That James Huntley the Third and his PR side-kick, Nicole. Talk about 'looks could kill.' I truly had no idea. I'm innocent!"

"You can't worry about everything, Stell," said Jeannie. "Have you seen your Facebook page?"

Stella fished out her phone then wished she hadn't.

"No," she groaned. "Message from Damian."

"What? Don't you even look at that. Give that to me. You need to block that man. Cheers!"

"How are the girls? How was your day?"

"Shhhhh. Only just got them to sleep. To Stellar!"

They swapped stories as they ate. Jeannie'd spent the day at a three-year-old's birthday party. Stella smiled and relaxed for a moment, banishing all thoughts of the mall for a while. Stock. That was what she must focus on tonight.

"And you should have seen Lucy's face!"

Jeannie grabbed her phone and flicked to her photos, showing her eldest daughter with chocolate icing all over her chubby cheeks.

"That's revolting, Jeannie!"

"Isn't it! And she still wanted more!"

"Too much of a good thing."

"What about Sienna?"

"Still has sore gums. You'd think all her teeth were coming up at once the way she's grizzling. I only just got her off to sleep when you turned up."

"My stall's right near a chemist, Jeannie. Let me pick up some more of those chewy things you can put in the freezer. I'll grab some tomorrow."

"You're a great aunty, Stell. I don't remember Lucy having so much trouble teething. Can't wait to show you your website. Matt reckons it's one of my better efforts, don't you dear."

The Matt and Jeannie team. They always made Stella smile. Radiant. Generous. Matt was a catch for her big sister alright - a farm boy living in a share house in Ryde while he did his electrical apprenticeship. They'd clicked the first night she'd moved in as a new student at Macquarie University. He'd ended up working on power saving technology, and had just been promoted to Australian Pacific manager of Reduxen. Even though he was away half the time, the couple had never looked back. Their happiness was like sunshine.

Sales were going well internationally. He'd flown back that morning from New Zealand where he'd signed up two new clients.

"Everyone's getting into it," he said. "It's not like I have to convince them. Energy efficiency's just common sense."

It was great to take the weight off her feet and totally relax, but she started to yawn. "Look at the time! I need to polish stock for tomorrow!"

Thank goodness Stella made so much stock before she'd left Perth. Once she'd made up her mind to leave Exos, she'd gone straight out and invested in as much silver wire and other materials as she could find. Gone were the days when she'd made things from offcuts of electrical wire and anything else she could find. With her savings, she'd been able to flash her card left, right and centre. Once things were going well, she planned to buy her materials in bulk, online, but right then she had to get busy and create enough jewelry to make her dreams come true. By working with silver, she'd be able to charge real money for her creations. Well, $50 for a pair of earrings was "real money" to her, even if it barely registered in James Huntley's budget.

"Gotta spend money to make money," she'd told herself when some of the totals shocked her. She reasoned she'd be adding value big time, earning back more than ten times what she'd paid. If she didn't believe in herself, who else would? Without her Exos wage there was no one to rely on but herself. It had been time to step up, pay up and get busy, and she'd worked day and night, squirrelling away her hand-made treasure for a brighter future.

She was glad she'd been so organized, with all her pieces sorted in portable trolleys.

Back in the living room, with the girls safely snoring in their cots down the corridor, Stella pulled out her jars of silver cleaning fluid and got to work making her creations sparkle, while Jeannie showed Matt and Stella the website she'd created. Jeannie was clever. Just as creative as Stella, in her way. They discussed pricing and online activity.

"You told me to go ahead, and I did. And guess what, Stell! Thirty nine online sales, just today!"

"You're joking!"

"Nup. And another one's just gone through. Oh no! Do we even have enough packaging to ship them in?"

"Unbelievable! Are you sure this is not too much for you to handle, Jeannie?"

Jeannie insisted she loved to help. She told Stella she'd missed using her brain, though she clearly adored staying at home with her girls till they were ready for preschool. She confirmed a few more online sales while Stella packed another tray of the Antoinette earrings, arranging them to catch the eyes of passers by.

Stella made a mental note to create more jump rings as soon as possible and order more findings. Thank goodness she wasn't trading every day of the week.

"What do you think about packaging up an 'Antoinette set' online?" Stella asked, explaining how Ruben Slavonicus had dropped in and accepted the first "set" for his girlfriend.

"Ruben Slavonicus interviewed you? Why didn't you tell us? He might have posted something on you." She searched her Facebook account and caught Stella's attention.

Suddenly, Stella recognized the familiar face of Antoinette Lacy, wearing none other than her own green earrings. And no. Was that herself, red earrings dancing?

"... Stella Rhys staged her own Heist, attracting the star's attention with her faux jewelry street stall."

There was leggy Antoinette, all teeth and bright green dangling earrings, and there was she, Stella herself, looking busy, slightly annoyed even, curious, trying to gauge what the reporter was saying. Now she was happier, and talking.

"I've always loved jewelry. Doesn't everyone? It's just a bit of fun, to brighten up your day or spice up the night. A bit of a novelty, you know. So we're not always 'same old, same old.' It makes us feel fresh. A bit of sparkle never goes astray. Jewelry makes people happy."

Ruben Slavonicus had crossed back to himself. She remembered it all now. What a day!

"Well, Stella Rhys has certainly given her own Stellar performance with her new Oxford Street Mall business. She's made Antoinette Lacy happy, and stock is selling fast. This is roving reporter Ruben Slavonicus, multimedia influencer."

"Amazing, Stell! You know Ruben used to work for a major newspaper chain. I think he has quite a few followers. No wonder everyone's ordering your stuff online. I'm going to retweet and like this everywhere right now. Wow. So many orders! They must have run that story in their earlier bulletin. Better brace ourselves. You are amazing, little sister. Incredible. Remember how I used to get you to do my school projects? Remember that volcano with the frothing lava, and the rocket. That thing was like a dolls' house inside, with the astronauts hanging upside down? I got an A+ for that one. And now on your very first day of business, look at your success. Anything you turn your mind to just works somehow."

"'Somehow' nothing! Damian and Exos didn't exactly work out for me. Look, Jeannie, none of this would be happening if you and Matt hadn't opened up your home to me, and you know as well as I do that nothing was falling into place while I thought I was in love with that wretched Damian. You and Matt made this possible for me. This is your doing, Jeannie."

Stella stopped for a moment and rested her weary hands. As she looked across at her sister, who was doing something with the back end of the website, a rush of gratitude came over her. Jeannie was more of a mother to her than Flame, always encouraging her.

Flame was big on sayings and short on action.

"You must always do what you love, my girls." Flame told them both more than once. It was certainly a motto Flame lived by. The only problem was that Flame loved many things. Too many things. Her loves were ever changing. Not Jeannie. Jeannie was steadfast. She always had her back. In the playground, in the camping ground between rental homes, and now, even here, though both of them were adults.

"I can't tell you how grateful I am to you and Matt, Jeannie."

"Stell!"

"No, hear me out. Damian was a mistake. I don't understand why I didn't just walk out sooner. I should have listened to you, Jeannie, but I wanted what you and Matt had so badly. I kept thinking Damian understood, that he really loved me…"

Jeannie turned from the computer screen and smiled back into Stella's eyes.

"You were due for a break. You just had some bad luck early on. All that's changing now."

"But look at you, Jeannie. You've been busy with both girls all day. You must be exhausted. And yet here you are, still slaving away for me, helping me when you should be getting some rest."

"We'll both get some rest soon. And I'm only too happy to see you succeed, Stella. You're so brilliant. You've always had that creative flair. I like making things, but I don't need to design them. You've always been the one with the bright ideas."

"But I'm not even paying you two rent."

"It's fine," said Jeannie. "You've promised me a share in the online profits. How generous is that! No. Let's get this business of yours going, and then we'll reassess."

Stella looked at Matt. He opened his palms, taking in their cosy townhouse.

"My wife's happy. I'm happy." And he laughed that great big laugh that made everyone laugh along.

Stella returned to her work. It would be Jeannie's birthday soon. How she'd love to surprise her - to buy her something really special, something of lasting value - a treasure that would always remind her how much Stella appreciated the love and support she'd lavished upon her all their lives. She made a commitment then and there. She would do it. Buy her something phenomenal.

Chapter 7

Next morning, Lucy toddled back and forth, chatting in her own language, bringing Sienna a steady selection of toys as she lay on her play mat chewing on whatever she could find. Stella loved this warm family time, before the working day began in earnest.

Four days a week, Stella disappeared to the garage for long hours to make and pack stock, but at this time of day, Jeannie was always glad Stella could help keep an eye on the girls while she checked her emails and social media on the big computer on the kitchen bench.

Suddenly, Jeannie's face fell.

"Sorry, Stell. There's good news and bad news."

Stella sipped the hot tea as she dragged a brush through her hair.

"Okay, out with it."

"The good news is your fan club keeps growing. There are another couple of hundred Facebook followers, and - see this! Another 26 online orders! Seriously? Must be Ruben's magic post. He already had a huge following, and his hashtags must have picked up a lot of Antoinette's followers."

"And the bad news?"

"Huntleys are fighting back. Take a look at this."

First there was Jeannie's post on Stella's behalf, linked to Ruben's story.

Great to meet Ruben Slavonicus out and about in Bondi Junction! Thanks for stopping by at Stellar, Ruben!

The post had 24 "likes." And then there was a comment from Huntleys: *All that glitters is not gold, except at Huntleys, where the diamonds last forever.*

"I don't even know why they bother," Stella said, shaking her head and furrowing her brow, puzzled. "Have you seen their stuff? Their least expensive item would retail at 10 times what I'm asking. I don't understand how they can even treat me like competition! My customers are completely different. My jewelry is affordable. Too affordable, so James tried to tell me. He reckons I'll go broke."

"It's okay. I've commented back." Pleased with herself, Jeannie took another big swig of tea.

"What?"

...because no one ever goes in there to buy them.

"Jeannie! That's just rude! You've made it sound like I'm saying that! Don't you think there's enough bad blood between us already with the Antoinette mix up, without you getting in there and stirring up things even more? Can you delete that comment? Please? It's just not necessary."

"They asked for it. What business do they have telling you what to do? All you're doing is running your business. Besides, it's the truth. You told me so yourself."

"Yeah, but that was just chit chat. Confidential. Not to be broadcast to the world. If I was a Huntley I'd be furious. We're in for it now."

"Nonsense. Controversies like this are great for both businesses. Gets people talking. Why would I delete it? It's got 18 'likes' already. No. Make that 21. And only one frowny face. From a 'Nicole.' Don't know what you'd do without me!"

At half past ten on Jeannie's orange kitchen clock, there was no more time for discussion. Stella ran her eye over the extra stock she'd put aside on the bench, ready for Jeannie to package and post from the online sales, then pulled up the handle of her wheelie bag, ready to haul it to the bus stop.

Part of her was bone tired, and the other part, elated. Stellar was flying. Maybe she'd have another sellout day.

Jeannie shoved a peanut butter sandwich and recycled water bottle her way and gave her a pat on the shoulder and kiss on the cheek. "Go get 'em."

…

Nicole gave Stella the ice queen treatment as she breezed past. No wonder she wouldn't nod and say hello, after Jeannie's social media dig. Too bad.

New leaves on the edge of the street tree glowed bright green in the late morning bustle. A couple of noisy lorikeets were thrashing about in the highest branches of a bottlebrush, feasting on the first feathery red flowers of the summer. When a bit of bloom and three narrow leaves fell down on her she had the idea for some new summer earrings, Australiana.

She pulled out her sketchbook and was capturing the shape of the leaves and flowers when, from the corner of her eye, she noticed an old lady in a black coat walk slowly towards her, bow legs encased in thick black stockings. She was bent with arthritis.

Arriving at Stella's stall, she hovered for a long time, silent, looking without touching. Stella laid down her pencil and gave the woman an encouraging smile.

"I'm Stella. Can I help you?"

The woman nodded and opened her black bag, rummaging inside and pulling out a man's handkerchief, faded with decades of washing. She held it reverently in both hands for a moment, before handing it over.

The bundle was soft as a whisper and warm from the old woman's hands. Something heavy and hard was wrapped deep inside the folds.

"May I?" Stella asked. At the woman's nod, Stella lay the soft material carefully on the bench near where she wrapped her own goods, once sold. In a reverse process, she unfolded the handkerchief, revealing a gleaming rose gold locket on a golden chain, somewhat worse for wear. Several of the links had worn through, and the chain was in pieces.

"This is very beautiful, very precious," Stella said, and the woman nodded. "This broken chain... You need it fixed. Is that why you've brought it to me?"

Again the woman nodded, holding up her arthritic hands in a shrug. "You make things. You fix for me?"

"I'm sorry. I can't do serious repairs. Not on something of this quality. Well, I could fix it, but it's so very special it needs to be repaired properly. You need a goldsmith."

The woman's face fell. Stella hated to disappoint her. Maybe she was still feeling guilty about Jeannie's Facebook jibe, or maybe it was the original Huntleys post about quality which gave her the idea, but she saw a way to make amends.

"Maybe you could take it into Huntleys, just here. I think they do repairs, on the second floor."

The woman stared at Huntleys, at the heavy doors and imposing facade. She was so small and frail and old and uncertain, Stella doubted she'd be tempted to make her way across to the entrance, let alone go inside.

"I've been in there," Stella said. "I was in there yesterday, in fact."

The woman held back, timid.

"Look," Stella said. "How about I come in with you? Would that help?"

The woman smiled, showing a cracked tooth, her face creasing, eyes shining.

"Just give me a minute or two." Stella wrapped the locket and chain carefully back in the handkerchief once more and handed it back to the woman.

While she nestled it back inside her black bag, Stella stacked her jewelry into her roller bag and hooked up her glittering clock signs on two sides: "Back in 10 minutes."

"Ready?" Smiling, she offered the woman her arm, and together they headed for Huntleys.

As she swung open the heavy door and held it for the woman to enter, the faint odour of brasso and expensive perfume ushered them further inside. The door closed behind them, shutting out the noise of the traffic and busy chatter of the mall.

Stella's heart picked up its pace, remembering her brush with James and Nicole's hostility, but she focused on the woman and her needs as she summoned the elevator. She couldn't allow negativity to spoil her venture. Six months. That was all she needed to prove to herself she could make a go of it and carry out her plan to use her talents to create a different life to Flame's. She would ensure she graduated from her stall and progress into something more substantial, into serious retail, online or in store. Prove she had a popular product. Make her name as a designer. Find funding for bigger dreams, expanding those online sales, or selling lines into established jewelers and upmarket department stores.

Now, where exactly had she seen the repairs section? Second floor? Sure enough, when the elevator doors opened, there was a salesperson slowly dusting and polishing the tops of the glass cabinets, and, behind her, in the corner, a long wooden counter.

Stella was fascinated. As they slowly made their way across, with the old lady's hand tucked into the crook of her arm, Stella was dazzled by the jewels she saw - chains of every length and variety, in gold and silver; bangles and bracelets, with and without gemstones; lustrous pearls - stud and clip-on earrings of every size, single pearl drops, symmetrical and baroque; and a whole display of sparkling pendants featuring jewels of every kind - birthstones, perhaps. Her designing mind jangled with new ideas. She could hardly wait to get back to her sketchbook and capture them.

She was so caught up in the wares, she barely noticed she was being studied just as carefully. In a long mirror on the back wall, she caught the

67

attention of an old man wearing a visor. Gold framed glasses magnified his blue eyes.

He'd been sitting on a tall stool, working on something, and he swivelled to the front as she and the old woman approached. He wore a denim apron, various tools in the pockets. Stella scanned his workbench, curious and envious in equal measure. Some tools were familiar, but well worn, used for a lifetime, and there were others she'd never seen before. She itched to inspect every item, every last corner of the place.

"I'm Stella," she introduced herself into the silence of the vast floor of sparkling but static jewels. The man's expression was welcoming, genuinely enthusiastic, so she continued to open up.

"I've just popped in with this lady because her necklace is broken. I do make jewelry and fix a few things myself, but not in this league. Really, I don't actually have the skills to repair something so precious. Would you be happy to take a look, please?"

"Of course! Of course. This is exactly what I love to do." He beamed and unrolled a piece of heavy black velvet across the counter. He was patient and intensely interested as they unwrapped the locket and pieces of chain. The old handkerchief was humble beside the majesty of the velvet, but the locket gleamed out at them from another era, glowing with its century of wear, winking across the decades.

The old man hesitated before touching it, as if asking permission. His gnarled fingers took to it as if he'd created it himself; respectful, loving even, cradling it. He raised his eye loupe with one hand to examine the hallmarks.

"Oh, this is a special one. I haven't seen one like this for many years. French. It has the boar's head. Paris, if I'm not mistaken."

The old woman nodded slowly and smiled.

"And this chain... It would have been for a watch originally. Ah. These were made properly. Made to last. 1890s, I would think."

She smiled again. "My husband's father's father's," she said. "A wedding gift."

He peered at the links through the thick lens. "Fourteen carat gold. Yes. I can repair this, though many of the links are very worn and it will take a while. It won't be perfect, not like new, but I can make it safe for you to wear again. When will you need this back?"

"My granddaughter, she's marrying in February."

"Oh yes. That won't be a problem. How long ago were you given it? Do you know any more about it? I would have seen the last one like this, maybe 12 years ago. They're not common, no, but they're memorable. You don't forget a chain like this. You were right to come here, Miss …

"Stella."

"Ah yes. Stella." When he gave her the full force of his eyes, they seemed so familiar she drew in a breath.

"You're…"

"Just call me Jim." He laid the piece down gently on the velvet and extended his hand to be shaken first to the woman, and then to Stella. He was utterly charming. There was no question James was a chip off the old block, and the old block was quality.

Stella could see the woman no longer felt intimidated and would be happy to leave her treasure with Jim. The warmth of the man put them both at ease. It was in such contrast to the formal exterior of the building and Nicole's hostility.

Her mind whirled with the possibilities of this place, and how extraordinary it would be to work with real pearls, real gems and precious metals, as Jim did, with the kinds of materials the pharaohs enjoyed. Not for the first time, she regretted not pursuing an apprenticeship in jewelry.

How she would have loved to stay and talk with Jim, browse properly through this floor of treasures, and learn more from him, but her jewelry wasn't going to sell itself. For once she was reluctant to return to her stall.

She forced herself to keep her mind on the job at hand. She must follow through with her plan. She must test her market, get to know her different kinds of customers, try out the popularity of her designs, gather statistics to prove which designs were selling best, and make her business pay.

If she wasn't careful, she'd flit from one idea to the next like Flame had done throughout her childhood. She didn't want that. She wanted to be fully self supporting, maybe even build a world-class jewelry like Huntleys. Why not? Maybe she had the talent. Did she have the determination? She must find out. She must channel all her efforts into making her stall a success. Everything else was a daydream at best and at worst, a waste of precious time.

"If you don't mind, I'll slip away."

"Please," the old woman nodded. Jim excused her with a warm smile, as if he was genuinely sorry to see her go. Understanding. Fine fellow. James's grandfather, she realized with a rush, banishing the impulse to imagine how James himself might look in 60 years. Ridiculous.

And Stella was out and down the staircase at a run, somewhat furtively, reluctant to run into James again, keen to make her business pay its way.

Half way down the final flight of stairs, just before she reached the foyer, she froze. She knew the set of those shoulders. James emerged from the elevator, slim black briefcase in one hand, busy on his phone.

"Yep, that's better now. What was that again, Scottie? … Ah. Okay…" Suddenly he halted, spun 180 degrees and began to bolt up the stairs.

Three or four steps up, and still listening intently, he only stopped as he was about to run into her, so close she felt the rush of air he'd created, could smell the pure wool of his suit and something else. Aftershave?

Halting mid flight, he narrowed his eyes, as if to say "you again."

Stella blushed from head to toe, though she'd done nothing wrong. Perhaps he thought she'd just been using his facilities again on the third floor. If only he knew.

He backed against the railing to let her pass, polite as always, and she inched down past his scrutiny, every part of her prickling at their proximity.

"Yes," he continued, stepping back to give her space like a gentleman, ostensibly ignoring her. There was certainly no smile as he continued his conversation with "Scottie."

She heard him race on up the marble stairs behind her as she rushed onwards herself, with a belated attempt at dignity, for the exit.

Noise. Movement. Heat. The mall claimed her once again as she ran back to her stall to resume trade, seagulls rising in a flurry of blinding white where they'd gathered beneath her workbench, down where someone had spilt half a bag of chips.

A headdress of swirling pearls suggested itself to her, and she grabbed her sketchpad, rapidly outlining the piece while it was clear in her mind.

Three tourists descended on her as she laid out her trays again. They were asking for Antoinette earrings. Word was continuing to spread. *Excellent*. She pulled out the tray of matching chokers and broaches and placed them near the earrings. Already the tourists were deeply engaged, mixing and matching possibilities.

Upselling, Stella said to herself. Jeannie loved sharing marketing concepts with her. She still wasn't sure what piggyback marketing was, but she loved the name of it.

"It's slightly cheaper per piece if you buy two, and cheaper again for three," she said out loud.

Chapter 8

All papers now compiled and ready in the briefcase, James arrived at Scott & Sons accountants in the city several minutes late, musing on how often he'd taken the grey lift to the 21st floor since inheriting Huntleys a decade ago at the age of 20.

As usual, Mr Scott the elder popped his head out to greet him, shake his hand and clap him on the shoulder. He seemed older this time, and a little stooped.

He liked Mr Scott, had known him since childhood. He remembered all the times he'd cheered him on with his son, Scottie, at the end of their cross country races in high school, when, faces bright red and chests heaving, they'd gulped for air in the final strides at the finishing line, always so closely matched.

Ron Scott had always said he'd been glad to take James under his wing when Jimmy was dying, and it was a great help to James that he'd known the Huntleys' finances backwards, having handled the accounts for decades. It was only natural that he would pass the Huntleys' business to his son to handle once Scottie completed his various accreditations. The boys remained firm friends. Scottie was always in the background if needed, ready to cast his eye over the books and offer advice.

"Going well, young James?"

"Well, that's what I'm here to find out."

"Of course, of course," Ron laughed at their usual greeting, knocking gently then opening the door to his son's office.

"On your own today?" Ron Scott the second, known by all as Scottie, rose from behind his grey desk, as he extended his hand.

"Scottie! Mate! Expecting someone else, are you?"

"Maybe that no-good brother of yours, or …?"

"Nicole's busy, mate." James did a quick scan of his old friend's office. Yep. The wedding picture was nowhere to be seen. A couple of years ago it had occupied pride of place. Now it was a distinct absence, but there was a new abstract painting on the wall behind Scottie, complementing a pot plant in the corner.

"So, how is Beck?" James asked outright.

"Queensland." Scottie stared out the window and drew in a long breath. "Divorce papers've come through."

"Sorry, Scottie."

"Nothing to do with you, mate. Nothing I could do either, as it turns out."

"'cept look after yourself." Scottie had hit the spirits hard for a while there. James had had to refuse his invitations to meet him at various pubs, reasoning that the liquid companionship was doing both of them more harm than good.

"Yeah. The rest's history, I guess. Moving on, now. So, how's Nicole then?"

"Angry," James muttered as he takes a seat. "Hoping you've got some good news for us, no doubt. Well, anyway, your office refit's looking good. Your business is powering, anyway."

"Yeah. Almost always does for accountants. People don't realize that when they run us down. Business good or business bad, there's always work for accountants. That's what my father says and he's right. Too bad it was all too boring for Beck."

"Not your fault, mate. She'll regret it."

"Nup. She's hooked up with some fancy builder from what I see on Facebook, building ritzy estates for retirees up north of Brizzie. Shows herself off next to his racy landcruiser and fancy speedboat pretty regularly. She'll never look back."

"Need to block that quick smart, mate."

Scottie knew James spoke from experience, but he shook his head.

"Nah. Good for me to see her and feel nothing. Lucky escape, I call it. Wouldn't want her back, anyway. Not now. Been too long. Moving on."

"Good to hear. Scottie. Nicole's around. You go for it. But I'm not your wing man. Look where that led last time. You wanna see Nicole, you call her okay?"

Scottie sat a little straighter opposite him.

"So she's free at the moment?"

"I'm not getting involved in this, Scottie. Not even a wink. This is for you to work out, mate."

Scottie definitely seemed happier.

"So what about your own love life, James? No wedding bells?"

"No news there. Gotta get the business back in the black." James tapped the top of the desk. Scottie shook his head and smiled. Since James's fiancee Helene had left him for a stock broker a year or two ago he'd been obsessed with getting Huntleys finances under control and looking up. Fair enough.

"Right-oh, then. On to business."

"Thumbs up or thumbs down?"

"Bit of both, you could say."

"Out with it."

"Well, business is tracking okay. Wouldn't say you're setting any records. But it's not too much lower than last quarter's results. The big problem's still your expenses. Jim's drawing a pittance as usual, but I have to be clear about this. Will and your mother…"

"What about them?"

"All this travel."

"You know my mother. Loves her travel. She's still decorating the Bowral place."

"In France?"

"Loves a good French antique."

"Hmmm. Might wanna see if she's ever coming home, James. Seriously. And what about Will? What's he doing in the US now, month after month after month?"

This time it was James's turn to whistle through his teeth and stare out the window. If it was hard to rein in his mother's spending, saying no to his brother was even more impossible.

"You know Will. Runs his own show."

Scott remembered Will. Sporty. Bit of a rogue. Popular with the girls.

"What's he doing again?"

"Finding new markets. Representing our brand."

"For Huntleys, or for himself?"

"Yeah, I know... Sourcing suppliers. Growing our customer base."

"In the US? Look. Your family's the biggest hole in your budget, James. Everything else is tracking okay. Well, not too badly, anyway."

"Nicole's had a few good ideas, revamping the website, getting celebs involved."

"Clever woman."

James smiled at his old friend.

"Always had a soft spot for our Nicole, didn't you?"

Scottie studied the spreadsheets, shuffled them a bit and handed a couple across.

"So will we say you're still solvent? You're going to talk to Will and your mother?"

"I'll talk to them."

"Frankly, Huntleys can't afford those open-ended expenses any more. You should know better than anyone there's too much competition. Asia, India. Imports. You can't afford it, and you're leaving yourselves wide open to extra tax liabilities. We're advising all of our clients with family businesses about this. You just can't assume every member of the family has the best interests of the business at heart. Gotta limit those personal expenditures. We'd advise offering a cumulative monthly limit, or a small salary increase to offset removal of all expense reimbursement, James. We've had to do it in our own business. Beck abused my account big time, I'm ashamed to admit. It's just a reality. Human nature."

James nodded. It made sense. Scottie was a great accountant. Already he was thinking how to broach it with his mother. Brother Will, though? Another matter entirely.

"Who's hitting it hardest, Scottie?"

"I think you know."

"Will's been in Vegas."

"Yeah." Scottie handed across the spreadsheets and a graph. Will's red expenditure line made an ugly red slash, dragging down the profits.

"Christmas is coming."

"Have to be a good one to offset Will's efforts, even if you halt him right now. Sorry, James. You're too kind to him, but it's gotta stop."

James nodded, grave. Will was a whole other story. If James's life had changed when their father died, and it did, Will's had changed even more. James had been practically an adult. Sure, he'd had to drop out of uni to take on the business, but Will was still at school. True apple of their father's eye, Will could never do anything wrong. His athletic prowess made their father so proud. Will swam, sprinted, hurdled, high-jumped and swaggered around in a perpetual glow of podiums, trophies, representative championships and sporting scholarship opportunities, bound for glory.

While James ran well in cross country, where he and Scottie forged their friendship, representing their school in the State championships, Will had shown true promise, basking in their father's and the school's glory from childhood.

As their father steadily shrank, physically and mentally, far too rapidly, James threw himself into learning about the business. He spent more and more time at his father's bedside, trying to glean the ins and outs of their family's livelihoods.

But when their father could no longer come to his games and carnivals, Will sulked and acted out, taking it all personally. His wins practically ignored for the first time in his life, he'd sought solace in parties, alcohol, drugs and sex, despite his young age. No one pulled him up on it. He had hero status at school, winning brilliant headlines and kudos, and he was almost 18 by the time Jimmy left them for good.

"Look after your family, son," Jimmy told James in those last terrible days of his life, and James was doing so, to the best of his ability. Scottie knew all this. He seemed to be watching James replay it all in his head as they sat and studied the spreadsheets.

"You know it's time, mate. Fix Will, or you'll all go down."

James glanced across at him and nodded slowly, then stood, wrapping up their meeting.

"Easier said than done, no doubt. Look after yourself."

"You too."

And James was out and down the stairs, all 21 flights of them, trying to block the black memories of his father's last days; furious at the futility of his brother's spending sprees; and brainstorming yet again how to tackle Will and his crazy lifestyle for good. It was grim, alright.

He was still brooding as he approached Huntleys, expression black with worry. If his eyes flashed fire at the distraction of Stella's bright stall and its flurry of activity outside his establishment, he was barely conscious of it.

And if Stella unknowingly drew his attention once more, with her dark hair drawn up in an emerald green ribbon in the day's heat, her throat and the delicate skin below her ear so exposed and delectable as he brushed past, a mere metre away from her; if her eyes sought out his, troubled at his scowl, concerned for him, still he stormed past her, wrenching open the doors to his building.

Finance meetings always did this to him. No matter how hard he worked and how smart, Huntleys consumed him and challenged him further. Did everyone's business pose so many problems? He'd have to confront his mother and Will. Sooner. Not later.

Up on the top floor, in the corner of his father's old office, behind the door where he kept coats and spare shirts and ties, he ditched his suit, changed into his board shorts and t-shirt and swapped the polished black leather shoes for runners, checking his watch. Huntleys had its compensations, so close to Bondi Beach.

He was out the door and off again, in the opposite direction, to strip off the runners, burn the soles of his feet in the hot sand, dive into the breakers and dilute his worries in the great wide ocean till he was exhausted and tame again and ready to face the future.

At her makeshift bench at her stall, Stella wrangled red and green beads and wire and spangles - trying out a Christmas brooch design. Fully focused, head down, she suddenly noticed James.

"Surf's up," he said, absentmindedly pushing his towel against the back of his neck.

Fresh and wild, his hair dark and damp, this merman was so different from the man in the grey suit, it took Stella a moment or two to recognize him. She could practically smell the sea and salt on him. She blinked, confused, but she'd know those blue eyes anywhere.

"Bondi," he explained. "The beach?" He waited while she registered, his eyes still dancing with the freedom of floating and diving in the frothy swell.

The man was a complete distraction, devastating up close like this. If James in a suit was eye catching, James the runner and swimmer was a full-on alarm system, flashing lights, bells and whistles. She practically had to close her eyes, block him out of her vision. How on earth could she concentrate on her customers? Maybe that was what he wanted, to distract her out of her mind, and then out of business.

A couple of beads detached themselves from her creation and rolled off the benching, bouncing across the concrete paving. She let them go, still mesmerized by his eyes and interest. She was speechless. Felt like an idiot.

"'Faux's still selling well, I see!" he tried again. He didn't seem hot and bothered, the way she was feeling. Did he even know what it was like to have to smile for customers even when you were exhausted? Stella was still puzzled. Was it an insult? She nodded warily.

"Getting ready for Christmas?" he asked, still trying to elicit a response, wondering a bit at himself. He didn't usually bother with small talk.

He gestured at her stall and she realized she still hadn't said a thing, fixated on the fine shape of his wrist so as not to stare at the rest of him.

"Pretty impressive all your work's original," he said. "You ought to think about using more valuable materials, getting a better return for your labour."

"Mmmmm."

"Come with me some time," he said. "Come swimming with me. Does you the power of good."

That smile. It seemed so genuine. She had no defences against this man.

"Yes. Bondi," she stuttered. "We went there with my nieces when I first arrived, a month or so ago."

"You're not from around here, are you?"

"Perth."

"So that's why I'd never seen you before!"

She nodded.

Huntleys door swung open and there was Nicole, this time in lime green. She scowled across at James, furious.

"Great for a quick break. Does wonders. See you."

And he was gone, swallowed up by Huntleys and Nicole. It took her more than a couple of minutes to settle down. She stooped and retrieved the escaped beads and tried to focus again on her work.

Chapter 9

That afternoon, Stella took an early mark. So far, Thursday evenings were quiet. She was better off taking a breather.

Back at the townhouse, Lucy greeted her with joy. She ran down the hall and returned, clutching a large envelope.

"Parsooo. Parsoo!"

"Parcel, Lucy. Thank you!"

She hoisted little Lucy onto her hip, planted a kiss on her chubby cheek and placed the envelope on the high window ledge in her room, above the ironing board.

Then they went together to the bathroom basin and lathered up the cake of soap for some serious handwashing, Lucy squealing with delight when the soap shot away and into the bath.

"Come on, let's wash this off, Lucy," Stella said, marvelling at the chubbiness of Lucy's fingers. "All clean."

"Aw keen."

"Very clean, Lucy. How about you go show mummy how clean your hands are!"

As Lucy toddled off, Stella closed her door, sat on the bed and opened the envelope. Inside was an official letter from Exos, several bills and a cheery card featuring a cat and orange geranium in a pot, both soaking up sunshine.

Dear Stella,

Richie and I miss you. We've had a passing parade of polite English language students next door. I'm getting better at saying "Ni hao" (is that how you spell it?) but it's not quite the same as having a bit of a chat with you. I think you might have forgotten to forward your mail. You'll need to go to a post office. I left out the Aherns catalogues, but here's the mail that looked important. Hope it's all going well for you,
Dulcie

Richie was Dulcie's fat tabby cat and the cause of their friendship. Always polite to Stella, Dulcie had invited her into her Perth apartment one day for morning tea complete with an embroidered tablecloth and fine china. Richie had kept to himself under a cane chair on the verandah among the geraniums, examining her with golden eyes. Stella agreed to feed him and water the plants while Dulcie visited her sister for 10 days down in Esperance.

Stella loved letting herself into Dulcie's tidy apartment, full of books and sunshine. The standoffish Richie eventually deigned to let her stroke his back and scratch him under the chin. Before long he was headbutting her ankles as she shook out his dry food and topped up his water bowl, and he would occasionally let loose a crackling old purr.

Stella smiled. Which letter to open next? What could Exos possibly have to say to her? She was done with Exos. Exos and Damian were in the past, where they belonged. She put the letter at the bottom of the pile and ripped open a credit card statement.

$14,784? No! Astronomical. Impossible. She'd tried to be so careful, keeping her expenses down, well below that $15k limit.

She crumpled the envelope and threw the statement on her bed, before snatching it up again. Yes. It definitely had her name on it. Riffling through the rest of the mail, she found two other statements, heart sinking as she recalled all her purchases.

She'd known that setting up a business would be expensive, and she'd tried so hard to keep it under control. She'd always been so careful with her money. Until she'd set up Stellar, she'd taken pride in paying off her credit card every month just before the payment was due. When she and Jeannie were children, pocket money was rare. What little she'd been given she'd saved and spent carefully. As a teen, she'd been aware of trends and fashions, but she'd managed to get "the look" with a needle and thread and some ingenuity, adapting simple black t-shirts from chain stores and pouncing on "finds" at the markets when not on duty with Flame.

A respect for money was one of the few things she and Damian shared. Both had single mothers, both moved school too often, and both grew up wanting a different kind of life.

Early on, as they'd lain on a rumpled king bed high in a Hong Kong Hotel, he'd confided how much it hurt to be called a "pov" at school, how it compelled him to outdo the rich kids in every aspect of their coddled lives.

"We're the same, you and I," he'd said, stroking her thigh as if it were the bonnet of a luxury car. "We understand each other, Stella. We're meant to be together."

At the time, she'd been thrilled, until she realized Damian's quest for money was ruthless and never ending, unlike her own. Stella's dreams were more nebulous. At first she wanted Damian. She'd dreamt of their home, their children, time together that was rich and full, not snatched from an already too-full schedule. Simple things. Pancake breakfasts around a big round table in a big old house with a verandah. A house they would own, not rent, where their children would have roots.

Damian had no time for such fantasies. He'd quickly move the talk on to the benefits of the latest BMW engine, or the possibility of skiing in Japan if they attended this conference or that.

This debt! If only she hadn't gone in too deep when she'd finally escaped him, escaped Exos. She'd been careful with her financial planning, as she was with everything to do with money. It was what had made her such a great office manager. The way she balanced Damian's books and office stock and payroll so successfully had been a great source of pride for her. She'd wanted to please him in every way, and since he adored money, he'd been pleased, alright.

As for setting up and running her own business? She'd known it wasn't going to be easy. Plenty of small businesses failed in their first year. Cash flow was a challenge for everyone.

But it hadn't stopped her. Finally, that day when she'd walked out, her old dreams resurfaced. They bubbled up from way back before Damian, before Exos, back from her youth and childhood, dreams of a creative life - an artisan's life they called it now - a simpler life, immersed in doing what she loved. She wanted to bring beauty into the world. She truly believed that everyone deserved to shine, that the act of giving and wearing jewelry brightened people's lives and they would value what she offered, enough for her passion to become her new career.

Simple! Too simple. She studied her statement and nearly cried.

She'd known it could be a challenge. She wouldn't be able to make money without spending some, too. And there would be plenty of unknowns. She would have to trust that her passion for what she was doing would carry her through the hard times, that she would learn from her mistakes, that if it was worth doing, she would make a go of it, eventually.

When she'd left Exos, she'd had too much time and not enough materials. Realizing she could make more money by working in silver, she'd bought up big, keen to avoid delays and simply begin. Maybe she'd have to rethink her pricing. Had James been right?

Then there was the fee to hire the stall from the council in Sydney, three months in advance, a real stretch.

Each figure had a story.

There was the Flame factor, always a wild card. From time to time over the years, Flame would phone Stella or Jeannie with what the sisters had dubbed "the ask," when their mother would seek "just a little bit of a loan" to tide her over. In conversation it would become clear she was on the move again, perhaps living in her car for a stint, or "just a bit short this month." Stella never gave her more than she could afford to give, as the "loans" were rarely repaid.

"Just keep it, mum," she'd learned to say. It made her feel good to help out Flame. She'd been a great mum in many ways. Her restlessness meant she and Jeannie saw more of Australia than most young people, and despite her failings, Flame was fun - more like a wild big sister than a mother. There'd been plenty of hugs and laughter in their childhoods, and freedom galore.

But Flame's many schemes made Stella wary of her own dreams. Flame's "investments," with and without various partners, had included planting garlic, milking goats, and even learning the celtic harp.

"Are you sure this is a good idea, mum?" Stella would ask.

"Why not? Life's for living!"

When she'd made her latest move, to the northern NSW coast, she'd asked for another hand.

"Thank you, Stella dear!" she'd managed when Stella had forwarded her $1,800 for another scheme, this time growing mesclun for local restaurants with someone called Grady. It had seemed a lot to Stella at the time, for little green leaves which grew by themselves anyway but Flame said some something about a cool room. Her approach was always big on faith and short on logic, so there was rarely much point discussing finer details. At the time, Stella was anxious to get her off the phone so she could continue stock piling product. She'd need to, to make up for the money she'd just given away.

Setting up Stellar wasn't cheap. She'd registered her business name, taken out third party liability insurance, then purchased the domain name for her website. Even though Jeannie built the website for her for nothing, everything else had added up.

Another unexpected cost was the loss of her rental bond. The agent fined her for leaving a tiny brown mark on the kitchen benchtop from when she soldered some links closed and accidently pointed her blowtorch away from the fireproof mat for a few moments.

And what was that figure? Oh yes. That whopping huge payment at the airport for her extra heavy luggage. Tools and silver. So much heavier than shoes. She should have known.

And then interest. Lots of it. She'd known she shouldn't have let her repayments mount up like this! It was punitive. Known she'd cop a slug of interest.

Her first thought was to grab the statement and share her woes with Jeannie, but she stopped herself just in time. Jeannie was already going out of her way to help her, offering her a rent-free bed and so much more. No. She would have to solve this herself. All the more reason to focus on her business and make it pay her way.

She drew in a deep breath. There was a lesson here. She must force herself to study her electronic statements more regularly, and reconsider every single purchase before she made it. Too much was at stake. She literally couldn't afford to let her finances come unstuck like this.

The Exos letter. She closed her eyes, drew in a deep breath and reached for it.

Dear Miss Rhys,

In view of your years of excellent service at Exos, we officially offer you a $25,000 bonus and a 20 per cent pay rise to return to work with us as Director of Exos Administration. We look forward to having you on our team again.

This offer will lapse in 28 days.

Yours sincerely,
Damian Beaumont
Managing Director

Damian had struck out the "Miss Rhys" with his characteristic thick black pen and hand written "Stella," and signed it simply Damian.

Twenty-eight days. They'd well and truly lapsed. There was no point even thinking about it. Besides. Damian and Exos were history.

Had she gone in too deep setting up Stellar? She'd gone in too deep with Damian, and wasted years of her life. Maybe it was a fault of hers, going in too deep. Maybe that was why Flame had kept moving all her life, escaping similar mistakes. Was Stella no different to her mother after all? The debt sat like lead in her stomach, with Damian's offer a dark cloud of temptation.

That letter. The "bonus." The bribe, more like. Did he think she could be bought, like one of his cars?

She grabbed Damian's letter, scrunched it tightly, then twisted it and threw it into the corner.

Should she get another job, here in Sydney? Most other people had jobs for a reason. She wasn't the only person who knew the fear of debt, who had shivered in winter without a proper coat and been afraid to eat the last few slices of bread, knowing there'd be no school lunch next day for her or Jeannie.

She could do it. Get her nails done again. Straighten her hair. Haul out an office outfit and high heels, and nod and smile and spend her days solving other people's problems, all for that vital slug of money every fortnight. Maybe she'd be able to make time for making jewelry at night and on weekends. Maybe. But her fingers were itching to create, all the time, not just after hours. And she'd come so far already. If she ditched it all now, she'd be no different to Flame, who always took the easier path to the greener grass.

She closed her eyes. There had to be another solution.

Like trading her way forwards, one piece of jewelry at a time. Surely it was possible.

Chapter 10

The next morning was surprisingly cool, so Stella hauled out an old black office outfit, teaming it with a green scarf and pinning it in place with one of her purple brooches.

She loved the freedom of being able to wear what she wanted, loved the new routine of snuggling her little nieces each morning, throwing all the washing in the machine and sharing tea and cereal with Jeannie before heading out for the day.

Her roller bag was heavy with polished stock.

Her fellow commuters were usually in a daze, scrolling through the news or browsing on social media, but when she swung into her seat as the bus lurched away, she found herself next to an older woman who was wearing one of her brooches, the pale blue version, nestled into a bed of silver wire pulled into a celtic knot. How extraordinary, to see her own creation being enjoyed! It suited this woman.

"Snap," she said, giving the woman a smile.

"Oh. I should have bought the purple one, too, dear. Looks lovely on you. I've had so many compliments wearing this one, I've barely taken it off."

The woman looked at her a little shyly.

"You're not…"

"I'm Stella."

"I thought so! I'm Beverley. I was too busy looking at all your other jewels to see you properly when I bought this. I love it. Do you make these all yourself?"

"Yes."

"So clever. Your stall's amazing, and your jewelry is absolutely beautiful. It would be such a shame if ..."

Stella's blood froze. That sick sensation, the alarm jangling at the centre of her being; it was back. She'd been so focused on trading and restocking, and now on her financial challenges. Was there another threat? Her response was urgent.

"If what? Have you heard something?" She searched the woman's face.

"Oh, I'm sorry. I hear all sorts of things. My husband works at the council. Shouldn't have said anything. Don't you worry, dear. Probably nothing. Now you have a nice day. Excuse me." Beverley gathered her bag, and Stella stood to let her out.

She pulled out her phone, thinking maybe Jeannie could phone the council and find out whether there was some kind of problem with her licence, but was immediately distracted by the latest social media tussle.

Huntleys: *Diamonds are forever.*

Stellar: *Fake gems glitter just as brightly, for a fraction of the funds.*

Huntleys: *Fake gems for fake love.*

Stellar: *Love isn't only for the rich. Lighten up and sparkle. Have fun with Stellar jewelry.*

Jeannie clearly had enough on her plate. *Just let her handle the social media stoush she's created*, Stella grimaced, turning off her phone again.

...

The mall had begun to feel like home. She must trade, trade, trade, and pay off that credit card debt. She waved at Fritz and then at Clint, a fellow stall holder who boasted a bag for every occasion. Clint, who came from a long line of farmers in South Korea, used to have a stall at Paddy's Market near Chinatown, but he'd told her he'd missed being outdoors. He was setting out all his wheelie bags and arranging the briefcases, which always fell over like dominoes. She gestured at the larger wheelie bag she'd bought from him and gave him a thumbs up.

Further up the mall, she could see Marita at the coffee shop setting out the chairs and tables, then pulling out the box of toys, ready for the playgroup parents. Some of them would wander past her stall later, maybe picking up a treat for themselves or each other. She made a mental note to create a little lucky dip for the children - maybe with some of those toothbrush bangles - so all of them might visit her more often.

Just then, mournful strains of slow jazz trumpet filled the mall.

Fritz greeted her with a dip of his hat and a roll of his eyes. His arm swept sideways, showing her the busker.

"Lennie," he told her. "'Nam."

She nodded and unlocked her stall, wondering just how slowly it was possible to play *St James Infirmary*, and for how long.

Lennie was still there when James turned up, dapper as ever in his pale grey suit. Stella was startled to notice a slight change in his routine. Instead of bounding inside Huntleys' ornate doors, he made a bee-line for Lennie. James reached for his wallet and pulled out some notes.

Lennie paused mid phrase and tucked the notes safely inside his jacket, nodding his thanks. To Stella's surprise, James stayed and exchanged some remarks, then offered Lennie a farewell handshake and another nod of respect before heading on up, head high.

Lennie's tune, when he resumed, was considerably more upbeat, something cheery, something dixieland, and the whole atmosphere of the mall under that cloudy grey sky had changed for the better.

She'd considered herself a good judge of character, thought she'd read James's thoroughly. She'd met his type before, people like Damian, privileged, blind to the needs of others, self-interested. She studied Huntleys' impressive facade, captivated by the current namesake. James was clearly far more interesting than she'd assumed.

Catching herself at it for the fifth time, replaying and reinterpreting all their encounters, she took some coins across to Lennie herself, just as he was packing up.

"Good morning?" she asked.

"Could say that."

"Oh?"

"Always good when James's about."

"You know each other?"

"About as much as anyone can know this lot, but he's the best of them. Oh, the stall holders, they're alright. It's them permanent shopkeepers who give me a hard time, always moving me along. Never James, though. Never too busy for a kind word. Generous, too. Told me his grandfather served. Shows a bit of respect."

Time disappeared as she wound more wire for jump rings and polished her silver bangles, the ones with the celtic catches, dreaming up new designs and selling more stock to tourists who kept posing for selfies.

At 2pm, she was practically panting. Even the seagulls seemed too hot to move, skulking beside the bin in the shade.

They were just moving away when an ice cream cone appeared out of nowhere. Was she hallucinating? No. It was starting to drip. Slowly, she turned. The hand and wrist were familiar, the shirt sleeve rolled up.

It was James, his white shirt blinding in the sunshine, a cone in each hand.

Spirits soaring, she couldn't decide which was more appealing, the prospect of the first mouthful, or the vision of James's lips already destroying the perfect swirl of his own. Could he guess the effect he had on her? She wouldn't risk a glance at his eyes. Practically drooling, she accepted the unexpected gift. Some drips start rolling down her wrist.

"But why? What's this?"

"You don't have these in Perth?" Was he flirting with her? She took a lick, the cool sweetness heaven in the heat.

She chased the runaway drips with her tongue. Messy. She blushed, and rushed on, turning away. She could hardly hand it back.

A minute later, done with it, she turned back again and met his eyes.

"Thank you. That was delicious and totally unexpected, but we need to talk, James, you and I. Right now."

"We do?" He was still finishing his. Distracting. She closed her eyes, blocking out the bright white shirt and his matching smile.

"I don't understand why you're being so nice to me in person when you're so aggressive online."

"Why not be friendly? You come into our business. Why can't I drop in on yours? That online stuff. Nicole does our PR."

"I only want to make a living."

"So do we."

And he was gone. Bright. Breezy. Into his air conditioned building, leaving her with a temper, a sticky hand, and the sun too hot on her head.

She washed her hands with some of her precious water and sat on the planter box, leaning into the shade of the small tree, defeated, heart still jumping.

Had she been too honest?

Chapter 11

At her stall, all was quiet. Stella had her notepad out, sketching, when a slim young man on an electric skateboard caught her eye, far away at the other end of the mall. She admired his technique as he wove in and out of the crowd at quite a pace.

His sense of balance was superb, his movements supple and mesmerizing as he bent his knees then raised himself to full height, hands and elbows tucked into his body then lifted high as if he were a skater on ice, doing a lap of victory. By dropping a knee or shoulder he could turn with ease. Beautiful.

Most surprising was his speed, even as he came towards the stalls, breathtaking. Stella was so swept up observing his grace, she didn't realize what was coming. He came past close, too close, and in one swoop, he grabbed her bag of takings and sped on, disappearing around the corner towards the railway station while she could still feel the sweep of air in his wake. The audacity stunned her.

"Wait!" she called out. "My bag!" But he'd already gone. She tried running after him but remembered she'd left her stock unguarded.

Anger. Shock. She shook her head, nauseous. She did a mental calculation. At least $400. Maybe closer to $600. More maybe. It had been a good couple of days, and she hadn't had a chance to get to the bank. At least she still had her credit card reader. And her personal credit card, hidden away for emergencies, secreted in her makeup bag where she wouldn't be tempted to use it.

"Did you see that?" she called out to Fritz.

He shook his head. "You call the police, yah. Have to make statement. Happened to me maybe three years ago, or four. Young people. No respect. Don't know how to work. Here. You need change?" Fritz pulled out some $5 and $10 dollar bills and brought them across to her.

"Heart of gold, Fritz. I've gone all shaky."

"You sit. I bring you lemonade. Sugar."

Within an hour, Ruben had arrived, thrusting his microphone first in his own face, and then in hers.

"I'm here at the site of the daring raid that took place in broad daylight here in busy Oxford Street mall at the popular new jewelry stall, Stellar. How are you feeling, Stella, shocked?"

"Yes, I ..."

"Riding a battery powered skateboard at break-neck speed, the thief simply helped himself to Stella's cash bag then took off towards the train station. What do you have to say about this?"

"I'd like him to bring it back, of course, Ruben. I've worked so hard to make Stellar a success and I need every dollar. Making jewelry is my dream, but I can't make ends meet if someone steals my profits. It's hard enough as it is..."

"Thank you, Stella. She's understandably upset. Stella's stall really brightens up the mall. I'm sure your customers would hate it if you had to close, so let's hope the thief reconsiders and you find your bag back here again. I'm off to the police station now to see whether the thief has struck elsewhere. If anyone saw anything, they can contact me. This is Ruben Slavonicus, multimedia influencer, keeping our streets safe."

"Good of you to mention me, Ruben. Is that thing off now? Can you tell me, how are you keeping our streets safe?"

"I'm the eyes and ears of this place, Stella. You know that. I'll post this, and we'll just see what comes in. Good luck with the police. Unlikely to get anywhere. You didn't get a picture did you?"

"No. He was gone so fast."

"Hmmm."

"Yeah. Well. Thanks again."

"Thanks to you, Stella. That's news, you know. Got a few more followers from the last time I featured you. I told you people love jewelry. And crime. This'll help spread the word about Stellar. You wait and see. This'll get you a bit more custom for sure."

"Thanks."

He nodded and was gone, off in the direction of the police station.

When Jeannie rang minutes later, Stella took the call.

"Saw it on Facebook. You okay, Stell? Want to lock up early and come home? Need a cuppa?"

Hearing the concern in her sister's voice made Stella burst into tears, surprising them both. It gave her some relief. Jeannie had her laughing soon after, saying Huntleys would think she'd done it on purpose for the free publicity.

"Don't you dare write that, Jeannie! Tell me you won't!"

"Just teasing. Sorry, sis. But seriously. Guess how many followers have just come in?"

"No idea."

"Another twelve. Just while we've been speaking. Ruben's right. Crime's popular."

"Well, followers are fine, Jeannie. But they need to buy stuff or I'm going to go out of business." She didn't add that she would soon owe another few hundred dollars if she couldn't make a decent payment off her card debt.

"Hey. You'll be okay. What about that cuppa? Early mark?"

"I actually need to stay and trade. Now, more than ever."

"Come home, Stell. Take a break. See the girls. Have some lunch with me and I'll drop you back in this afternoon when I go grocery shopping. Matt'll be back. He can mind the girls while they sleep."

"Okay. Thanks, Jeannie"

Still feeling empty, Stella locked up and headed for the bus stop. Jeannie was right. She needed a break.

Lucy jumped up and launched herself at Stella for a hug, then toddled away and returned clutching a small pile of books. Stella was only too pleased to draw her onto her lap and read to her. Lucy's chubby legs jiggling with anticipation, settling as each story began. Stella helped her to turn the pages. The bright books with their simple stories comforted her, particularly *Old McDonald's Farm*. Even Sienna joined in, with a kind of happy yell, whenever they sang together. After four times through the same book, they were all ready for lunch - leftover spaghetti followed by jelly.

Matt walked in with his suit bag while they were eating, back after another week in Singapore. He ran through the shower and returned in shorts and a tee shirt, ruffling everyone's hair. The girls held up their arms for cuddles and he took one daughter in each of his own, planting big kisses on their cheeks till they squealed to be put back down.

"So, what's this I hear about a robbery?" said Matt, taking a seat at the table. "You okay, Stell?"

Stella nodded. "A bit shaken, but at least no one was hurt."

"Stellar jewels must be really hot property if people are stealing it." He sprinkled a hefty spoonful of grated cheese over his helping. "Great. Leftovers. My favourite. I'm so over room service."

"Lucky you," said Jeannie.

"Hey! Let me babysit tonight," said Stella, pleased to see Jeannie and Matt reach for each other under the table. "You two don't see nearly enough of each other. But I have to tell you, Matt, he only stole the cash."

Matt whistled when Stella described it again, causing Lucy to blow through her lips, too, and make everyone laugh.

In the car, Stella was almost tempted to tell Jeannie of her financial woes, but thought the better of it. She'd reported the robbery to the police, and there wasn't much more to be done, except trade, trade, trade. The weather was fine. That would help.

Fritz waved her over when Stella dropped her off.

He had a new bag for her.

"From Clint. On the house, he said. Gift. For you. A bit shy, Clint."

Stella waved over at Clint and blew him a kiss.

"You okay, Stella?"

She nodded, full of spaghetti and love. She still felt sick when she thought of the money she'd lost, on top of that astronomical debt, but as long as her stall could stay trading, she would gradually trade forwards, wouldn't she?

Fortunately some customers arrived to take her mind off her woes, but although they looked and took photographs of themselves at her stall, they didn't buy.

All afternoon she thought of her debt and Damian's letter. Damian's $25,000 was such a dangling carrot. It would solve her financial problems immediately, but there was no way she'd go back. She'd rather starve.

She forced herself to count her blessings. Wonderful Jeannie. She closed her eyes in gratitude at her sister's generosity and encouragement. They shot open a moment later. Jeannie's birthday! It was coming up, and she'd made a vow to surprise her this year with something truly beautiful, a lasting treasure. It was a long-held dream to give Jeannie a "proper" gift. All their lives they'd traded practical, low-cost gifts, like socks and underwear, or secondhand treasures, or things they'd made themselves, making the most of what little they had. This year would be different.

She wanted to give her something that would have value no matter what the future held - an heirloom like the locket the old lady carried closely, into her old age.

Well. She couldn't let the robbery stop her good intentions. Why let the thief steal her sense of purpose as well as her money? No. What was $500 here or there? Petty theft was a temporary inconvenience, a mere blip on her financial fortunes - poorly timed for sure, while the credit card debt grew like a cancer - but ultimately insignificant, or so she hoped.

This gift meant so much to her. She had to have faith in her dream. Sales were good. She would earn back the money soon, wouldn't she?

And even if she ended up having to return to Exos to clear the debt, the gift would remain to remind them all of her venture out east, perhaps to be reactivated some time in the future.

Yes. She wanted the best for Jeannie. Quality. *Huntleys!* She laughed at herself. Was she being softened up by their social spin? Doubtless there were other great jewelry stores in Sydney, but the one thing she could say for Huntleys was it was conveniently located for her. She wouldn't be wasting much time.

Stella was absolutely determined to find something of true beauty and value for Jeannie's birthday, and soon.

Next morning, Stella scanned the mall. *Quiet.* A few older men chatted at a coffee shop, some office workers were smoking outside their building, and a few pigeons pecked at the pavement, strutting about for each other.

She locked up shop then gave Fritz a wave.

He raised his eyebrows.

"Going shopping," she said, eyes shining with resolve. She'd been planning this treat since her first day of trade, longing to explore all those treasures inside Huntleys and select something just right for Jeannie's birthday.

She'd allowed herself half an hour to browse. What was the point of being in business for yourself if you never gave yourself a break? Matt was planning a surprise birthday party for Jeannie that weekend, and Stella didn't want to put off her gift hunting a moment longer.

She planted her big straw hat on the hook at the side of her stall, hung a big, sparkling "back soon" sign across her Stellar sign.

"Thanks, boss!" she said to herself, peering in at one of her mirrors, pushing her hair into shape.

"Well, you deserve it," she told her reflection, double checking her choice of clothing for the day; a simple, scoop necked, pale blue polka dot cotton dress, practical yet feminine, and just right for this weather. She was wearing a small string of faux pearls alternating with fake sapphires, each separated by a run of silver chain. In each ear was a small half pearl stud and droplet of a faux sapphire, swinging on a length of fine chain. It was a new design she'd put together the previous Sunday afternoon when Jeannie and the girls were having "quiet time" and Matt was out doing the week's grocery shopping as penance for being away so often. It meant there'd be a few more corn chips and chocolates than Jeannie normally wanted in the house, but it was a small price to pay. Matt would demolish them soon enough. Stella finished the earrings. Now she wanted to find out how they felt in her ears. They swung a little as she walked. They felt good.

She headed across to Huntleys, stopping and turning before entering. There it was, small but definite, her own bright mark on the world, with its lights flashing, exclaiming "Stellar" to the world - this start of her dream come true - her way of making a living from what she loved.

She glanced along the mall at the other stalls. There was Clint, using this quiet time to chat with Fritz, the two old men of the mall with their backs to the morning sunlight, nodding and gesticulating about something.

There was Donna, further up the mall, setting up late today, unpacking her new stock, hanging it up to swing a little in the breeze and catch the eye of the lunch crowd to come. She and Donna met a week earlier when a rogue wind unleashed a whole pile of her scarves, scattering them along the mall like bright sea creatures. When the first one came billowing past, Stella reached out and caught it, then all the others. Donna, chasing them from the rear, insisted she select one to keep, though she'd selected a sunhat instead.

Donna saw her about to enter Huntleys and gave her a wave. She waved back. How fond she'd become of her new part of the world in such a short while, including the other stallholders! Good people, trying to make a living.

She savoured the anticipation. What a treat to see some real jewels, and study some fresh designs by master jewelers! As she swung open the front doors and noticed again that faint whiff of furniture polish. Should she start here or go straight to the upper level, either in the elevator or via the old staircase?

In the foyer, peering around in the sudden dimness to see if there was a guide to what to find on each floor, she stopped. James was coming straight towards her.

"Stella," he said smoothly, extending his hand, charming but aloof, superior. She couldn't help but admire how perfectly his suit fitted, a dark blue one today, with a hand stitched collar.

"To what do we owe the pleasure of your company, Miss Rhys?"

Was he mocking her? Dumb struck, she regarded him. Did he greet all his customers this way? Or was he insinuating he didn't want her custom?

"There are public facilities at the end of the mall," he added.

Her eyes flashed fire. How dare he!

"I know, thank you, and I haven't used your facilities since that first day, thank you very much." She was offended by his barbed comment. Why had Jeannie had to be so aggressive on social media? This was awkward. "You might think it's extraordinary, James, but I'm actually here as a customer. At least, I was planning to browse and to purchase something.

Is that alright with you? Or do you only sell to movie stars and the rich and famous?" How dare he insult her like this! If he treated all his potential customers this way, it was no wonder his store was practically devoid of them.

He stiffened and looked away from her. Good.

"Oh, you're famous alright, Stellar. Quite famous."

Compliment or insult?

As his eyes grazed her necklace and earrings, she blushed. But she couldn't let herself be intimidated. She had every right to be here. She'd planned this treat for more than a week, and she wouldn't be bullied out of it by some clueless heir. She must stand up to him. Call him out on his rudeness. Defend herself, and attack if necessary. Stealthily.

"Really? I'm famous, am I? Maybe you'd like to tell me about it. I have half an hour. Come for coffee, James?"

"Unfortunately, it's not possible today." This time, he seemed embarrassed. Good. "Another time perhaps. I'm just on my way out." He stepped backwards, ushering her into the main part of the store and gesturing to one of the staff.

"Lorna, can I ask you to come and assist our customer, please? Lorna, this is Miss Rhys, a fellow jeweler. We couldn't be more pleased to welcome you." Was he mocking her? She retained her dignity, explaining her quest to the young sales assistant.

"I'd like something for my sister," she said, turning sideways at James to ensure he heard. "It's her birthday this weekend. I have an *open mind* about how much to spend."

"Lovely," said Lorna. "Well, welcome. It's mostly watches and everyday pieces on this floor. Upstairs we have our VIP selection. Do you have in mind what you'd like to buy? Would you like to just browse, or can I show you something in particular?"

"I'd love to browse, thank you, Lorna. How about I call you once I've had a general look?"

Chapter 12

Stella adored jewelry, and always had. She could have gone elsewhere, and she might yet, but with so little time on her hands, Huntleys was it. She took a look at the lockets - hearts set out for valentines and young lovers.

They were sweet. Some were old-fashioned, etched gold, and others more modern, exaggeratedly puffed up and shiny, and there were some outlines, strung through with their chains, and even a variation of the hearts broken in half, for sweethearts to share. Several were studded with small gemstones. They were pleasant enough, but there was nothing outstanding, and certainly nothing here was suitable for sisters.

She moved on to the pendants. The gemstones were tiny compared to the ones she worked with. Of course, these were real, but they were starved of life, stuck there in their cabinets. The settings were far from inspirational. It was a disappointment. She found herself frowning.

She moved to another cabinet, hoping to find something more interesting, something more "Jeannie." Strings of pearls. Good quality, yes. She could see their lustres, some pale pink and green, others more creamy, but the prices were astronomical. And truly. Her own supplies might not be the real thing, but to her mind, they were every bit as beautiful.

Over to the watches she wandered, but watches were something she could find anywhere, in any magazine, or any other jewelers, or even a department store these days, and how many watches did one need? Jeannie used her mobile phone to tell the time.

She couldn't hide her disappointment. She shook her head at Lorna, walking away.

"Nothing today, miss?"

"No, thank you, Lorna."

She was surprised to find James still in the foyer.

"You're not pleased with what you've seen," he said. Was he wanting her reassurance? She couldn't make him out.

She stared at him before answering.

"Perhaps there'll be something suitable on the next floor." Could he really care about her opinion? James was clearly more complex than she'd first imagined. Was there something vulnerable about Mr Perfect after all? She decided she liked him better for it, and smiled.

Taking it as an invitation, he began to speak, following her up the stairs.

"I've cancelled my appointment. I'm interested in your comments. You clearly have a real eye for jewelry and for what the market wants."

"Oh?"

She quickened her step, keen to see what the next floor might offer.

Again, he opened the door for her, and for just a moment she allowed herself to feel accompanied, truly welcome. It was a rare sensation. Her meetings with Damian had always been clandestine, furtive. There'd been business trips in distant cities, a day or two of meals together in impersonal hotels, when she'd allow herself to imagine her whole life might one day be shared with him, but never something as simple as just being together.

Jim was in the section at the back, head down, intent on his work. Or was he nodding off?

But it was the centre of the room that caught her attention. There was a new cabinet, up on a dais, brighter than all the other cabinets, gilded and lined with lights like the mirror of a Hollywood actor.

Past sparkling polished glass counters laden with engagement rings, gold chains and platinum ones, and a few spotlit gemstone pendants, she was drawn to the new cabinet. Inside it, black velvet rose up in three tiers on four sides. At the centre of each tier was a single item.

She drew a breath. Behind her, James was poised, watching her reaction.

Time stopped. She stared at the cabinet. She walked around it as if in a trance.

On one side were rubies, on another, sapphires. Then there were diamonds, white and hard and fiery in the professional cabinet, blazing like stars against the black velvet.

But. On the final side. There was no denying it. Huge. Green. Emeralds. Her cry rang out across the entire hushed floor. Jim looked up sharply.

"This is my design, James!"

James stepped back, like a magician, his arms wide, triumphant, looking at her as if he'd accomplished something magnificent.

She could scarcely breathe.

She approached the cabinet and studied the jewels. They were spectacular. It was true. She could barely imagine how much they must cost, this size, half the size of her own, yet in real gemstones. Every detail was the same, yet these jewels had a class and quality far beyond the faux ones. These were truly beautiful. They were great pieces, heirlooms of the future. Any star would want these. Any wife or mother or lovestruck teenager, any sister or working woman or grandmother. They were masterpieces.

On closer inspection, every setting mirrored her own designs. She pointed at the sapphire rosette choker.

She was in a dream. "That one," she said.

James extracted a key from his breast pocket. "Allow me," he said, unlocking the cabinet. From beneath it, he pulled out a swathe of black velvet, laying it gently on the counter top, as if he'd done this countless times. He'd probably been helping out since he was a child, she reasoned.

Maybe he'd done this every school holiday and every trading Saturday and every other day of his life. His hands were so smooth, so clean. He wasn't the jeweler, that was for sure. The manager. The owner.

Was he taking extra care for her, or did every customer receive this special treatment?

Gently, he lifted out the dancing blue piece and placed it on the velvet in front of her, then waited, hands behind his back so nothing distracted from the beauty of the piece itself, waiting there to be claimed.

She gazed at it there between them, mesmerising, this thing of her own imagination, more beautiful even than she envisaged it could be.

She put down her heavy bag of cash beside it, then stooped to place it between her feet on the floor. On the counter, the object was still there, James behind it, his face inscrutable.

"This is very beautiful," she said, picking it up and twisting it backwards and forwards in the light, watching it shoot sharp sparks from every facet.

"It's a new…"

"… *my* design," she cut him off, her voice every bit as sharp as the platinum setting. But something was different at the back of it. Her tension dissipated as she explored it. She was intrigued. It had a tiny clip. Ingenious. The piece could be worn as a pendant, a choker, or even a brooch.

"Oh. This is clever. Who …? How?"

"Jim's the goldsmith. I'll introduce you." James gestured, and Jim prepared to come across, slowly removing his magnifying headset and apron and pulling on a formal jacket.

"Your design skills are excellent, Stella," James said. "I was going to show you this display, but it's not quite complete. Jim's been working on creating some rings to match. Rings are his specialty. Jim, this is Stella, from the mall."

"I believe we've already met." Jim's blue eyes sparkled as he took Stella's small hand in his own, strong and gnarled with a lifetime's work.

"You brought in the lady with the broken locket. So, it *is* you. You're the one whose work James brought to me? The one with the earrings Antoinette loved so much? James is right. You, my dear, are extremely talented. I don't say this to many people, but I haven't had such joy creating a set for many, many years."

"But … but…," Part of her was horrified. Furious. Fighting for control. But part was proud. Amazed. She couldn't attack Jim, such a gentleman, so sincere in his praise. She would have to save her fury for Mr Perfect. "I'm honoured. Thank you, Jim."

"Don't thank me, my dear. You're the one who deserves all the thanks. Stirred us all up with your shop in the mall. Stellar. Clever. Yes. Very clever." He took a breath. "Excellent. Now if you'll excuse me, I must finish this repair by lunch time." And he took her hand again, as if he were going to kiss it. He bowed instead and returned to his counter.

Disoriented, she turned back to James.

"Don't get me wrong, James. It's very flattering. But can you really just copy my designs like this? Isn't this breaching copyright?"

He drew back, defensive.

"Jewelers have been gaining inspiration from each other since the dawn of time, Stella. You'll find your own ideas have stemmed from others. There's rarely anything so original it can't be traced back to someone else's work, to another design era or culture. The human body remains roughly the same, as do the ways we adorn it. And as you see, Jim's made a few changes, due to the different properties of the materials, and to use some of the gems we had in stock."

"So..." It bristled to be buying her own design. Shouldn't she be using every cent to pay down her debt? But how she wanted that little choker! Couldn't put it down. It would be perfect for Jeannie. She'd adore the fact it was a proper jewel - something of true value, that would last forever. And the fact it was based on her own design made pride surge up through her from her toes to her fingertips. She stood taller.

"So, how much is this?"

"Be my guest. Take it. You must have this one."

Stella was angry now. She wouldn't let herself be patronized. James Huntley, with his manners and his class… Did he think she was a charity case? She'd been treated that way before. School mothers taking pity on her when she and Jeannie and Flame rolled into town, so obviously lacking in normal things, like black lace-up shoes. Jeannie never minded when a friend handed over something spare, but Stella always found it awkward. For a moment she remembered how relieved and grown up she'd felt when she received her first regular pay cheques and could finally pay her own way. There was so much to be said for holding down a real job, whatever the limitations. Her wage was lifeblood to her, a reassurance she was valued, and an insurance for all the days ahead. The Exos letter inviting her back still weighed heavily on her mind. Every day she wondered whether she shouldn't just go back, face up to Damian with all his imperfections, clear her debt and recalibrate her future.

No.

There it was again, that tug of independence, the voice inside her urging her to have the courage to forge her own way. Maybe there was more of Flame in her than she realized, that call of the wild, the winds from afar that fed her dreams of a more creative life. She had her pride.

James stood as she turned the jewel over and over in her hands. Her voice was quiet.

"You think I can't afford it. You've told me already. You think I'm going broke." Her contempt for him could not be greater, her voice ice. Even if he was right, she was over being treated like the poor girl. *Why shouldn't she be allowed to shop in a place like Huntleys?*

"No…"

"I asked, 'how much is this one?' Don't you want a sale?"

"It's retailing for $1,199, but for you, Miss Rhys…"

"I'll buy it."

She stooped and lifted her bag again. She brought out a few notes from the day's sales, a few 20s stacked like slices of smoked salmon. That way she would only be putting a few hundred on her credit card.

She counted them out in front of him, and handed them over, seeing again all her eager customers, and all those days and nights out west working like a madwoman creating stock until her fingers ached and eyes watered. It was a small fortune. But she wouldn't accept his charity. He was just a merchant after all. She was a designer, a creator. He'd said so himself. She might have an insurmountable debt but otherwise, she was free as a bird, living her dream. She stared at him till he dropped his gaze.

"Well then, Stella. Would you like it gift wrapped?"

"I would."

He had the grace not to recount the money in front of her. He brought out a leather case and nestled the jewel inside it slowly, as if it were priceless, immeasurably beautiful. And it was. To Stella. She was thrilled to imagine how Jeannie would react when she opened it.

He brought out tissue paper, finely watermarked with the age-old Huntley's H insignia, then he placed it in a paper gift bag, shiny black, with the gold H on two sides, and handles of rounded gold trim.

Although there were a few normal cash registers, James rang up this part of the sale on an old cash register, expertly tugging the crank and working the levers, till the tray shot out with a bang and the dinging of a tiny, tiny bell. He hand wrote a receipt in a book with carbon paper, placing it inside the bag.

Their fingers touched with a zing and their eyes caught again as he handed it all across to her. A grandfather clock clicked.

What did she see behind his eyes? Audacity? Shame? Remorse? Pity? Pride? There was no question the display looked brilliant. Was he pleading with her? Was he measuring her naivety? Did he really think he could steal her design with no consequence? Was Huntleys so desperate for fresh ideas they had to copy the works of a street seller?

What might he be seeing in her own eyes? Pride? Contempt? Fury? Confusion? Triumph? Satisfaction?

She held his gaze, trying to fathom it.

"I believe in 'win win' transactions, Stella," he said, breaking their stalemate.

"Do you, James Huntley ... the Third?"

What must it be like to grow up rich, she wondered. To inherit a whole business, functioning if not thriving. To own a multistorey building and all its contents, not just the use of a few square metres for a few months?

"You underrate your talents, Stella," he said. "You're underselling yourself out there in the mall."

She was silent, astonished.

"Your designs are outstanding. Fresh. Every one of them. Did you design this piece?" he gestured at her neck, and she felt the warmth of him, so close, the almost-touch of his hands on her decolletage in the still air of the showroom. She held her own fingers to her necklace, remembering the piece, the faux sapphires and pearls, interspaced with chain.

What was this? It felt good, but dangerous. It felt like seduction. Was he flirting with her? Weren't he and Nicole an item? The last thing she wanted was another affair. She closed her eyes, clenched her fists.

"A bit late for flattery, don't you think?" Her voice was low, quiet, controlled, each word a barb. "How dare you steal my designs!"

He stepped backwards, withdrawing his hands. "I thought you'd be pleased. Imitation is the most sincere form of flattery. Besides. This is actually an ancient design. Not yours at all. And you'll see we've made modifications. Improvements. There's no copyright issue, if that's what you're wondering."

"We'll see about that."

She turned on her heel and marched out, her footsteps echoing across the checkerboard floor.

Back at her stall, Stella wondered what she'd done. *$1,199!* With all her debt!

But every time she thought of the piece, she was thrilled. She knew she'd bought something she truly treasured, so she knew Jeannie would adore it too. On the other hand, the money had all gone to Huntleys, while her own debt had grown considerably. She shook her head at herself, at her pride. She felt ill.

Stella's phone rang, interrupting her reverie. An unidentified number. Normally she ignored those calls, but she thought it might be the police. Maybe they'd found her bag!

"Did you get my offer?"

Stella was speechless. She knew that voice. Too well.

"We need you back. Exos needs you."

"I ..."

"And you need us." Had Damian been stalking her? Social media was like that. You never knew who was watching.

"How did... You didn't arrange that robbery did you? Damian?"

"You were good here with us. You were meant for this role. The team misses you."

"I ..."

"Come back to us, Stella. That bonus. We're doubling it. For you. $50k." Silence.

She could imagine him waiting, eyes hooded.

"You can't just ..." Bile rose in the back of her throat. He might not know about her credit card debt, but he would know that most sole traders struggled in their first year or two, and that many collapsed. How dare he tempt her like this! Why couldn't he leave her alone? Suddenly she guessed. It might have been that little chat she'd had with the office assistant just before she'd left.

111

"She won't sleep with you, will she? Lexie." She spat it out, lips tight with hate.

Damian stayed silent.

"I want the money, Damian, but I don't want you."

"Don't be so quick to decide," he said. Conciliatory. "Maybe you do still need us, need me."

"Never. Not any more."

"Come on. We belong together, you and I, Stella. We're two of a kind. Remember? I remember. So. How's your little business?"

"I could ask you the same thing."

"Keep it as a hobby. That's my advice. Shame about the robbery. Not easy, is it, being in business? Now you've tried it, got it out of your system, you can come back to your real career. Office manager. You were good at it. Excellent. The best. I know you miss it."

"I don't miss it. And I don't miss you."

She hadn't meant to even answer. Why couldn't she just hang up? She wasn't done with Damian after all. She wanted him to know the depth of her contempt for him.

"How's your new PA, Damian?" She regretted her question the moment it was out of her mouth. She should have shut down this conversation before it even began, but she wanted to shame him, to lash out at him somehow, excoriate him with the depth of her hatred.

"Fine. Perth's fine. The office. We miss you."

"Well, I'm fine, too," she lied. Her finances were far from it. Her burgeoning debt made her reel. "I don't miss Exos. Nor you. At all."

"Think about what you're saying, Stella. We had something special, you and I. Offer's still there. In fact, I'm prepared to more than double it. $50k. And the payrise. And that title. Office Director. But it won't be forever. Come back now and you could hit the ground running. Big conference in California coming up shortly. You'd love it. But that's my final offer. Think about it."

"This is about your damned pride, Damian!" she said. But he'd already hung up. She felt sick. What Damian hated most was losing a deal. Why couldn't he just accept he'd lost her?

Bastard. When they'd first met, back in the days she'd just left school and was temping where he was working, she'd once confessed to him her childhood dream of going to Disneyland. Did he think she was still that young, still that shallow? Was she really that impressed by money and the things it could buy? Not any more.

Her fingers were white on her phone, tight with anger. She'd been so dazzled by him back then, so grateful he'd even stop to talk to her. He'd been reeling her in even then, with his talk of their similar childhoods. Had her own poverty been so obvious? He'd had a sheen about him, of the up and coming go getter. How proud he'd been of his first Rolex - so *not* about telling the time.

"We'll go places, you and I," he'd said to her once, leaning his forearm on her desk so she'd notice it. He'd worn it like a talisman, as if it made him better than all the other middle managers, gave him the confidence to hand pick his future slaves and then never set them free. $50,000. Did he actually think she was for sale? Was she? *Maybe…* The idea disgusted her.

Stella was so preoccupied she hadn't paid close enough attention to a group of school girls who'd been admiring her stock. They'd turned their backs and were already at the other end of the mall when she noticed three of her rings were missing. She clutched the edge of her counter, furious. What a day. What was the saying? Caveat emptor? Buyer beware? More like "seller beware." She wasn't going to tell Damian about it, that was for sure.

Even when she'd hung up on Damian she could still picture his superior expression. He might like to make her think he understood everything about her and always knew best, but she was wise to that now. She shoved her phone down onto her counter as if it was red hot. Maybe it was.

Damian knew his offer was tempting her. Bonus? Bribe more like. Money for sex. Money for slavery. Money to tempt a girl who'd grown up with so little of it she was still in awe of its power.

Not the best of days. And when she arrived home, another credit card statement was waiting for her on her bed that evening. Imagining little Lucy delivering it there for her softened her rage. She tiptoed in to see the girls that night, stayed and smelled their washing powder fragrance, listened to their soft snores, gradually calming herself down.

Chapter 13

As if to echo her mood, a southerly swept in overnight. Unwelcome. Bitter.

Worried about her finances, Stella was up all hours polishing her dwindling stocks and trying to make a few more of the simpler things, some twisted wire pendants of celtic knots, quick but effective, and reasonably lucrative. And replace those alphabet rings the schoolgirls found so attractive, and make a few more. Who knew. Maybe those girls would start a trend, increase demand for her special rings. She might as well think positive. At least they'd wanted her work.

Her makeshift workbench was in Jeannie and Matt's cramped garage. Matt had rigged up some bright lighting. She hadn't noticed the time - well past midnight. Her neck ached from working such long hours. All the while, unbidden, memories of Damian kept resurfacing.

When she'd finally got to bed, eyes streaming from exhaustion, her mind was roiling, the dread of her credit card debt making sleep impossible. What was she doing with her life? Had working with Exos really been so bad? Maybe if she just went back to Perth for the three months, banked the bonus, and then worked strictly 9 to 5, building up more stock after hours, she could return to Sydney again and make it all work.

No. All that was over, and good riddance. What she needed to think about was making more stock, selling more stock. Paying off her debt. Create. Sell. Survive.

She rose and went to the kitchen for a drink of water, passing the girls' bedroom and listening again to their quiet noises of simple, untroubled slumber. If she hadn't come east to chase her dreams, she never would have been able to spend so much time with them, never would have witnessed Lucy's joy toddling up to her in the mornings with a book for them to read together. And little Sienna's gummy smiles melted her heart every time.

She was loved in different ways here in Sydney, in healthy ways that left her free to be herself and live her own destiny, however challenging that was proving to be.

The fridge was full of chicken wings. Of course! Jeannie's birthday party was on Saturday. She pulled out a mixing bowl. She'd make that cake for her with cinnamon and instant coffee between the layers. It was easier to slice if it was made a couple of days ahead.

A darker dawn than usual fooled her body clock.

Half asleep from only a few hours of sleep, Stella rushed and fumbled through her routine. She'd grabbed the first thing at hand, a summer frock from earlier in the week. There'd been no time to eat breakfast, let alone hear the weather report or check her weather app.

The icy breeze shocked her as she jumped off the bus and set out her goods. Sydney's southerlies were intense. As the wind rattled her displays and sliced through her clothes, she was cross with herself. She'd seriously underestimated the strength of this cold snap.

Clouds built. As the wind steadily strengthened, bringing with it the smell of the open ocean, Stella shivered in her summery dress as she carefully positioned the trays.

She would have to try to get away to buy a warm scarf from Donna, but there were still some half empty trays, and she was finding the earrings particularly fiddly to position with her cold fingers.

A dog walker pounded past, pooches of all sizes straining at their leashes, frisky with the extra smells as the breeze intensified. It was fresh alright. Wild.

There was a rumble of thunder. At a stronger gust, three empty coffee cups skittered past. Stella had to hold her skirt down.

No sign of James, she noted. Good. She'd been there more than a month, and he still couldn't resist offering gratuitous advice as he came past. Who needed another insult on a day like this? She was still smarting from having to buy back her own design the day before. Thrilled that Huntleys had seen the potential in her design, but desperate to pay down her debt. Saturday would be a write-off. Debt or no debt, she was determined to give up a day of trade to stay home and help host Jeannie's party.

Stella's sign was threatening to blow off, and she resolved to purchase some stronger hooks if she could find a quiet moment.

James appeared in a fine Burberry coat, like some kind of English squire who'd lost his horse.

"Rain's coming," James said. "Can you protect your stock?"

She glared at him, so perfectly presented, so totally prepared for every situation himself, then up at the clouds. She wasn't expecting rain. She had no idea how she could protect her displays. The stock was waterproof, but not the velvet trays. She might have to close up and go home.

She put her hands on her hips but couldn't think of a rejoinder. He was right. She should have considered this. He was making her feel like a fool.

If I'd wanted you to weigh in with your opinion, I'd have asked for it, she thought, but really, she was more cross with herself than with him.

Trust James to point out the obvious then disappear into his beautiful dry building.

A heavy drop of rain hit her forehead, and then another and then buckets of rain tumbled down. The soggy fabric of her dress clung to her skin, freezing in the stiffening wind. Frustrated, she rushed to cover her wares.

How foolish of her to forget a coat and umbrella. She scowled up at the sky.

There were no customers in sight, but for the coffee club parents with their babies and strollers, who would sometimes call in on her stall on their way home or before heading into the shops or yoga. They were gossiping away at the café while some of the older children scribbled with crayons at a small table.

Her dress was soaked. Teeth chattering, she gazed at the clouds. At least the rain had stopped.

There. *What would James know? Just a passing shower.*

James emerged again, debonair as ever, curse him. This time, he was brandishing a fine black umbrella as he swung open his door, and strode towards her. *Really?* Could he be bringing it for her?

As she pushed back her wet fringe, she imagined the toasty warmth of Huntleys' interior.

A flash of red caught her attention - one of the children.

"Mummy, mummy, I'm a winner," he was calling, frisky in the wind. Oh no! He was dashing towards the kerb!

Without thinking, Stella lurched forwards to catch him, her hand reaching for his shoulder, but she was unprepared and he was too quick, his sweatshirt slipping away from her grasp.

"Lucas!" his mother screamed, too many metres behind, busy with a baby in a stroller.

Panic in her throat, Stella sprinted after the child. He was heading straight for a line of traffic as the lights turned green. The menacing hiss of the wet tyres was terrifying. Time slowed. The cars were coming closer, the bus gathering speed.

The child was so tiny in his little denim pants, his face alight with excitement as he twisted back to look at his mother, oblivious to the danger. He would go over the curb, topple under those tyres ....

Without thinking, Stella threw herself at him, grabbing the top of his soft arm and yanking him back into the safety of the mall - just as she twisted her ankle on the wet curb and went down. Hard.

The pain took away her breath.

"Stella." James's deep voice was so close it reverberated against her chest, as her ankle shot pain up her leg and lodged in her gut. She'd crumpled into the gutter like a piece of cardboard. Brilliant. Ouch.

"It's okay," James said, soothing. "The boy's safe. He's with his mother."

That was a relief, but she could barely breathe for the pain, and the traffic was so close it roared and hissed like a monster!

With her wet fringe in her eyes, she couldn't see properly. The pain stabbed at her, and then panic. Had she broken something? How could she trade with one leg out of action!

Gentle fingers smoothed the hair out of her eyes. James's strong arms cradled her, his presence an immense comfort as the pain just keeps stabbing, stabbing, shooting up her leg.

"You're okay, Stella."

A tender touch at her temple. Could she believe this?

James was holding her; James in all his fine clothes, down here in the gutter with her, stormwater swirling all around them and traffic roaring past.

Within the black frame of pain and confusion, his tender embrace was a balm.

This man was so achingly beautiful up close, a blazing distraction from the throbbing pain.

His eyes, bluer than ever, were boring into hers, intense with concern. She could see every eyelash, even a tiny scar on his wet cheekbone, maybe from chickenpox. Could Mr Perfect have once been a boy? Could it be that he cared for her? She closed her eyes again, ashamed. She'd been so sure he'd hated her. It was true his every comment had seemed insulting, but how could she have thought this man hostile? He was here. For her.

Or maybe he'd do this for anyone. Save a life.

She went to move, but the pain made her cry out. He held her closer. Wet James Huntley. This man smelled divine. Warm and wonderful. Strong. Irresistible. How could so beautiful a man be real? Those chiselled cheeks, those parted lips, so close, tender with concern. For her. Maybe she'd died and gone to heaven.

"You're hurt."

"I'm going to move you further off the road, Stella," he said, breaking their gaze. "It's too dangerous."

The rain fell heavier now, the world growing darker still as the storm intensified. The pain in her ankle spiked as he moved her, then receded to a throb, dwarfed by her intense awareness of him, closer than ever, warm, protecting her, helping her.

"Mmmmm," she moaned as he held her closer, one arm beneath her knees.

What was this agony, to be so close, and not to kiss?

She tipped her head back, then, willing him with her eyes, inviting him, daring him.

His eyes flashed fire.

And then. Ecstasy.

Those lips, brushing hers, were softer than expected, so tender and warm in this cold, wet wind. Yes! But oh. Less than a second. An explosion of possibilities, too quickly extinguished.

"You're bleeding, Stella. I must get help." *Damn him. Damn this broken kiss.*

She turned her head away, wretched. The pain in her leg returned with a vengeance.

"You're okay," he said. "You'll be okay." Except she wasn't. All she wanted was to kiss him again and have him kiss her in return, kiss away the pain, kiss away the rest of the world.

He was fiddling with his phone.

She panicked. In the driving rain she couldn't see what was happening. "The kid!"

"He's fine. He's with his mother."

"My stall!"

"It's okay. Nicole will look after it all."

Great. Nicole's got everything then. Delicious James, and all my worldly fortune.

She would have to shake off the pain, push him away and get on with her life.

She struggled, but he held her fast.

"That's inadvisable, Stella. You might be badly hurt. There's some broken glass here. Stay still. I'll take you in to Emergency. We'll get this seen to right away. Is there someone I can phone for you?"

"Jeannie."

"What's her number, please?"

She could never remember it, so she reached for her pocket, but pain darted up again through her leg and she cried out.

"Let me," he said.

"My pocket."

He was searching for it, brushing her waist, her hip, her thigh. Intimate. She was almost sorry when he located it and extracted it from her sopping wet pocket.

She caught his eye, and both of them blushed.

He knows. He feels it too.

It was right there between them, stronger than the cold wind, brighter than the pain and louder than the sound of the rain and hissing tires. *Desire.*

Go on. Kiss me again, she willed him, but he blinked and turned away, then handed her the phone.

"Jeannie?"

"Stell! What's up? You've been retweeted by Harrods. It's incredible. Talk about star power."

"I'm in the gutter."

"Not for long, baby sister. Not with me managing your social."

"No, Jeannie. I'm about to go to hospital."

"What?"

Stella thrust the phone at James, closing her eyes as the pain surged.

"It's James Huntley here, Jeannie."

"James Huntley? What have you done to my sister?" Stella could hear Jeannie's frosty tone, suspicious, hostile.

"There's been an accident but Stella's okay. I'm taking her to Prince of Wales Emergency, Randwick."

Blue shirts. They were moving her. James was holding her hand. She never wanted to let him go. The pain was excruciating. Someone was giving her an injection. She kept her eyes on James's, such a deep and beautiful blue.

Chapter 14

Amid the hum of the hospital air-conditioning and smell of disinfectant, Stella's heart lifted to see Jeannie waiting for her on one of the beige emergency waiting room vinyl chairs, flipping lazily through a gossip magazine.

Awkward on crutches, Stella eased herself down beside her.

"Hey, little sister! Knew you'd be okay Are they done with you?"

Stella nodded.

"Sprain. Bit of a gash. Wish I'd seen that broken bottle in the gutter, but it's all sewn up now and they've jabbed me with a few injections, Tetanus, I think. Whatever. Still a bit numb."

"That's okay. Just sit for a minute. No rush. Still raining out there. Matt's looking after the girls. Take a break. You've had a bit of a shock. Hey! I hear you saved a little boy!"

Stella remembered the flash of red, the child's t-shirt, her frantic dash to stop him…

And then, the swirling storm water and a kiss, a delectable kiss and basking in the warmest sensation of being loved and cared for…

"Jeannie! My stall! The takings!"

"It's okay. Don't worry about a thing. It's all locked up in the Huntleys safe. The guy who called me was looking out for you, alright. You didn't tell me you had a fan…" Jeannie was smiling.

Stella started to pull herself up on her crutches again. Her ankle was throbbing and she wanted to get out of there, to get her life back in order.

"Hey, relax, Stell. Slow down. Everything's okay. I've only been here an hour. Can't remember when I last read a magazine. Besides..." Jeannie was smiling again, that smile she used when she knew something Stella didn't.

"What is it, Jeannie? Don't tease me."

"You didn't let on at all."

"About what? What's up?"

"James Huntley."

"What about him?"

"Met him just as you went in. Gave me his card." Jeannie looked like the cat that got the cream, or the older sister who had something she didn't. She pinched the card between thumb and forefinger and moved it slowly back and forth like something precious. The raised gold lettering caught the light, and Jeannie held it just out of reach.

"Tell me, Jeannie. Take pity. I'm injured, dammit. How much more pathetic can I get? It's cruel to take advantage of someone in hospital!"

"Calm down, calm down. Alright, I'll tell you, but I don't see why I should, since you've barely been levelling with me."

"What do you mean? Jeannie, stop it!"

"Rescued you, told us not to worry about a thing. And he's rung me twice while you've been here, to see how you are. You have a big fan, Stell. You never told me he cared about you. I thought you two were enemies."

"We ..."

Jeannie leaned towards her, one eyebrow up, smiling.

"What?"

"Why didn't you tell me, Stella?"

"Tell you what?"

"He's hot. He's hot, full stop. And he's especially hot for you, little sister."

"Stop it. What is this?"

"James Huntley. All this time I've been slinging it to him on social. I had him pegged as fat and middle aged and grumpy. Instead, I meet him here and I think he's the doctor. He's tall and toned and tanned and ... really rather nice. Not nice like my Matt, mind you, but not bad. Not bad at all. And you. You never let on once that you liked him, not at all. And you never said once that he likes you. He's crazy about you. Wants you to phone him by the way. Left me his card. For you."

She held it again like a trophy, teasing. It caught the light, the gold edges and raised gold H glowing like strips of gold.

Stella took the card, closing her eyes, remembering the wet morning, the dash to save the child, James's warm embrace, and then that instant of a searing, delicious, broken kiss.

"Come on, Stell. Fess up. I thought it was war between you two."

War. Practically. Except ...

"Any chance of a cup of tea?"

"Yeah. I'll be a few minutes. But you don't get out of it. Here, you can use my phone. Lover boy wants to hear from you."

Stella looked at the number on the card, glanced at Jeannie's phone, and hesitated. Maybe it was all better as a dream. This was so awkward. She didn't even know if she'd just imagined the kiss. Everything happened so quickly. Still. At least Jeannie was out of the room. She'd just make it a quick call. Get it over with.

The phone rang twice. "You're okay then?" he said, his voice full of concern, warm as tawny port. "Good of you to call. Do you need me to come and get you?"

"No. Thank you." She cleared her throat, awkward as a schoolgirl.

James cleared his, too. Maybe it was a mistake to ring. They were strangers, practically rivals, from Nicole's point of view, anyway. What would Jeannie know? Had they actually kissed? Maybe she'd just imagined the touch of his lips as some kind of wishful thinking. Or maybe he thought if he used his charm she wouldn't sue him for breach of copyright. Deep disappointment attacked her very core. She felt like weeping.

She hadn't told Jeannie yet about the way Huntleys stole her design. She didn't want to spoil the birthday surprise. Yes. That was it. James was just being charming so she wouldn't make trouble. Despicable.

"Gotta go," Stella said as Jeannie walked back in, balancing tea in paper cups.

"See you," James said levelly.

"See you." Whatever that meant. Tea. As she reached for the tea in its flimsy take-away cup, Jeannie leaned over her to give her a gentle squeeze, smelling like fruity shampoo and vegemite sandwiches.

Stella burnt her tongue on the first sip. And she ached all over.

"Jeannie! My takings. My bag. Where's it gone? Do you have the money?"

"Relax. I told you everything's okay. Take it easy! It's fine. Your hero rescuer has it all in hand. He asked me to remind you that Nicole got your bag, and it's in the Huntleys safe with your stock."

Stella ran a finger over the raised gold lettering and copperplate font of the card. Old fashioned, it oozed status.

"So, come on," Jeannie prompted. "Tell me about the hottie!"

Stella looked away and bit her lip, all her senses remembering in a rush. *Essence of James.* That broken kiss. She hadn't imagined it. No way.

"Yes, little sister. He was here with you till I got here. Very, very attentive, Stell. Very concerned about you. An absolute gentleman. Crazy about you. Not crazy *at* you at all! Come on. Explain."

"Mystery to me. Maybe he finally worked out his competition was about to be eliminated… Any port in a storm? How am I to know? You've seen it on Facebook. Huntleys has only ever been hostile, hostile, hostile. Then, suddenly, Mr Nice Guy. Mr Hero. Mr Save the Day. I don't trust him one ounce and nor should you, Jeannie. And you should know better than to judge a book by its cover."

Jeannie held her tongue, encouraging Stella to say more.

"Well, I'll admit it's quite an attractive cover. Very attractive, even. Yes. Anyone might find James attractive." Jeannie remained silent, smiling. "Look. He might have good manners and he stopped me getting run over, but don't read too much into it, Jeannie. Please. You shouldn't tease me. Come on. Even if he did rescue me, it doesn't necessarily mean a thing. He might be spoken for, for all I know. He spends a lot of time with that Nicole person, the PR agent, partner, whatever. And you've seen all those hostile tweets."

"We give back as good as we get…"

"You do. I have nothing to do with it. You enjoy it, Jeannie, I swear it! Mild-mannered Mrs Matt Lipson, former marketing executive and mother of two is actually a social media warrior! One of those trolls. Savage! Is it really necessary?"

"Now you're just changing the subject, Stella. Or are you actually asking me to back off on James Huntley. I knew you were interested in him. I just knew it."

Jeannie's little know-it-all smile was starting to annoy Stella. She sipped her tea.

"Sorry," Jeannie said. "I shouldn't have teased you, Stell. I'm just so bloody relieved you weren't hurt badly. But you do need to rest and recover. Let's get out of here. I'll go get the car."

Between stretches of blissful, deep and restful sleep, Stella woke often. While her ankle ached in dull throbs, there was a more insistent sensation, a searing need she couldn't quell, an aching emptiness within, a need for James, damn him.

It was her body, remembering the bliss of being held, the warm security of it. And that kiss. Like the sweetest syrup, but just a drop. Just a promise of more to come.

She dreamt impossible dreams, waking to chastise herself. She should be thinking of jewelry, not the delectable shape of James Huntley's jaw and throat, carefully shaven. The man was simply a distraction!

When Jeannie brought in a breakfast tray, Stella gave her a grateful smile. She shrank at putting weight on her ankle. Her stall would have to wait.

"Take a few days off, Stell. Let yourself heal. I'll keep the door closed so you don't get too disturbed."

"I love the girls, Jeannie. Keep it open. They can visit me any time."

Not expecting Stella to still be home, they took their time. While she waited for her little visitors, Stella sighed and flicked through the news on her mobile phone.

That's when she saw it; a photo and a snippet. Click bait.

"Huntley heart breaker," the headline shouted. It was the photograph that first caught her eye - of a couple's picture torn in two, a dark-haired beauty holding a guitar and a tall, confident man, his high forehead and handsome smile so like James's.

> *Huntleys House of Diamonds heir Will Huntley has broken up with US singer songwriter Holly Breen who is reportedly at a retreat.*
>
> *The first known US celebrity to have her heart broken by the handsome Aussie is giving 'no comment.'*
>
> *Huntley leaves a string of broken hearts across the globe including Irish actress Maeve Dawson and the daughter of Italian opposition leader Rosa Bianchi, who is reportedly suing her former fiance for breach of promise after he failed to show up at their wedding.*

"Great family," Stella muttered, throwing down her phone in disgust. Forget daydreams and all distractions. What was she thinking! Forget James Huntley. She had plenty on her plate without him. She must heal her ankle and get back to work, to clear her debt, focus on her business and make it a success. But first? Jeannie's birthday party.

"Shhh. It's mummy's special day," said Stella, luring both girls into her room early on Saturday. "Let's give mummy a sleep in. Bring me every teddy and every book. Let's read to all the teddys."

Then she kept the girls busy making cards till almost nine o'clock, bringing Jeannie tea and toast on a tray with the Huntleys bag sitting casually on the side. She let Lucy and Sienna push in ahead of her, waving their cards, and they sang Happy Birthday.

Jeannie made a fuss of the girls, cuddling them up beside her in bed and admiring their drawings and messages, the hot tea safely out of reach on the chest of drawers. Her eyes kept returning to the little gold and white bag.

"Stella! That's not what I think it is, is it?"

"Could be a little something for the best big sister in the world."

"Stella! Huntleys is over the top. Tell me it's just the bag."

"You saying my sister doesn't deserve quality?"

"Well…"

Stella couldn't wait any longer. She handed Jeannie the bag, smiling as the girls watched on and Jeannie pulled out the tissue wrapped jewelry box.

"This is heavy, Stella. I'm hating this. I can't believe this."

Lucy put her arm through the ribbon bag handles and admired the swinging bag. Sienna tried to eat the discarded tissue paper, which Stella rescued, swinging her youngest niece up in a hug to distract her.

Jeannie looked at the box for ages before opening it.

"I hate to think what this cost you, Stell."

"Today's actually about you for once, Jeannie."

Jeannie's face broke out in an enormous grin. She leaped out of bed.

"OMG, Stella. Oh. My. God. Gold! This looks *real*. Will you look at this thing!" Jeannie held the heavy jewel in her palm, turning it as it flashed and sparkled in the morning light. "Did you design this, Stell? It's a lot like your brooch."

"That's what I thought when I saw it, but it's actually better. Did you see the back? You can wear it as a pendant or a brooch or even a choker. I'm going to modify all my brooches now so they can be adapted, too. Charge a bit more for them."

"I love it. I absolutely adore this thing. But you're way too generous, Stell…"

"Don't you dare talk to me about 'generous,' Jeannie, taking me in, working with me. I couldn't have a better sister if I tried to design one. Oh. And you're wearing that out to dinner tonight, after your party. You and Matt are going out. On me. And I'm babysitting."

"But your ankle?"

"That's the whole point. I'm staying home anyway. We'll put our feet up, won't we girls?"

Once she was dressed, Jeannie kept rearranging the jewel ahead of her party, on a chain and off again, on a ribbon at her throat and then pinned to her top. Stella smiled every time she saw Jeannie checking herself out in the mirror. She'd made the right decision. Whatever happened, she'd delivered some solid joy alright. She couldn't be more thrilled.

Matt flew in that morning, coming home via the shops, with ice and cold drinks. By the time the chicken wings were sizzling on the barbeque, the townhouse was full of Jeannie's friends, Stella tossing salads and adjudicating minor toddler squabbles and generally assisting.

Jeannie's new jewel was a hot topic.

"This is one of Stella's designs," Jeannie said proudly. "She's actually got some of her work here if anyone wants to have a little look."

"So you're Stella of Stellar?"

"Did Antoinette really buy your earrings? You wouldn't have any more of those, would you? I wanted to get some red ones. And some purple ones?"

"Do you take cash?"

"You could do this, you know. Sell this like tupperware, at parties at people's places." She could. Anything was possible now she was her own boss.

Wine and bubbly. Cake. Tea. Coffee. Washing up. More bubbly. It was almost seven o'clock before the last toddler was rounded up and all the friends departed.

"Now. Out you go," said Stella.

"I can't eat another thing. And your ankle? It must be killing you."

"I'm okay. I'm sure you two need a romantic wander on the beach together. Why not? We've got this. Haven't we, girls?" Sienna was already almost asleep, and Lucy was still on a sugar high, racing around collecting plastic cups and putting them in the bin. They'd both be out like lights within half an hour, and Stella not far behind them, glad to put both feet up after all that hopping around the house. Today hadn't been easy, but what a joy!

"Best birthday ever, Stell," said Jeannie, her face glowing. "Thank you, Matt. Thank you, Stella. Thank you, my babies."

Chapter 15

A few days later, extricating herself from the Uber with her crutches, Stella felt a rush of pride. Her stall was so tiny, yet somehow defiant. Bright. Brave. She had to succeed. Since leaving Exos nearly four months ago, she'd already achieved so much. She was bringing in good money every week.

While she hadn't made nearly enough to pay off her debt, and the theft had set her back, money was still coming in – through Jeannie's online sales and directly into her own hands – and, best of all, she was doing what she loved.

And Huntleys – one of the best known jewelers in Sydney - had so much faith in her designs, they were copying them. It was an endorsement, even if she wasn't too sure of the legalities.

There it was, the Huntleys building, so substantial, so solid. Hope surged that her own business could become so successful. Maybe Stellar, too, could sustain and nurture generations. If the Huntley family has done so well, surely she, too, could power ahead, fueled by her own talent and determination.

Right now, though, she set off gingerly, placing most of her weight on her good foot. Progress was slow. A spark of pain shot up from her bad ankle. Was she really so invincible?

A vivid memory of the accident returned - the blind dash of the child, her need to save him, the scream of the brakes, the child's soft warmth as she'd pulled him to safety, away from the cold hard metal, just in time, the excruciating pain. The blood streaming from her ankle in the rain…

A shiver of pure fear seized her as she stood, remembering. What if she'd left her run a second too late? What if a car had been going faster, or had skidded on the wet road? How had she not run headlong into it herself?

How had James been there at the kerb so quickly? He must have been coming around the corner as she'd chased the little boy. She remembered now. The umbrella. Had he been bringing her the big umbrella?

Such a close call. She rubbed her hand down her bruised hip, and limped along on the crutches. She would never take her ankles for granted again.

James's dash to save her returned to her mind again and again. It was plaguing her. Despite his audacity in copying her designs, and despite the gossip piece about James's playboy brother, she knew she must at least thank James for his kindness. Whatever their business rivalry, he'd done the right thing by her. And if she was honest with herself, there'd been that kiss. A hot kiss. The start of something five star. Something unfinished.

At the very least, she needed to retrieve her cash and stock, and thank him for taking her to Emergency. It was only right she should see him, at least briefly, however awkward it might be.

The mall hadn't been the same without Stella busy at her bright stall. More than once, James caught himself lingering at the staff room window, peering down, watching out for Stella's dark hair and bright eyes. He remembered the first time they'd met. Her spark. Her feisty resistance to being pushed around.

James was accustomed to being in charge. He'd grown up empowered. He knew what authority was, what it was to be a privileged white male. Tall, strong, good-looking and wealthy, all his life he'd been treated with respect. People took him seriously. Once he'd inherited the business, they'd looked up to him even more. Not that things had always gone smoothly for him, not back then and not now. He'd had his share of hurt.

Losing his father so young was a blow, Helene had run a mile once she'd worked out Huntleys finances were in trouble, and Will had given him headaches all his life by doing the wrong thing, but for the most part, things had gone his way, fallen into place, run smoothly enough.

Not that PR stunt. While Nicole had been furious and still held a grudge against Stella, James was philosophical. *Win some. Lose some.*

He smiled, remembering. Stella had put her case clearly. And she'd benefited, that was for sure. But she hadn't actually done anything wrong. She'd had a right to be there.

He could now admit to himself he enjoyed seeing her every day, stopping for a chat, surprising her with that ice cream. She'd accepted it so warily. As if it had strings attached. Why shouldn't he give her an ice cream? She'd been out there all day in that searing heat, practically wilting. An ice cream was exactly what she'd needed.

And he genuinely admired her designs. Jim had that kind of talent. He'd probably been born with it, and had honed it every day of his life. That was how he'd been able to pick up on Stella's design ideas and create those new pieces so quickly. And they were selling well, not just to Stella herself.

She hadn't seemed entirely pleased to see her design for sale in the display case, he remembered. Imitation was a form of flattery, wasn't it? Rivalry in the jewelry trade was rife, as in any industry, a fact of life. Her eyes had flashed fire and fury. And then she'd insisted on paying full price. She was determined, alright. Formidable. *Admirable.*

Yes. He'd been surprised how much he'd missed her presence. Every day.

It still horrified him to think how close he'd come to losing her, how he'd brought her the big umbrella, only to see her almost run over. Thank God he'd snatched her away just in time.

She'd shown such courage. Small but strong. Except she wasn't. She was soft, too. When they'd been down there in the gutter, when …

He'd just been glad her takings and stock were well protected in Huntleys safe. It was the right thing to do. In fact, he'd shifted them up to the smaller safe in his office.

So when he'd happened to be at the staff room window again, finishing a coffee, and he'd chanced to see her struggling out of the Uber on crutches, he was down those stairs and out in the mall in a heartbeat, ready to assist.

The protective aura of James enveloped her again, impossible to ignore. She wanted to stop right there and turn to him, to feel the warm, reassuring strength of him, and just be held, to let the horror of the accident begin to seep away and escape her body for good.

But she just couldn't do it. Wasn't being this close to James also a danger? It was every bit as real as falling into the gutter ahead of oncoming traffic. No. She must caution herself, to keep her distance. A man had never been part of Stella's new plan.

Her whole aim now was to become totally self-sufficient. She must never allow her future and her happiness to depend on someone else. She knew she could rely on herself. Men were too likely to distract and disappoint her.

She understood now that much of Damian's power over her was physical. The last thing she needed was another relationship like that. She pulled herself under control, and glanced at James again, guarded, wary.

No. Wildly attractive or not, James Huntley was just a distraction from her long-term goal.

"It's okay, Stella. Let me help. I won't bite."

She stopped in her tracks. If he was trying to put her at ease, he'd used the wrong words.

"You've been very kind, James." Her voice was measured.

"Nonsense. It's what anyone would do."

"That's just not true. But look. I've come to retrieve my stock and bag."

"You saved the little boy's life."

They entered the foyer and James summoned the elevator.

"Is he okay?" If she held her crutch at an angle, she could keep her distance. His proximity was intoxicating. *Essence of James. Danger zone.*

"He's fine. You blocked his fall with your own body. It was very brave of you. You have many talents, Stella Rhys."

If she leaned against her side of the slow old elevator and studied the floor, she could avoid seeing him in all those mirrors, could hide from his compliment.

James was quiet. Respectful.

"Speak for yourself," she said, meeting his eyes despite herself, heart flipping again.

She had to glance away. *Too high a voltage.* She must retrieve her things, thank him, and that would be that. Anything else was simply not part of the plan.

In the VIP room, James offered to rest her crutches against the wall as she settled on the ornate deep blue velvet couch. He asked her to wait a few moments.

When he re-entered, he was carrying her heavy bags.

"Business is good, I see."

"Look, I need to thank you, for taking me to the hospital, for keeping my things safe."

"Please. It's nothing. Don't forget you're one of our customers, apart from everything else. We look after our customers."

"James ..."

"Alright. Repay me by having dinner with me," he said, pleased with himself. "We might even enjoy ourselves. We can talk about trends in jewelry design. Or maybe something completely different. Are you a cat person or a dog person? That sort of thing."

"That's a very kind offer, but it's me who should be offering you dinner, James." What was she doing? She'd told herself she wouldn't fall for him.

She had a business to run, and more than a week of trade to make up for, and her ankle was still throbbing. Imagine the agony at the end of each day.

She was in no position to invite him home, where she could put her foot up in comfort. He'd have to share dinner with Jeannie, the babies, the bottles and probably Matt. *Too late.*

"I accept," he said, his smile so joyous she couldn't help but return it.

"But can it wait? Till, say, Friday? I need to rest and recover a little. It's only sensible." She was gabbling. It was the only way she could create some distance between them again.

She was back peddling. She simply couldn't fall into the same trap she'd made for herself with Damian, completely relinquishing her own plans and dreams to become the robot lover. What did she actually know of James, except that he kept company with movie stars and was in some kind of relationship with Nicole the PR person. And he'd laid his charm pretty thick on Jeannie. And he had a playboy brother. *Danger.*

Yet, there was that bounce in his movements again as he offered her his hand to help her stand up from the couch. There was an invisible hum between them, that lovely temperature of his skin against hers. She winced as she put her weight on her ankle and he stepped closer to help support her, placing his arm around her waist. It felt right there. Too right.

"Lean on me." His voice was deep, kind and reassuring, with no shortage of the masculine charm and strength she so missed in her life. "Just let me help you."

"I'm fine, thanks," she said, turning away from those eyes so full of concern for her, and those lips, way too close to hers. His breath was on her shoulder. How easily she could turn to him again.

She'd almost forgotten that complete feeling of trusting another, that way of moving together so closely. But had Damian ever been this caring?

She closed her eyes lest he sense her longing. She was almost in tears. He was so considerate, so genuinely caring. *Nicole's a lucky woman.* What business of hers was the company James kept?

They made it to the elevator. Too soon, it opened and she had to enter it without him.

It was like leaving part of herself behind. The best she could do was turn awkwardly and hold out her hand for a farewell shake.

James held it alright, a touch too long, long enough for that pulse of interest to flicker and deepen between them, but as he leaned forward, the doors closed.

As she descended, alone, Stella counselled herself to get back to her patch of the mall as quickly as possible and literally mind her own business. Friday was all of four days away. Anything could happen.

Chapter 16

Back at her stall, Stella laid out her wares in as tempting a fashion as she could without having to hop too far. Some browsers approached, including a diminutive older woman with a large black bag.

"Something for yourself?" Stella asked.

"I don't know." She was like many of her customers, those with time on their hands, window shopping and happy to chat.

"This one reminds me of when I was a girl," the woman said.

"Oh?"

"Except it was much smaller. It had little opals inside. There was a matching set of earrings. It was my mother's, bought for her by her mother, bought right here, at Huntleys. I'll show you. I'll bring it tomorrow."

"I'd love that," Stella answered, intrigued. How she loved her work. At times like this, her imagination flared. She could create a series of tiny globes, each with different jewels inside, and there could be sets to mix and match.

She'd been dreaming of different pieces, of a set inspired by fruit, and another of various animals. She'd love to create a flower set, an alphabet set, and a set for the four seasons. She'd even wondered about some space jewels, inspired by the planets.

It reminded her she'd dreamt up some "get well pieces" while at the hospital. Swinging pill capsule earrings and a stethoscope brooch. She reached into her bag for her notepad to jot down her ideas. She pushed her hand around inside the bag, feeling for it. Where was it?

Had it disappeared when she'd rushed to save the child? Her heart pounded. *All her ideas! Lost!*

She fought to still her rising sense of panic. They were just ideas. They came out of her head. She could sketch them again.

For now she must think only of her customers; forget the missing sketchpad; forget James Huntley. Only Stellar mattered.

That afternoon, a vaguely familiar woman appeared with a stroller. Holding her hand was a small boy with a bright bunch of flowers. He thrust them at Stella.

"We can't thank you enough," the woman said, eyeing Stella's bandaged ankle uneasily. "You saved Lucas's life."

Stella bent down to accept the gift.

"Thank you," he said, looking up at his mother to check he'd said it right.

Stella smiled. He was angelic. Contrite.

"They're so beautiful! Thank *you,* Lucas." And to his mother. "That's really not necessary. But I appreciate it."

The woman was still staring at Stella's ankle, frowning.

"We're so sorry you were hurt. Lucas has promised not to run away like that again."

"Well, that's a good idea," Stella told him, reassuring his mother she was okay before they moved away.

"You have another admirer, I see." James stopped by on his way into Huntleys, nodding at the bouquet.

"Lucas. He's three." Despite her reservations, Stella actually found herself laughing and fluttering her eyelashes at James. She couldn't help liking the way he was making her feel special. He noticed, amusement flickering in his eyes. *Was he flirting with her?*

"I hope he's not invited for dinner as well..." *Definitely flirting.* She liked the way she and James were testing the distance between each other, like a bird stretching its wings before taking flight, or the sun slowly rising. Yes. She always wanted to be closer to him.

"Nope. Just the two of us."

James leaned towards her. Was he going to touch her forearm? Was he actually a little shy? He pulled away, but he held her eyes with his own.

"Looking forward to it." He swung his hand up in farewell instead, but the smile they exchanged made her catch her breath.

Oh.

What was she going to wear?

And she still hadn't solved the problem of where they would go. With her credit card debt, swanky wasn't possible right now. For an instant, a vision of fish fingers hovered in her imagination and she laughed. Absolutely not.

With her ankle still in a boot, high heels were out of the question. Amused, she remembered all the missing shoes of her childhood. This would be the one time in her life when just one shoe would be perfectly appropriate.

Stella suddenly knew the solution. A picnic! Flame made an artform of picnics. They'd enjoyed one at least once a week when she was growing up. They required little preparation and no washing up.

"Let's dine in the great outdoors," Flame would say as she'd picked the girls up late from school. They'd find their way to a lookout, or a beach or a park, with fish and chips or a pizza, or sometimes just dips and crackers and a bag of carrots. One tub of hummus could go a long way.

Flame even knew how to picnic in the rain. Stella remembered them all whisking away broken glass and rusty bottle tops and hiding under a picnic table in a park as rain plummeted down around them. Even now she couldn't eat corn chips and salsa without remembering the smell of rain.

She might need something more sophisticated than corn chips for Friday night, but she liked the idea. Would James?

She texted him before she changed her mind.

Picnic dinner on Friday. Meet me at the stall after 7pm.

Looking forward to it, he replied.

Good. So was she. Though strange nerves pulsed through her. That was silly. She was just thanking him for being so nice to her when she'd hurt her ankle, wasn't she? It wasn't like it was a date.

Next day, Stella closed her stall for a few minutes to visit Donna.

"Need your help, Donna. What've you got? I need something really…"

Donna held up her hands for more clues.

"Sexy? Date?"

"Sort of. Something fresh. For a picnic. I want to look …"

"Sexy." They laughed. Did she? She did.

"But subtle." Stella wasn't ready for another relationship. Or was she? She certainly didn't want things to move too fast. She'd jumped into becoming Damian's mistress without a second thought. Surely she was wiser now.

The two of them rummaged, Donna finally holding up a silk scarf in black, purple and crimson. It was much more frivolous than the simple outfits Stella usually wore. When Donna tied it around her waist, Stella did a light twirl and felt the power of the thing. She clicked her fingers, like a flamenco dancer, or Carmen. It had a holiday vibe, and if James felt like a flirt, she'd be ready. So far, he'd only seen her in simple cotton frocks. This could be fun.

At the last minute, she selected a pair of flat slip-ons studded with diamantes, for $30. They were practically plastic but they added some glamour and had plenty of room for her super boot. Then Donna threw in a short black cardigan, beaded, for her shoulders. It was classy. It would sparkle in the dark.

"No, no. You keep it," she insisted. "Stallholders' deal."

"Well, I owe you your pick of earrings, Donna."

As Stella paid up, Donna frowned.

"You know, Stella, I've been meaning to talk to you."

"Oh?"

"Maybe I shouldn't say anything. Maybe it's nothing."

"Tell me?"

"Well, my cousin works at the council. He tells me things sometimes. He said he saw something. About your stall."

"What?" A cold chill washed over Stella in the balmy afternoon.

"Apparently, even with a licence, we can be closed down if one of the permanent traders launches a complaint."

"But I've done nothing wrong!"

"I know you haven't. It's probably nothing. Forget I said anything. Have a great night, Stella."

Stella pushed Donna's comments out of her mind, dashed around to buy a basket and a couple of glasses and small plates and a platter, then found some delicacies. Finger food. Stuffed olives. Dolmades. Prosciutto. Fancy crackers in a tin from Fortnam and Mason, and creamy blue cheese. Liqueur chocolates. Would it be enough? Sultana grapes. Cold white wine.

They'd need something to sit on. In a homewares store, she headed for the beach towels, thinking she could use one as a picnic rug, deliberating for a moment or two, then snatching up the purple one to match that flamenco scarf.

"I adore this one," said the sales assistant as she rang up the purchase. "Lush purple. The color of seduction."

Stella laughed, then blushed, and rushed to the bathroom to change, give herself a squirt of perfume and a few dabs of makeup, and pull her hair up into a high bun. Purple Antoinette earrings completed the ensemble. Why not.

James turned up at 7pm on the dot, in casual trousers and a fresh cotton shirt with the sleeves rolled up. Casual James was like something out of a David Jones catalogue - designer understated - yet he wore the clothes with complete ease.

His eyes lit up as he took in her face and outfit, lingering in just the right places. *Good.* It thrilled her, made her heart pump. It was a thank you picnic, and she wasn't interested in a relationship right now, but that was no reason she shouldn't enjoy it.

Besides, maybe that was just standard Huntley charm - the way he enticed his customers to pay so much for their baubles. For an instant, she wondered whether Nicole knew about their outing, then pushed her out of her mind.

"So. Where are we going?" he asked, eyes holding hers as if it were the most important question in the world. "I've got the convertible."

"Harborside picnic?" she asked. She tried to hide her own sense of anticipation, to keep her expression neutral, but his smile was intoxicating. How easy it would be to simply lean into him and kiss those lips! If she was honest with herself, spending time with him would be no hardship, none at all.

Not. A. Date.

So now, with James swinging his keys, she was ready.

Adrenalin was surging. The prospect of a picnic had never been more appealing.

"Where to?" he asked. This time when he looked her up and down, and she shivered, she cautioned herself. The man's brother was a playboy. Maybe they both were. Just a thank you picnic, and she could go back to designing her planet set. Or maybe the season set. That was it. Keep her mind on her higher calling.

"You know this city better than I do. Somewhere scenic. I'd love to see the water, James. I haven't actually seen much of Sydney. I mostly just make jewelry and sell it…"

It was a beautiful evening, beginning to cool down. She studied his handsome profile as he considered some options. Evidently there were quite a few, and she wondered for a moment just how many picnics he'd had with how many women. Then again, she was hardly a blushing teenager herself anymore. Or was she? Had she ever been this excited about a date? *Not a date.*

"Been to Parsley Bay?" he asked. "South Head? Beach Paddock? I'd take you to Bondi, but swimming at sunset's best left to the sharks, and if we're after somewhere secluded... it's the opposite." His eyes were liquid with possibilities. They drifted to her lips.

"You choose," she said. "After all, this is all about thanking you for caring for me after the accident. Remember?"

He took the picnic basket from her and ushered her towards the convertible, a little vintage E-type Jag, British racing green, auto shabby chic.

"Mother's," he offered by way of explanation, as he opened the door for her and she slid in. The smell of leather enveloped her, the walnut dashboard a work of art. Stella ran her hand across its smooth surface as James leapt in on the other side and started up the engine, a throaty throb that sounded like adventure.

"She's in France," he added, glancing as her fingers caressed the wood.

How easy it would be to drop her hand to his thigh, she thought. *Maybe later.*

"Mmm?"

"I promised I'd give it a run now and then, but it's garaged in Bowral, a couple of hours south. Have to take it back again tomorrow. Feel like a country run?"

"Maybe. I ought to work. Saturdays are quite good." What she really needed to do was create and sell enough stock to pay off her debt, not goof off with a playboy.

"Pick you up after the lunchtime rush, then?" he said, both hands halting on the wheel, turning to give her his full attention before pulling out of the kerb.

For a moment she remembered Donna's comment. Was there really another great cloud hanging over her business? Big debt, and now, some question about her stall? She didn't want to think about it. Not right now.

"Hey. We don't have to talk about work. It's a beautiful night and you're about to show me Sydney Harbour in this fabulous car. Your mother has great taste. You grew up here, didn't you?"

"Born and bred."

"Come on then. Give me the tour."

Chapter 17

James swung them down Ocean Street under a glorious green canopy of plane trees. When they stopped at lights, Stella was acutely aware of his hand resting on the gearstick, so close to her knee. She calmed herself by turning the other way and admiring the classy home wares and fashion on display in the windows of the small shops.

As they accelerated again, her hair escaped the bun in the mild evening air, she clutched it to hold it out of her eyes, and he glanced across at her with a grin.

James's 10 out of 10 smile was catchy. The corners of her lips floated up in an answering grin, and she threw back her head and laughed. It was lovely being driven around by James in this extraordinary car.

He looked across and laughed along, as they scooted along the edge of Rose Bay past mansions on one side and the yachts and pleasure cruisers on the other.

The car engine sang like Shirley Bassey as James changed gears and they vroomed up the "s" bends of New South Head Road.

...

James couldn't remember when he'd had so much fun lately. How relaxing it was to leave his work worries behind. He could finally let himself dwell on Stella and that incredible kiss.

"Family home was up that way," he shouted above the sound of the engine and rush of air, pointing up to the top of the ridge.

"'Was?'"

"Sold it a few years after my father died, when we'd all left school."

"Sorry. To hear about your father." He tensed as her hand touched his thigh, then relaxed. Yes. This Stella…

They'd stopped at a set of lights. He put his own hand over hers, gently.
…

When he lifted it to change gears, its absence was a loss, so she removed hers from his thigh again after giving it a quick squeeze. It was firm, muscled.

"Do you work out?"

"Runner. I don't run as much as I used to do. Ran all the time when I was a kid. Ran to school, ran to soccer training, ran to see friends, to the library, to the shops. Represented the State in cross country for a few years there. I know this area so well. Strange to show it to a newcomer. I keep forgetting to point things out, like the playing fields, the golf course. We've already passed my old school."

Suddenly he pulled off the main road and dived down a side street, past more manicured gardens and fancy fences, then down to a park on the edge of the water.

"Lots of places I could take you, but that ankle's still sore. You won't want to walk too far. This place is good. Great view. Quiet. We'll have it to ourselves."

When he shut off the engine the silence roared. She was doing better without crutches now, and he drew her arm around him and put his own supporting arm around her shoulders. Slowly they walked together down a path towards the edge of the water. Crickets stilled and resumed their chirrups again as they passed. At last, with a welcoming whisper, came the hush of gentle waves against the shore.

The cut grass smelled sweet, so far from the traffic. All lit up, a huge cruise ship slid out of Sydney Harbour, lights reflecting in the glossy water in front of them, as it headed back to sea. The breeze brought wafts of jazz from the band on deck.

Stella flicked out the beach towel on a flat patch of soft grass, and James placed the picnic basket on one edge, suddenly grabbing her around the waist and clasping her close. He swayed her to the beat of the band, and when she laughed, he pulled her off her feet and spun her around with him. A good dancer as well! Bonus. Her flouncy scarf-skirt swung out as he set her down.

"Enough of that. I promised to take you to dinner, and really, you've taken me. The least I can do is offer you some wine for starters."

"Sure. Thank you. Need a hand?"

"Screw top. Easy. Margaret River Sauvignon Blanc, sir?"

"Why thank you. Pretty good restaurant."

"Best table in the house, for you."

"Best company for sure."

"Flirt. Fairly limited menu, though. Stuffed olive?"

"Love a stuffed olive."

"Antipasto? Fancy crackers? Cheese?"

"Love a fancy cracker."

They touched their glasses together before they sipped.

"Beautiful wine."

"You've had it before?" Dumb question. Playboy family.

"Not this one."

"I suppose you've been to Margaret River."

He had. With Helene, as it happened. She'd complained the whole time she couldn't get decent phone reception. For him it had been part of the charm of the place, escaping everything else. Just being there.

To his astonishment, as he sipped the cool wine he found himself telling Stella all about Helene, the daughter of a family friend; how they'd invited each other to their end of school dances at their parents' suggestion and

149

had ended up at the same uni, studying different things, but running into each other often enough to be considered a couple. A few years later, they'd gone to so many friends' engagement parties and weddings together, they'd been on the point of getting engaged themselves.

By then his father had died and he'd taken on the business. At first Helene had been thrilled, but she'd shown no interest in retail and was jealous of all the time he'd had to devote to the business, learning all about payroll and supply chain, balancing the books and dealing with the employees and customers. The last straw had been when she'd finally realized he wasn't just an heir who could go around spending a fortune on her.

"Yep. Helene only wanted the good times. Turned around and targeted one of my old uni mates whose father owned a big freight company."

Stella carved some cheese for him, placing it on a biscuit and handing it across.

"Broke your heart?"

"Not really. I don't reckon she had my heart in the first place, now I think about it. More like left it cold. There hadn't been a lot of loving in our relationship. Not through thick and thin or anything. As I said, Helene was only there for the good times. Turns out there's no shortage of company like that."

"Playboy," she teased him with an edge of challenge, topping up his wine. She was beautiful in this late dusk, her curves emerging from the shadows, arms and shoulders bare, with that low cut top and the flash of scarf. Alluring.

"It's my brother Will who's the big playboy. Not me. So go on," he said, drawing up his knees and topping up her own glass. "Your turn. Do you always buy Margaret River wines for your beach picnics?"

Stella took a sip. What question was he really asking? The view was mesmerizing as the last notes of twilight faded in the west, beyond the bridge. She usually felt sad as the final golds and pinks of the sunset drained away, but this evening, all the street lights, headlights and windows across the water sparkled like fairy lights, while the red and green channel markers created such a cheerful display, she was enchanted.

"What was that?" They were both sitting now, leaning closer to each other as they shared the food. He'd been sincere with her. "Do you rescue a lot of women, James Huntley, the Third?"

"Should I?"

"I'm glad you rescued me."

"It was very difficult," he smiled.

"It was. What about your suit? I bet it shrank. You were wet through."

"There were compensations if I remember correctly."

"There were?" Was he talking about the "almost" kiss? It burned there between them. Maybe it hadn't been an accident on his part after all.

"You know there were."

"Maybe I've forgotten."

"I remember."

"Mmmm. Maybe you need to help me remember."

"Mmmm. Maybe."

So close already, she could sense his warmth in the cool night air, warmer still as they leaned in closer.

His lips tasted every bit as good as the wine, and this time, there was no rain, no pain and no need to stop. *Oh.* In an instant, the stars, the sparkling surface of the water and the humming dusk were sucked into the vortex, as his hand came gently to her shoulder and brought her closer, and she wove her fingers into his hair, hand on his neck to kiss him more deeply, and one sweet moment became the next, as their bodies opened to each other, so alive, asking and responding.

James, James, James. This man was delicious. *More.* She wanted more.

Yes. But … Something. What was it? *Careful.* She'd wanted to be careful. Not rush in as she'd done with Damian, to her lasting regret.

151

"Wait," she said, dizzy, breaking away.

"Really?"

"Really. Chocolate?"

"Chocolate?"

"Yes. They're in here somewhere." She burrowed in the basket, catching her breath. Yes. This was better. She needed to use her brain.

"I need to ask you something, James."

"Ask away."

"Do you know Donna? Another stall holder. She sells hats and sarongs and things, past Fritz."

"Well, I've seen her there. Yes. I didn't know her name. And I've never been on a beach picnic with her, if that's what you're asking."

"No. That's good to hear. I was just... Well, Donna told me she heard something. About my stall. Heard someone might want to close me down."

"Go on..."

"Well, can they do that? I've got a licence. Isn't that a guarantee? I've paid a small fortune. I had to pay six months in advance. How can anyone shut me down? Don't worry if you don't know... I wondered if you might have heard something..."

His dark silhouette was devastating. All she wanted to do was lean back in there again, and mend that broken kiss. But she did have to address this problem. Maybe he could help, and at the very least, it gave her a chance to collect herself again, not go to putty in the dark. Her body was protesting, quietly crying out for his.

James sat up, touching the back of one hand to his lips.

"Stella. The only way a stallholder can be shut down that I know of is if a competitor lodges a complaint." He sounded serious.

"But my only competitor is ..."

He sat up on his haunches.

"I haven't launched a complaint against your business," he said. "Did you think I did? Is that what all this was about? Is this why you came out with me tonight?" His voice was short, angry.

"No. This was about thanking you for your help the day of the accident. What else would it be? But if you think I want Stellar to close, you're wrong. I can't afford to stop trading."

She began to pack up their picnic, snatching at the towel and shaking it.

James stood silent, so she stooped and tossed the empty wine bottle back in the basket, hastily wrapping the cheese and standing tall to confront him again. Was he telling the truth? Or was he just like Damian, manipulating her for sex?

The wine went to her head and she spoke out loud.

"Huntleys tried to push me around since the very first day I opened my stall. You've always resented me being there. You're forever putting your nose into my designs and telling me what I'm doing wrong, how I'm pricing myself too low or how I should be using mass production, but what gives you the right, James Huntley? What? From what I can see, Huntleys isn't doing so well. You're hardly in a position to tell me how to run my business."

James stood, still as a sentinel.

"Is that what you think of me? Go on. Or have you quite finished?"

She felt spent. She marvelled at his self control. She could sense his mood, a kind of black despair. She was torn. Ashamed. She'd said too much. Accused him of lying. Told him his business was failing. Now she wanted to comfort him, kiss him again, anything to stop this confrontation. She hated it. There. Sex. Men. Relationships. Fraught. Too hard. Wrong wrong *wrong*.

And he'd just opened up to her about Helene. His familiar silhouette against the night sky was so controlled. It was all she could do not to go to him and put her arms around him. How she'd love to rewind the clock, unsay her words. Her body was crying out for his. She didn't want to fight like this. She wanted to be back in his arms, not standing here awkwardly, their picnic feast in tatters between them, the magic of the night ripped apart by her words. But she couldn't unsay them now. Wasn't sure she wanted to. The prospect of her stall having to close horrified her. And if it *had* been Huntleys...

"I'll take you back." His tone was terse, controlled. It was a monotone. Robotic. Devoid of emotion.

"I didn't mean that about your business," she said. She wanted to rescue the situation if she could. It came out lame.

"You're right about my business, and that's not the half of it," he snapped.

"You can tell me, James."

"Why would I tell you anything? You're just like Helene. Only interested in the good times. And you've just told me you have no respect for my comments. You think I'm just a liar."

"That's not true and it's not fair."

"Maybe it is. Maybe it isn't. We'll go now. You've taken me for dinner alright, Stella Rhys. And now I'll take you back."

Chapter 18

"Where am I taking you?" James ventured as the residential and office towers of Bondi Junction rose up. His voice was a monotone. No smile. He'd do the right thing and nothing more.

The evening's promise was ruined. It surprised him now much he missed their earlier, easy company. Acutely.

"I'd appreciate a ride to my sister's place, please, James." Formal. Prim. Nothing more from her, either, then. "Randwick. Carrington Road, please."

He sprung around to the side of her car to let her out, standing well back, avoiding her eyes. There would be no kiss, such a loss. Like part of him was missing. He'd hoped for a different ending.

"Thank you," she said.

If his body was still longing for hers, he ignored it, turning to the boot, retrieving the picnic basket. What had it all been about? Business?

Their hands brushed as she took the basket, but she kept her eyes down.

"Thanks," she said again, but without a trace of warmth, as she opened the door, stepped inside and closed it.

James was surprised at his disappointment as he drove away.

He really thought he'd got over caring what women did or didn't do in his company.

Served him right for expecting something more of Stella. He'd hoped she might be different, but she even named it, the fact his business wasn't doing all that well at the moment. So. She only cared about his money. Same as Helene. For all her free spirit, flat sandals and untamed hair, she was no different. Curse them all.

As he accelerated out of Randwick and back to Bondi Junction, he couldn't help noticing the balmy evening, the beauty of the brightest stars as they punched their way through the ambient light of the city streets.

He could still feel Stella in his arms, her unruly hair brushing against him as they'd explored each other's bodies in the soft seclusion of the shoreline. Despite himself, he shivered, clenched his teeth. She'd kept him wanting more alright, and why?

Had she assumed he was trying to close her down? Had she used her body like a weapon, a bargaining chip? What a fool he'd been to stoop so low.

If he'd just wanted sex, he knew how to find it any time. So what had he wanted from this evening? He'd wanted more. Respect maybe. Understanding. Acceptance. A soul mate, even. How high his hopes had been.

He shook his head bitterly as he parked the car under his apartment, staring at the bland grey concrete that surrounded his life. He punched in the numbers of the ordinary elevator to his characterless penthouse.

He poured himself a whisky and stood at his balcony, studying the dark water and city lights.

He couldn't bear to look back at his empty king-sized bed with its fresh sheets, and the silver champagne cooler he'd set up on the marble kitchen bench with so much hope, earlier in the day. It was a beauty, a gift from his mother the last time she returned from the south of France, a flea market find, the ultimate bachelor's accessory.

What had his mother said to him when she'd handed it across like some kind of trophy during her most recent visit? "Bon chance pour l'amour, mon fils." Pretentious nonsense. She'd even had the gall to hint she was ready for grandchildren. Maybe if she stopped spending the family fortune on French antiques he'd have a hope of making the business boom and actually attract someone suitable.

He fought with himself as Stella came to mind unbidden, with her bright eyes and sass, not to be pushed around. The smell of her, the whisper of her hair against his cheek, her smooth skin, the soft weight of her in his arms, like she belonged.

Absentmindedly he picked up the cold, heavy cooler, testing its weight in his hands, the cold burning his fingers. Replacing it, he reached for the whisky and wandered over to the sliding doors, opening them to step out onto the balcony and stare at the night.

Someone.

Someone like Stella, so different to those shallow women he usually met, the fawning sycophants who targeted him for his name, and the spoilt ones he went to school with, always too self-obsessed to settle to anything, always off to the next best party.

This Stella. Feminine yet firm. Direct. She had grit. Determination. He would never forget her eyes.

Smart. Independent. Creative. Imaginative. Energetic. An ideas woman. Stella could do a lot more for Huntleys than provide his mother with the coveted grandchild.

He swirled the whisky in the glass and downed it. The lights of the last ferry of the evening winked as it sauntered down Sydney Harbour.

When he finally flopped onto his bed, he couldn't stop his mind turning it all over and over. What had gone wrong?

Stella had been worried about that comment she'd heard, about her stall having to close. Had she assumed Huntleys would do that to her? Had she suspected him? Had she tried to seduce him, to bribe him, to stop a potential closure? Was that all she'd thought of him, that he could be charmed and manipulated! Would she really use her body as a weapon?

157

But why would she even think he'd want to close her down? Hadn't he made it clear how much he admired her skills? He'd even taken inspiration from her designs. Oh. Maybe that had been part of the problem. But jewelers always did that. Like fashion designers. It worked both ways. She could be inspired by their designs, too. Maybe she didn't realise that. She'd only been trading for a few months after all…

Saturday morning James was wearing his sunglasses as he entered the mall, nursing a hangover, but not altogether despondent. He made for Stella's stall, prepared to be friendly despite that lacklustre farewell the previous evening, but he was in for a surprise.

There was no sign of her, nor of her jaunty diamante "back in 10 minutes" signs. No sign of her at all.

Except for the day she'd been in hospital, every Thursday, Friday and Saturday since she'd opened, she'd been there. This morning though, even though it was almost 10am and the mall was full of shoppers, Without Stella's flashing sign and glittering wares, without her bright personality, the mall was bland. This morning, especially, he'd had plans, things to tell her.

Uncharacteristically rudderless, he wandered across to Fritz's stall to enquire. Maybe he'd heard something. But no. Nothing. Fritz had just shrugged.

Nicole was up in the staff room, humming to herself and checking the quality of her latest nail polish, pale brown.

"There you are, Nic. Stay right there. We need to talk."

Unusually content, she glanced up at him and gave a little smile.

"Good night, then?" he asked her.

"Yeah. Surprised myself."

"Wanna tell me who? Is it who I think it is?"

"Scottie." Her smile was full now.

"My old mate? Finally?"

"The very one."

"Well, Scottie'll be pleased. He's had his eye on you since you were about thirteen."

"I know. He told me. Sweet."

"I remember you telling me he wasn't exciting enough for you," said James. "Something changed?"

"Dunno. Sick of being treated badly, maybe. Thought I'd see what it's like to be dated by someone who likes me for a change."

"Be gentle with him, Nic. Scottie doesn't have a mean bone in his body. A genuine nice guy. Hate to see you hurt him."

"Yeah. Sweet. Divorced. We talked about all that. I'm sick of it, too. People treating me badly. Sounds so simple really. We could just be nice to each other."

"You should," said James, opening his laptop.

"So, what about you? Hot date last night?" Nicole opened a packet of biscuits.

"None of your business."

"Sure, James. Why don't you just admit you've got the hots for her?"

Jim came into the room behind them and switched on the electric kettle.

"Nicole, my girl! James, my boy! Keep your voices down. You sound like bickering children. What's this? What's this?" Jim was making himself his usual 11am instant coffee, adding two heaped spoonfuls of sugar and stirring the brown liquid noisily against the edge of his sturdy old mug.

"Just asking James about his date with Stella."

"Who?"

"Stella from Stellar. Faux jewelry," Nicole clarified. "You know, the stall down there with the brightly lit sign."

Jim moved to the window and peered down at the abandoned stall, nodding and turning back to them.

"Stella. The bright one. Fresh ideas." He turned and pinned his grandchildren with his blue eyes, rocking backwards and forwards on the balls of his feet as he sipped his sweet coffee.

They stared back at him, as if they were being compared, accused of not being up to scratch. They weren't the ones lacking in effort. What about Will, James wanted to say, but the comment would have sounded as childish as Jim had just suggested.

"While you're both here, I need to brief you," said James. "On our latest figures. Scottie reckons we need fresh ideas fast."

"He was telling me the same thing," said Nicole. "Well. Stella stole my best idea. Antoinette. Can't say I've forgiven her, actually."

"I've met this Stella," said Jim. "Met her. Yes. She brought in a customer for us. Brought in a repair, then rushed away before I could thank her. Isn't she the one whose designs you got me to create in real gems, James? The one who came in again recently. Ended up buying one of her own designs, didn't she? Isn't that right, my boy?"

James nodded, feeling churlish. Wished he'd convinced her to take it for nothing. Then remembered her coldness. He had to fix their misunderstanding. Surely that's all it had been.

"Actually. Stay right there," Nicole said. "I've been meaning to show you both something. Should have done something about it sooner, but it's been ages since we've all been together. I found something amazing."

She dashed out and returned a few moments later, laying a sketchbook on the old formica table.

It was a simple thing, but the moment Nicole opened the cover, it had them riveted. They leaned in for a closer look. One bold design after another stared out at them as she turned the pages, alive with pencil drawings. Elaborate pendants, enamelled cufflinks, paua shell tie pins, gemstone earrings, opal shirt studs, and luminous pearls, arranged in brooches, earrings, drops and strands.

The designs leapt off the pages, one after another, each carefully labelled, each daring, unusual and utterly beautiful.

"Where'd you get this?" Jim's voice was hushed.

"In the safe. I thought maybe one of you put it there. Maybe someone came in wanting an apprenticeship, or a supplier left it behind."

"When did you find it?"

"Earlier in the week. Maybe Thursday?"

James spoke quickly, eager.

"That stormy day. When I took Stella to the hospital. You came and grabbed her bag of takings, remember, Nicole? I think this is Stella's. Did it fall out of her bag?"

"This is good. Good strong design." Jim was still flipping through the book, pointing to each page. He was up to a series of rings, each more unusual than the last.

"This Stella," Jim said. "She has a gift. A gift. Ah. What I could teach a young jeweler with this sense of design..."

Jim twisted away, drained his mug, rinsed it out and banged it upside down on the edge of the old sink to drain as he'd done for 60 years. He looked back at his grandchildren.

"Well? What are you waiting for? Won't she be wanting it back?"

"I'll go," James said, fingering the keys in his pocket. "I'd offered to take her for a run to Bowral, anyway. See if I can find her."

Stella's sketchbook burning in his hands, James was off down the stairs at a run, back into the Jag and pulling away from the kerb within minutes. He'd forgotten to ask Jim and Nic whether they knew anything about an official complaint about her stall. Next time.

Chapter 19

There was an insistent knocking against the fuzz of a dream. Stella was at a beach, in the froth of a wave, warm, happy. Hawaii. Swathes of pearls were around her neck.

As she came up out of the dream she wondered again where her notepad could be. She wanted to capture the lavish bounty of the arrangement, like froth and bubbles. Sea foam. So many pearls. How many strands? Some big, some small. She wanted to float back into her slumber to check. So many beautiful visions ...

"Knock, knock, knock." Stella woke to the reality she'd only been asleep for an hour or two after tossing and turning most of the night, worrying about ... fixating on ... James. Worried she'd been mean to him. Worried her stall would close. She should have just gone to the garage and worked like an idiot all night. Not wasted time worrying and then sleeping in instead of selling more stock as planned, to get ahead of her debt. What a waste of time!

"Sorry, Stella." It was Jeannie with a cup of tea for her. The room was too bright. She wanted to sink back on the pillows, put one arm over her head and drift back to sleep again.

The clock must be broken. It couldn't be nearly noon. Had she slept all this time? She sat up, pushed the hair away from her face. Thought of James again, the loss of him, the look in his eyes when he'd assumed she'd been accusing him of closing her down. Felt miserable.

Jeannie had come in and closed the door. That was unusual. She was still holding the tea, so Stella sat up, held out her hands for it, blinked a few times.

"Stell," Jeannie whispered urgently. "Hot, hot, hot visitor. James Huntley. Vintage e-type Jag convertible. Top down. Thinks he's driving you to Bowral?"

Stella burnt her mouth on the tea. Maybe the end of their beach picnic was actually a nightmare. Or maybe she was still asleep.

"What?"

"He's in there with the girls. And the piles of ironing. James. Why didn't you tell me, so I could clean the place up a bit?" Was Jeannie a bit keen? She was smiling at her. Stella frowned and sat up straighter in the guest bed she'd called her own for months.

"James the hero," Jeannie said excitedly in a singsong voice. "King of Jewels."

"Shhh. You're spending too much time with nursery rhymes, Jeannie!"

"Well, he rescued you, didn't he? And you can't deny he's good looking. Not to be disloyal to Matt or anything, of course. And I suppose you already know all about the car."

"Settle down. It's his mother's, and I've never cared about such things." Confused, her emotions were a jumble. Still angry at James for not understanding she didn't want her business shut down. Relieved she hadn't frightened him away for ever. Curious.

"Sure you do. You care about design. It's a classic. In *my* driveway. I told him you were 'busy,' but he says he'd 'prefer to wait, if possible, please.' So *polite*. Says he has something he thinks belongs to you. Want me to offer him coffee? Slowly? Give you time to get dressed?"

Stella groaned. It was difficult to ignore the spike of excitement in her chest. Maybe it was just the caffeine in Jeannie's strong tea. As Jeannie closed the door, she leapt up and threw on a fresh t-shirt and denim skirt, dragging a brush through her hair. She didn't want to appear too keen. She brushed her teeth, splashed some water on her face and rolled her eyes at herself. He'd have to take her as he found her.

If she was taking her first day off, and she'd already slept through half of it, she was determined to enjoy every minute of it from now on. Damn the lost revenue and the credit card from hell. Savour the moments. She took a deep breath and stepped out.

She peeped her head around the living room door to see James surrounded by her nieces. Sienna had pulled up onto his knee and was swaying there. He had one hand hovering behind her back, ready to steady her.

Lucy was in earnest conversation with him, bringing him another teddy to add to the pile already in his lap. He was nodding earnestly. Maybe a lifetime of serving customers had done him some good, she mused.

Just then, Jeannie entered with a large frothy coffee for him and a couple of blueberry muffins, and he smiled appreciatively.

"Got one for me, too, Jeannie," Stella asked, scooping up Sienna and giving her a big hug, then hiding her face in her smallest niece's tummy as she giggled and tried to pull her hair.

"Good morning," James said.

"Afternoon." Stella looked across at him now, guarded. However good he might be with her nieces, their parting the previous night had been poor. Lacklustre. But those eyes! What was he even doing here?

"I have good news for you, Stella. I wanted to reassure you straight away."

"Oh?"

Lucy was watching their exchange. "Oh? Oh?"

"Exactly, Lucy. Got a cuddle for me?" Stella held out her arms as Lucy toddled across.

"Nicole found a notebook. We think it's yours."

"My notebook! So good of you to bring it back to me in person! Thank you!" It was impossible to stay cross with James.

164

"Still coming with me for that run back to Bowral?"

"Now?"

"Sure. We can be back by this evening."

"Oh? Oh? ..." said Lucy, watching Stella's expression.

Jeannie entered with two more coffees and took the free armchair.

"Matt bought my engagement ring at Huntleys," she said, smiling encouragingly at James and Stella. "Amazing old place."

James took another sip of coffee, pinning her with his eyes. "... except that 'no one ever goes in there'...?"

Jeannie blushed, mortified, but she was no shrinking violet. "Yes. Well. You saw that. Of course you did. Just defending my sister. Nothing personal you understand. She works so hard. It's only natural I want to see her succeed. You know? And it's not as if Huntleys has been perfectly silent."

"True. That's Nicole. Marketing."

"Well. I suppose you all work hard at Huntleys, too..." she offered.

"Not all of us," James said, somewhat bitterly. "And you're right. Footfall's right down. A lot of shopping's gone online, as you'd know, and Huntleys needs to recognize that. Can't get stuck in the past. There's a lot to be done. We're ready for some fresh ideas."

Jeannie stared at Stella and widened her eyes.

"Sometimes business plans need to change," Jeannie said, nodding significantly at Stella, who remained pan-faced, non-committal, ignoring the excitement in her chest for the fifth time that morning.

James reached inside his jacket and pulled out the sketchbook.

"So. This is yours?"

Stella reached for it, relieved, and brought it back to her lap, turning the familiar pages.

"Nicole found it in the safe. I have no idea how it got there. Unless maybe it fell out of your bag that day..."

"Thank you." It was practically a whisper. Her book was like an old friend. "I wondered where it had gone! Not that I've had much time to sketch. But I was only missing it again this morning, strangely enough."

James was looking at her keenly.

"You do realise how talented you are?" His voice was deep, serious.

Jeannie had shrunk to the side of the room, swaying to keep Sienna quiet and kissing the top of her head, looking eagerly from James to Stella and back again.

"I should hope so," Stella said, giving him her clear attention. "That's why I opened my stall."

"Of course. Yes. What I meant was, in the industry, there are makers who assemble the jewels, but there are also designers..."

They were silent, regarding one another. Interested, wary.

"More coffee anyone?" Jeannie ventured.

Stella was still silent, looking at James, reflecting. Silence. Silence.

"No, thank you. It's been delicious but I must get going." He smiled and stood, then smiled expectantly at Stella.

"Coming for the run? Bowral? Remember?"

"Yes," she said after more silence. "I think I will after all, thank you. Looks like I'm taking a day off. Might as well see a bit more of New South Wales while I'm over here."

He picked up a wariness from her as they finished their coffees and muffins. That lovely free feeling of easy togetherness of the early evening still lay shattered between them, despite the fact her stall was safe and he'd brought back her precious sketchbook. It might be hard to win her back, but he was going to try.

"Let me be your guide for the day, then," he said, standing. "Southern Highlands, here we come. Thank you for the coffee and cake, Jeannie. Delicious. Can we bring you back some shortbread?"

"I'd love some. How did you guess? Thank you. Need to pack a snack?"

"We'll grab something on the road, but thanks anyway."

Jeannie watched as they left, Stella standing back as James opened the car door for her like a gentleman.

Chapter 20

It was a blue sky day with a stiff westerly as they headed out of Sydney under the airport tunnel, then burst out into the sunshine in the classy old car, southbound.

The road was new, flat and straight. As they zoomed past suburbs and farms and forests, Stella marvelled at the scenery, enjoying the warmth of the sun and the proximity of James's shoulder. He drove safely, she noted. Not slowly, but he didn't show off, despite the fancy car. She felt safe with him. She studied his handsome profile, a quiet joy beginning to glow inside her. Yes. She could definitely get used to this.

"I wasn't kidding about the fresh ideas," James said, as they settled to a steady 110km an hour past Campbelltown, the old engine purring, sun glinting off chrome. Jeannie was right. The car did have style.

"Oh?"

"We're open to them."

"I see."

"You've clearly been talking to Jeannie about Huntleys," said James.

"We talk in the evenings when the girls are asleep. Matt's away a lot. Australasian rep."

"You talk about Huntleys?"

"All sorts of things," said Stella. "Jeannie helps me assemble some of my jewelry if she's in the mood. Handles all my online sales. Social media. She does all of that for me. I'm so lucky."

"Nicole does it for us."

"Your PR agent."

"My sister."

"Your sister!"

"You sound so surprised!"

"I thought Nicole was your girlfriend actually." Her voice was quiet, and Stella had to turn to look out the side window to hide her sudden flush. Yes. She was embarrassed she'd read Nicole wrongly. But, more than that, it meant James could be truly hers one day, in a way Damian would never be. It was exhilarating. It was frightening.

"You're kidding."

"I'm not. I guess that explains why you're so close, and why she's so passionate about the business."

"Actually, she's more interested in PR than in jewelry."

"Really?" Stella turned to James, studied his profile and hands on the wheel, fine hands. Strong. Yes. Sexy. She shivered and watched the road unwinding up ahead.

"Yeah. All that 'Antoinette' business. That's where her heart really lies. Celebrity endorsement. All of that was her idea."

"It was a great idea."

"Well, it worked for your business, anyway."

"It did. I can see now why she was so furious I got in the way."

He glanced across at her. Her elbow was on the edge of the window and the sun lit up glints of red in her dark hair as it flicked about in the breeze. She'd slipped her feet out of her sandals for the journey and had one foot tucked under her skirt and the other leg dangling, almost completely healed. The swelling had gone and the bruising had faded. It was a shapely ankle, he decided, with a rush of desire. She seemed relaxed, content.

As if she knew what he was thinking, she turned to him and slowly smiled, and the bolt of happiness that struck him threatened to make him hoot out loud and steer up into the blue sky.

The engine hummed along and they were silent as the paddocks widened out and they saw more and more sheep and horses.

"We're making good time," James said. "You wouldn't think it today, but sometimes this road's bumper to bumper. Do you like waterfalls?"

"Love waterfalls."

"We'll go through Bong Bong, then. Stop at Fitzroy Falls for afternoon tea if you like."

"Sure."

The silence was shocking when James parked at Fitzroy Falls. Stella was glad to get out of the car and stretch her legs. She was shy with him again, this stranger.

"Might stop in at the visitor's centre and freshen up," she said, fingers unable to untangle her messy hair. He watched her attempt, eyes amused. Her breath caught as she held his gaze.

"You do that. Hungry?"

"A bit."

"Meet you in the information area if you like. There's a little cafe near the information desk. I'll pick up that shortbread for your sister. Jim likes the stuff, too. Want something? The wattle seed biscuits aren't bad. Not real bush tucker, but pretty good."

James was holding a small paper bag and was studying an information board about lyre birds when she emerged. She came and stood beside him, acutely aware of his tall presence, wondering if he'd put his arm around her if she stood close enough.

"That tail's the most beautiful shape," Stella said, reaching for her sketchpad and capturing the sweep and proportions of the different feathers. "We don't have them in the west."

"We might see one. More likely to hear it though. You're never sure what sound it'll be making. Mimics other birds. Can even imitate the roar of a truck. Here's the other one we might see. The bowerbird. Look at the trouble the male goes to attract a mate!"

A poster showed an elaborate display of long grass shaped into a bower, decorated with an array of bright blue objects, including a drinking straw and blue peg.

Stella turned a page and was sketching again, quickly depicting the glossy black head and beak and the perfect positioning of the deep blue eye, totally absorbed in her work. As she made a final stroke of the pencil and snapped the book shut, she became aware of James close behind her, looking down over her shoulder, so close she could almost feel his heart beat, way too close for comfort. Or was it? She closed her eyes and leaned back against him till his chin capped her crown. He brushed his cheek against her temple and she let one of his arms come around her, gently, as they stood. It felt so right. Delicious.

A family banged in through the door. "Can I have an ice cream?"

"Mia! Don't touch."

"Me too. I want an ice cream."

"Do you want an ice cream?" James whispered in her ear as they pulled apart and she laughed, snatching up his hand and leading him out past all the souvenirs and into the fresh air and sunshine.

"That was so lovely of you to bring me an ice cream that day, James," said Stella, squeezing his hand as they started along the bush track, breathing in the smell of eucalypts and moist soil at the edge of the creek. It reminded her of some of the wilder places they'd camped when she was a child. It was a smell of freedom. "So, you like the bush?"

"Love the bush. Love the beach, too, and it's closer. Getting a break from business is important. Come back refreshed."

Yes. Fresh. That's how this felt. Apart from Jeannie's birthday and the quick hospital visit, her days and weeks had been almost the same, selling all day and creating for much of the night, chasing success.

"Usually I fly past this place, trying to get back to Sydney as fast as possible," James said. "So I'm glad to stop today and show you around. I covered a few miles back in school days, cross country running. You never forget the smell of the bush, all those shades of green and brown. The sounds." A whip bird called.

They were silent for a while, taking it carefully. James offered his arm on bigger steps and rocks, easing her journey on her damaged ankle as they enjoyed the sounds and smells of the bush, the darting wrens and native flowers, the vistas of cliffs and eucalypts. It was peaceful, the air so fresh it almost hurt Stella's lungs.

They stopped near a lookout and James placed the bag on a bench.

He'd brought some cool water, and Stella drank it greedily, grateful for his thoughtfulness.

"So I hope you'll think about it."

"Sorry?"

"Coming and working for Huntleys."

"What?"

"Doing some design work."

"Where did this come from?"

"We can teach you things. Jim's a proper goldsmith. He can offer you an apprenticeship."

Speechless, she studied the vast valley before them, the depth of air, the fine white line of the distant waterfall, and the play of rainbows in its spray.

Into the wilderness, he spoke again.

"You should be exhibiting at shows. You have serious talent, Stella. I can take you to gem shows, introduce you to suppliers. You could be representing Huntleys at international shows, go in some competitions.

You met my grandfather, Jim, up on the second floor. He was blown away by your designs in the sketchbook."

"You looked at my designs."

"Nicole showed us the book this morning. We didn't know it was yours till we started flipping through it and worked out how it must have got there. Where'd you learn to draw like that?"

He was looking at her, studying her reaction, worried. This was not going as he'd planned.

"You'll want to think about it, of course."

"Of course."

"Biscuit?"

Absentmindedly she broke off part of a biscuit.

She remembered again the warmth of James's lips around her fingers the previous evening, and brought her attention from the huge view to his eyes. They reflected her concern.

She was speechless, totally floored. She'd come east to control her own destiny. Not to work for another handsome man. She already had a plan. She was barely three months into it. Flame would have said "yes" on the spot, but Flame was a rudderless ship on the ocean of chance. And because of Flame, Stella couldn't be more cautious. She'd shrunk from change all her life. Having worked like a slave for the past few months, she'd need a good reason to throw Stellar to the winds just as she was starting to build success. The offer had come out of nowhere. If her heart whispered "yes," her head was saying "no." The last time her heart had its way, it had been Exos and Damian. *Look how that had turned out.*

"How long do you think it'll take us to get back?" she asked. "I didn't achieve a thing this morning and I really have to create more stock."

"A few hours. It's about 45 minutes to mother's from here. Once we've swapped the cars we can head north again."

173

Cynthia Huntley's place was a low-lying homestead with bull-nosed verandahs on three sides and perfect symmetry. It was architect designed, solid, with a feature stone fireplace and several sets of French doors, in the style of a small country manor, perfectly tasteful. Pruned hedges lined the front garden, and the climbing rose over the front gate was bursting with amber blooms.

"It's charming," Stella said.

"Mother would be pleased to hear you say that."

"Would she?"

"Planned the garden herself. She loves it best in spring with the wisteria in bloom. That's around the back along the lavender walk."

"Did you say she's in France?"

"Yes." He couldn't help sounding a bit bitter. "In Provence. Prefers it there, I guess. Excuse me."

He reached across and extracted a set of keys from the glovebox.

"Why don't you go in and take a look, maybe put the kettle on? I'll swap the cars."

As James disappeared down the long driveway, Stella made her way along the path, enjoying the fragrance of more roses, mostly white. On the porch there was actually a "bienvenue" welcome mat, and she smiled, locating the right key.

As she swung open one of the double front doors she was struck by the other-worldly interior with its stone flagging and tasteful antique furniture. Linen. Marble. If it smelled a little musty, it looked fabulous. It was like wandering into a *Côté Sud* magazine, a showcase house, nothing like the crowded apartments and cheap, worn-out rental houses of her childhood.

She found the kitchen, light, bright and classy, with marble topped benches as smooth and creamy as a wedding cake and a magnificent set of antique copper saucepans of all sizes marching along one wall. She didn't have to be a great chef to appreciate the designing eye behind the effect.

The kettle was hidden under a white roller door with a plethora of other kitchen devices. As she filled it from the fancy tap and switched it on, she took in the view of a courtyard, complete with an ornate stone fountain.

A glorious green-tinged light flooded in through French doors all along the back wall. The courtyard was covered with wisteria vine, a few purple and white sprays still hanging.

Stella turned another key and swung open one of the French doors, wandering into the shady light and space, and breathing in deeply the fragrance of lavender and wisteria.

She headed down a meandering path towards what must be the garage. It was a substantial building, with a similar roofline to the house and space for at least three cars.

"Kettle's on," she called out to James, who was busy replacing the roof of the Jag.

He nodded at her as he closed one set of garage doors and opened another, revealing a red Alfa Romeo.

"Your car?"

"Will's. I drive a sensible car."

"Oh?" She wandered closer. He was watching her running her hands through the lavender.

"Cut some flowers. Take them back with you if you like. Gardening gear's over there." James nodded at a third area, a wall of windows and a long workbench flooded with northern light.

Stella had a sudden vision - of how it might be to work there awash with natural light, sketching, beading, designing, creating prototypes. After months of camping in Jeannie's tiny spare bedroom, the sheer amount of space around her was shocking; made her giddy with new possibilities.

James was still watching her, quietly.

What was it someone once said? Free speech with friends is a joy, but a loving silence, divine?

175

She glanced back at him, and they shared the tiniest of smiles, before she slowly turned to the task at hand.

Tidy shelves held secateurs and a basket, and she headed back into the garden, filling it with blooms before returning to the kitchen to plunge the stems in water as quickly as possible and investigate tea options.

By the time James came in, she'd managed to lay out cups, saucers, some UHT milk in a matching jug with the sugar bowl and steaming teapot, all on a round marble table in the corner of the kitchen. It was more like a conservatory with its abundance of french windows festooned with garden greenery. She'd put three of the white rosebuds in a cut crystal vase in the centre of the table.

"Having fun?" James asked.

"It's like playing house."

"Nice to be here when it's not entirely empty."

"How often do you visit?"

"About once a month. A local gardener comes in, too. I never have time to enjoy the place. It's more like a duty. You can see I've failed to keep the fountain working."

She peered out at it. On closer inspection, it was full of green sludge.

"How long will she stay - over there?"

"Who knows. But it can't go on forever."

"Why not?"

He looked across at her. Stella. He was tired of playing games, tired of keeping things to himself. Stella was a good listener. She might as well hear the truth. Maybe she'd stop accusing him of being a playboy.

"She and Will and their jaunts; they're bankrupting us."

"What?"

"Exactly what I said. It's only taken about five years for them to spend most of the family fortune. Mother sold the Bellevue Hill place and built this, and we bought an apartment each for Will and Nicole and me off the plan, and a car each. That got rid of about half of it. We own Huntleys, but it's an old building. You've seen it. It needs maintenance. And there are all the staff. Lorna, Charlie, Ming. They're like family. Can't lay them off. We'd be alright if mother would settle back down. Will's the big worry."

"Want to tell me?"

"He never got over dad getting sick and dying. Of course we all miss him… But Will needed him most; always needed his attention and praise. He was the favourite. A rising sports star. Plus, Will was the baby of the family. Always a bit spoilt."

James sighed. Stella waited.

"In theory he's finding new markets and new suppliers for us in the US, but he's been in Vegas for the past six months, and you know what that means."

"What does that mean?"

"Gambling."

"Really?"

"Must be. Where else does all the money go?"

"Can't you stop him? Surely that's not fair. You and Nicole work hard. Why should he just play?"

"Agreed." He rested his teacup in his saucer and reached for Stella's hands, holding them. His eyes caught hers. "It feels so good to tell someone the truth. Nic knows, and our accountant, but mother doesn't want to discuss it. Won't hear a word said against him. But can you keep it to yourself, please, Stella? Huntleys has had enough bad press over the years. Will's misbehavior is legendary, but we don't need it broadcast."

She looked away, then back into his handsome face, creased by worry. She had a sudden impulse to cup his face with her hands, smooth away those lines with her thumbs. Simply kiss him. Wasn't today meant to be a holiday? For her? Why not for both of them?

"It's okay," she said. "I can keep a secret."

His relief rewarded her. The worry lines eased.

"Knew I could trust you," he held her hands, ran his thumbs across them, then let them go. "Well, you wanted to be getting back, didn't you? Mustn't keep you waiting."

James sprang to his feet, grabbed the cups and swished them quickly with detergent and hot water, then propped them upside down to drain dry on the creamy marble counter.

"See you out the front in five? Feel free to have a wander around the house while you're here. You'll find plastic bags under the sink, if you want to take some flowers back."

Stella emptied the teapot in the garden, rinsed it and turned it upside down with the teacups and empty milk jug by the sink. She locked the back door then took a quick tour of the other parts of the house.

Some of the furniture was shrouded in dust covers and the blinds were drawn, giving the place a feeling of emptiness, but there was a beautiful living room with a wide marble fireplace, three chandeliers and gilt mirrors against one wall, Versailles style. Again, the sense of proportion was perfect. Calming. Classy without being imposing. Lovely.

There was a baby grand, closed, with a cluster of silver-framed black and white photographs on top. She peeked at pictures of three generations of Huntleys. The wave at James's forehead was unmistakable even as a toddler. There was one of the three children together in their school uniforms, and another of them all at high school age.

She leaned in to study Will, a younger version of James, but a bit broader and stockier. In both pictures he was staring off to the side instead of smiling at the camera, a maverick even then, anxious to get away and do his own thing, she surmised. There was James again with a mountain bike, at 15 maybe. Wild hair and a grin to match.

She realized with a start that her five minutes must be well and truly up, and retreated down a long hallway of cream carpet to the front door, locking it behind her. She'd forgotten the roses. In she went again, pricking her hand on the thorns as she grabbed them and wrapped them hastily in a plastic bag she'd found under the sink.

By the time she was back at the front gate, door locked behind her, and breathing in the heady scent of the roses, there was still no sign of James.

He had told her to wait there, hadn't he?

Another five minutes, and she was beginning to worry. Was there some problem?

Footsteps crunching down the drive eased her mind, and he came into view.

"Sorry, Stella. It's Will's car. Temperamental bloody Alfa. That's why I need to give it a run every so often. Keep it running smoothly. This time I can't even get it to start."

A wind had come up from the south and clouds were building. In her denim skirt, she was starting to shiver.

"I've cleaned the spark plugs. That usually does the trick. But I might need to change the fuel filter; maybe drain the oil. Total bore. How urgently do you need to get back to Sydney?"

"Oh."

Stella had thoroughly enjoyed the change of scene and James's company. It was the weekend, wasn't it? She was her own boss. If she couldn't take advantage of her autonomy now, when would she ever have a weekend off? Sure, she had her debt to consider, but there had to be some benefits of taking all that risk.

"That's okay," she smiled. "Later's fine."

James smiled back. He looked relieved.

"Thank you. Might as well make yourself at home for a while. I'm really not sure how long this will take."

She looked at her watch. Five o'clock already. "How about I fix us some dinner?"

"Sure. See what you can find. Freezer's usually pretty well stocked. Here, I'll show you. Thanks for thinking of dinner. We might as well enjoy our visit."

As they walked back together to the front door, naturally in step, she allowed herself to fantasize it was their own house.

"If this were my house, I'd set a fire," she said. "Looks like a cool change is coming. Can you smell rain?"

"I can. Beautiful smell in the country. Every farmer's best dream. I'll bring some wood in from the shed when I've got the oil draining. Maybe you could gather some kindling before the rain gets serious. Should be plenty out near the orchard."

Orchard. Of course. Why not?

"Which way?"

"That way. And there's the pantry. Deep freeze is at the back."

Chapter 21

Stella followed James part of the way to the garage before branching off to the orchard. As more clouds gathered and the world became grey, little lizards scurried ahead of her. Some wallabies watched her from the other side of a paddock before bounding away.

As James had said, there was no shortage of twigs, and she quickly gathered an armful before returning to the house. She was almost there before the heavens opened, dumping huge, cold drops of rain. Leaning over the kindling to keep it dry, she ran the rest of the way, throwing open the door and standing, dripping, just inside. She was drenched, but she'd kept most of the kindling dry.

Shivering, she placed the sticks on the tiles and found a teatowel, French blue and white, depicting Notre Dame and other cathedrals. She mopped her hair, neck and arms to sop up the drips, and removed her sandals. Her feet were muddy now. It seemed like sacrilege to use the towel on the floor, but maybe she could take it home and wash it and give it back to James before his mother returned. For that matter, she might need a proper shower, and to borrow some clothes.

First, she took the twigs through to the living room and kneeled at the hearth, scrunching up some newspaper she'd found in a copper bin beside the fireplace. She snapped the twigs into suitable lengths and balanced them against each other, smallest first, the way Flame had taught her. Memories of childhood camping trips came back. It hadn't all been bad.

She washed and dried her hands on a creamy hand towel in the nearest bathroom, as stylish as the rest of the house. It was brand new, though the style was old, with a large clawfoot tub, and brass and marble accessories. Here, the window looked into a kind of lightwell full of ferns. Another beautiful room. How on earth could James's mother stay away?

It didn't take Stella long to find a stash of frozen beef bourguignon in takeaway food containers in the bottom of the freezer, and a packet of pasta in the walk-in pantry. She put on water to boil, threw the casserole in the microwave and went hunting for cutlery and glasses.

Sure enough, there was a dining room with a whole sideboard laden with antique silver and crystal, but this room was too formal and cold.

Stella opted instead for a marble side table in the living room. She removed an ornate porcelain figurine of a woman in a long dress, placing it carefully beside the photographs on the piano.

She moved the little table closer to the fireplace and set it with a silver candlestick, the little rose vase, cutlery and crystal glasses. She and James should be comfortable enough sitting on the hearth rug, their backs against the closest couch.

With most of the furniture still draped, this made for an intimate setting, a picnic by the fire. Two picnics in a row with James. She had to pinch herself. Was this real?

By the time James entered, wet from the rain and smelling like engine oil, the fire was burning cosily in the grate. He added some thicker pieces of wood and placed the rest on the hearth for later.

The aroma of the casserole made Stella's mouth water as she found some frozen french bread and defrosted it in the oven. It too smelled delicious.

James looked down at his wet clothes.

"Smells so good! Thank you, Stella."

"Been fun. Like I said, it's like playing house. All care. No responsibility."

"Well. While I'm such a mess, I'll duck back to the cellar and find some wine to go with this meal you've whipped up for us. Do you like red?"

"Sure."

While he was out, there were several serious flashes of lightning and a huge rumble of thunder.

When he came back in, he was dripping wet and the power had gone off. He held up the wet bottle like a trophy, grinning like the kid in the photo.

She clapped and they laughed. She found another teatowel and helped to mop him down. Up close, he smelled like rain. Delicious.

She shivered.

"You're wet, too. Cold." He held her by both shoulders and considered her. "You're about my mother's size. There's a tonne of clothes here you could borrow. Mother's wing is that way; her dressing room is on the left."

"Oh, no, I …"

"What? You're going to stay wet all night? And get sick? No way. Mother's half a world away. There's no shortage of dry clothes. She's certainly not using them. Maybe leave the ballgowns where they are, but otherwise, go for it. I'm going to freshen up myself." He pointed up a hallway, then headed in the other direction.

James was right about his mother's clothes. Her dressing room was a dream, spacious and well stocked, everything carefully color coded, and hanging according to size. Stella would have grabbed jeans and a fresh t-shirt if she could find them, but there was nothing quite so simple.

She was struck by the quality as much as the quantity. Beautiful silks, cottons, linens and wools. Exquisite textures. Suits and other carefully blended ensembles. Was there nothing plain? What did she wear in the garden? There was half a wall of shoes. Everything looked new.

Stella settled on a plain black turtleneck cashmere sweater and black slacks, not unlike something she'd normally wear, then contemplated the bathroom, another affair in marble and shiny brass. The products were an education. There was so much French on the bottles in the shower it took her a while to recognize the shampoo and conditioner, but their smell was divine, as was the moisturizer, and she emerged in a fragrant puff of steam and padded off down the hallway in the fresh clothes, feeling as if she was in an advertisement for a health spa.

James stood by the crackling fire, taking the top off the bottle in the old fashioned way, using the corkscrew with finesse. There was a gentle pop of cork. Victorious, he turned his attention to her, smiling his approval.

He wore clean, close-fitting jeans, a fine blue sweater and that smile. She wanted to run her hands all over him. Forget dinner. But she was suddenly shy, and so was he. Why else would he talk about the weather?

"Bit of a wild place, Kangaroo Valley. Storms whip up from nothing and they can be quite severe. We might need to hunker down for a while. Cheers."

"Cheers. You can see I'm really suffering." She felt like a kid. The fire was warm and the wine smooth, maybe a little too smooth. Through the rich red liquid, the flames leapt. She was so happy to be close to James. He smelled fabulous and she was more relaxed. A whole glass was gone before she remembered she needed to drain the pasta.

"Back soon."

She found a tray and loaded it up with everything she could find. Salt. Pepper. Casserole in wide pasta bowls. Bread. Olive oil in a small bowl.

"*Here with a Loaf of Bread beneath the Bough,*

"*A Flask of Wine, a Book of Verse, and Thou…,*" James greeted her as she entered. He was topping up their wine glasses.

"*Beside me singing in the Wilderness,*

"*And Wilderness is Paradise enow.* Omar Khayyam."

"And you say you're not a player, James Huntley."

"What does that make you, then, Stella Rhys? How do you know that poem?"

"My mother loves it. Says it practically every time we have a glass of wine, and that's at just about every meal. Enjoys life, my mother. 'Rich in the things that matter.'"

"Wise woman."

"Single mother."

She hadn't told him much about herself or her family. Maybe she'd open up if he didn't push her too far.

"Cheers again. I'm enjoying myself, Stella. For once I'm glad Will's away and his car's a crazy Alfa that won't start."

They laughed and touched their glasses together. He was even more handsome in the intimate light of the candle and fire. She bit her lower lip.

Wind howled outside.

"We might need to stay the night," James said. "I've tried to drive in weather like this and copped a branch in the windscreen. We love these country roads, but they can be dangerous."

"We might."

"What a great cook you are!"

"It was really difficult pressing 'heat' on your mother's microwave! Want some more?"

"Sure. I'll get it. Want to help me finish it off? It'll go off if we don't finish it."

"Well. Okay. It's delicious."

Stella swirled the wine in the glass as the flames danced, resting her back against the nearest sofa. Cosy. Relaxing.

"Given any thought to joining our business?" James asked, as he settled himself next to her, handing her a plate.

"I've given your business lots of thought," she answered carefully.

"Oh." They were two different things, but he didn't want to state the obvious. Wanted to draw her out.

"Trouble with Huntleys is, it's a bit exclusive. These are just my ideas. I'm not criticising, just sharing."

"Go on."

"Well, people love jewelry. But only the wealthy must feel like they can afford Huntleys jewels. And, believe me, I've been studying the crowds. There aren't that many truly cashed up people walking through Bondi Junction. Rich people, I mean. People like your mother. And I bet she chooses to buy her jewels in Paris, because she can."

"True."

"So if you want to make Huntley's a destination in itself, you've got to make it world famous. And the fastest way to do that is to open it up to more people, and go online. Turn it inside out. You want people to love the place, to feel like it's theirs."

"And?"

"I reckon you can do it."

"You do?"

"Those doors of yours. Why are they always closed? Prop them open. Make the place totally welcoming. It's a beautiful building. You want people in there who love history and architecture as well as jewels. Put it on the map for lots of people, for lots of reasons."

"Alright. What else?"

"Well I don't want to be rude."

"Go on. I'm all ears. Everything you've said makes sense so far. It's so good to discuss this with someone I respect. Someone who understands jewelry and cares about the customers. Growing up with it, it all just happened around me. Maybe I would have learned some theories at uni, but you heard what happened. Never got to finish."

A pang of sympathy rose in her for his own unfinished ambitions. Maybe he could make time for uni in the evenings once things were on an even keel again.

"Okay, James. Here goes. You've got loads of space in there, and you're just not using it. I know about cities. Every square millimeter costs a bomb to own or rent. Why don't you make it work for you? You've got every piece laid out on every floor with about a metre of space around it, but at my stall, people love to crowd around and riffle through it all. The more packed my trays are, the more they love it. It's the 'hunter gatherer' instinct. Maybe you've been appealing to hunters who like wide open spaces. But you've got to appeal to the gatherers as well."

"'Hunters and gatherers.' I like it. You've given this a lot of thought."

"It's one of the reasons I came out east. To test my ideas and watch how buyers behave."

"So… what you're saying is we need more stock, and a greater variety of stock for a greater variety of customers."

"Exactly. And why not? As I said, you've got the space for it. Make the space pay, why not? You could even bring in guest jewelers to exhibit in your space. Host designers from all over the world if you wish. Big names. And little names. Mix 'em up. Get people talking about Huntleys. And get some rent in for your space at the same time."

"There's certainly no shortage of styles," James mused, picking up on her ideas. "We could have vintage 60s in one corner - all those bright orange and lime green triangles. Yes. And art deco in another. And antique watch chains and collectors' items on another. Mother might be interested in sourcing that, in France."

"And why not offer workshops for aspiring jewelers, and master classes for people already in the game who need fresh inspiration? You could make them like mini-conferences, with themes. Like 'fire and ice,' and 'fruit of the fields,' and 'the planets.'"

"I like the workshops idea. Everything from beading to the lost wax method. Cloisonne. We could get some archaeologists in to give talks on jewelry through the ages."

"Exactly. Great idea. And you can write up all that stuff on your website and Facebook site. Get Ruben in to do some regular features. He could interview the designers, feature a jewel of the week, a gem of the month. Have you and Nicole thought about podcasts? Jim could talk about some of your most interesting vintage pieces. There's no end to what can be done, James. Even Jim's a hidden treasure. Share him with the world. Why not? Most jewelers these days are like all the others. They're franchizes. I guess they don't have much freedom. But Huntleys is unique. You're a lucky man, James Huntley, the Third."

Stella suddenly gave a yawn, though the ideas were still flowing.

"And you heard how Jeannie spoke so warmly of Huntleys because Matt bought their engagement ring there? There must be so much brand value you could stir up! Make it work for you. Why not? Are you keeping a database of your customers? Send them wedding anniversary vouchers with discounts. And what about… *yawn*… Valentine's Day? How about Huntley's hearts?"

She yawned again and rested her head against his shoulders, enjoying his strength and warmth.

"Too much wine."

"You're extraordinary, Stella Rhys."

The buzz of James's voice humming through his body right into hers was lovely.

The wind whistled outside, slapping wet leaves against the French windows. As the flames leapt up and gave off heat, she turned to study him with those dark eyes. *Those lips, slightly open. So close.*

One brush of his lips against hers, the smell of her, and his fingers were in her hair, cradling her head, pressing her closer, and she was up on her knees, her hands on his shoulders. He laid her down on the Persian carpet in a tumble of dark hair and kissed her again, deeply, tasting her, running his lips across her jaw and down to the soft skin between her neck and collar bone, and she was pulling him closer, running one hand under his shirt, her fingers cool against the heat of him.

Had Helene ever loved him like this, hungrily, generously, the whole of her suddenly opening up to him, willing him onwards, welcoming every inch of him, her hands as eager as his to touch and hold and cherish? Never.

Down on the rug, as the flames illuminated the planes of their faces and her soft curves against his strength, they were finally free to find each other and surrender, to lose themselves in the wonder of each other, until they were satisfied and the fire burned low again.

Chapter 22

Stella emerged from a dream, aglow with contentment, wondering why every part of her body was humming.

She could see his forearm and hand, still in sleep, exquisite as a detail in a Michaelangelo. James, the golden man. Memories of the previous evening swirled and settled. Bowral. James's mother's house. The fire, the sex. Great sex. Now she practically purred.

She almost laughed at herself. Since when had Damian ever done anything but roll away from her and retreat to his own room, once satiated?

James. She wanted to feast her eyes on him as he slept, revisit that beautiful body, but by the time she twisted around, his own eyes were blinking, then fixing on hers, and there was that half smile of his, so sexy.

Sex with James had been an utter revelation. Damian had always prided himself on his prowess, but it had always been all about him, she understood now, whereas James had actually cared about her own enjoyment, had insisted on caressing her, again and again.

It made her want to ...

"What's the hurry?"

"Oh."

"Are you hungry?"

"For you, actually."

"Excellent."

It was cold above the quilt, so they burrowed underneath as she relished the welcoming heat of his body and the way he reached for her, like something valuable, irresistible, necessary. *Wonderful.*

…

It was still wet outside, the stench of oil from Will's car's burbling engine competing with the smell of rain. Branches and sprays of leaves were down all over the place.

James pointed at an echidna at the edge of the drive as he opened Stella's door. It was sinking itself into the soil, spines protecting its underbelly. They watched as it all but disappeared, a small Australian miracle, going about its business.

He reached across to squeeze her hand and steady her as she slid into the low seat, and the feeling of being cherished rose inside her like the sun.

Just then Stella's phone buzzed and without thinking, she reached into her bag for it.

Damian.

Damian. She thrust it back into her bag, heart pumping.

James was silent as they joined the road. *Maybe Damian was her brother. Her husband?* What did he know of her after all? It wouldn't do to become too attached. *Too late for that.* His eyes caressed her. He was warm from their love making, confident. Stella.

Her phone bipped with a message. *Would she read it?*

"Everything alright, there?"

Stella sighed and looked out the window.

He was still elated, humming with contentment. These country roads were fun to drive in Will's car. The storm of the previous evening had washed away the dust. The summer gum trees were beautiful, sloughing off their old bark, freshly watered. It was full steam ahead, a turn for the better in his life.

191

"My old boss, back in Perth," she blurted out. "Damian. He wants me to come back and work for him. He's offered me an outrageous sum of money."

"Tempted?" he tried to keep the jealousy out of his voice. He had no hold on Stella Rhys, though he'd like to think there might be a future for them.

"He led me on for years. I was in love with him. We had an affair. It's over."

"Good to hear," he said, though he wondered. He'd seen what outrageous sums of money could do for people, for Will, for example. Will was always for sale.

"All those ideas of yours," he said. "Last night."

"Yes?"

"So, when are you joining Huntleys?"

Stella's answer made him want to slam on the brakes.

"To be honest, I drank quite a lot of wine, James."

It hit him in the pit of his stomach. This was rejection. Again. Surely she couldn't be backing away. Not after their easy banter and all of their sharing, not after the hot sex. Had he not been considerate enough of her? Not from the way she'd clung to him and whispered his name. Not from the way she'd stayed with him, allowing him to stroke her, cherish her. No. They'd been right together. Perfectly attuned. Experienced. Honest. Mutually satisfied. More than that. They'd fulfilled every promise of that first snatched kiss in the gutter, finished what they'd started down beside the water. They'd hurried, and then they'd gone back for more, more slowly. So what was this sudden pulling away from him? Didn't his offer make perfect sense?

Noticing he was gripping the wheel too tightly, he deliberately unclenched his hands, along with his jaw. He needed to explore this. Not panic. Go gently. Something wasn't right. Whatever it was, he needed to find out.

"You gave me one brilliant idea after another."

"Ideas are cheap. It's the execution that matters."

"You're talking to a long distance runner, Stella. I know all about the long jog. All about the middle mile. Been in the middle mile for a few years, truth be told. Till you turned up outside my door."

She smiled at him and reached across, tracing the back of her finger down his stubbly cheek. When he tried to bite it she moved her fingers to his thigh.

"Hey! Want us to have an accident?" Good. She was still attracted to him. This wasn't a physical barrier. He was reassured.

"Of course not!"

"You're going to, aren't you?"

"Join your business? Maybe. But maybe not. I have to tell you this, James. You've been straight with me, but I haven't shared my story with you yet."

"Tell me. I'm listening."

"I came across the country to be my own boss. It's really important to me. I wasted too many years slaving for a boss I loved who never returned my attention. There are things I need to achieve for Stellar."

"So how do I repay you for the ideas you shared?"

"With hot sex," she said and he raised his eyebrows.

"Seriously, though, there are plenty of ideas you could share with me, too, James. Like what are some good competitions, what gem shows might be worth visiting. And suppliers. Show me your world, James. And if Jim's going to be offering workshops, maybe I can be his first customer."

"And maybe you'll get sick of staying outdoors. Maybe you'll consider becoming our first ground floor tenant. If you're not ready to come and work with us."

"Maybe."

Stella twisted away from him to look out her side window. Why couldn't she just accept his offer? There was no question she was attracted to him. She could barely keep her hands off him. And every moment, the feeling was stronger. It scared her.

Because there it is, she thought. *Impossible.* She really had wasted too many years adoring the boss. It would be the hardest thing in the world to be working so closely with James every day without knowing he would always return her love, without reserve. The last thing she wanted was to end up subservient again. What if she was just another promising young jeweler in a long string of them hired by James - so hard to resist with his manners and sex appeal. She knew how that felt - to be just one in the lineup of Damian's never-ending supply of PAs.

She would not do it to herself again. She would not expose herself to the agony of sharing the man she loved with any other woman, day after day, ever again.

No. Now, more than ever, after this brilliant weekend together, she needed to keep her distance, retain her independence, keep hold of her own dreams and make them happen.

As gorgeous as James Huntley might be, in bed and out of it, he wasn't the main game for her at the moment. Unless he was totally committed to her and her future, as well as his own, he was simply a distraction.

The last thing she wanted was to get all starry eyed and helpless. She'd been there before. Knew it wouldn't do either of them any good.

No. She had her own business to build, with her own talent, energy and ideas.

Besides. If she thought about it, and she did, she was the one who'd been making all the moves. She'd kissed him in the gutter that day she'd twisted her ankle, and again at the edge of the water at their picnic. And last night, beside the fire. He'd been keen, but she'd been keener. *Dangerous ground, alright. What if he was only going along with her because he wanted her ideas for his business? Flattering her to get what he wanted.*

No. If Stella just ended up adoring James while she worked for him, she might as well have stayed at her old job in Perth.

Chapter 23

J ames, too, was subdued. He couldn't work Stella out. As they left the windy country roads and slipped onto the highway, he went over it all again. She'd wanted him alright.

Yes. But now? She was keeping her distance. Silent.

Maybe she's dwelling on the Huntley business challenges, he thought. Regret settled on him as he overtook a couple of caravans, a large removalist van, and a refrigerated semi trailer. Why did he tell her those things about his business being on the brink of bankruptcy? Why did he share so much with her!

Well. Too late now to take back those words. He had work to do.

He needed to rein in Will's spending for starters, and his mother's. And he needed to work out how to pitch some of Stella's ideas to Nicole and Jim. Show her he was an action man who could bring her ideas to fruition.

This run into the country had been a delightful interlude. The best. But real life approached and it demanded his attention. He now had something to prove to her - a business to get under control, and a host of initiatives to inject new life into Huntleys under his watch. Just let Stella Rhys see what he could do.

His mind was so full of the next steps he barely spoke on the way home, just as Stella seemed deep in her own thoughts.

She broke their silence as they purred into the outskirts of Sydney.

"Design comps?"

"JNA's been a big one. International. All they need is a drawing on a normal sheet of paper. Scale is always 1:1. Any of your drawings would be up to scratch. Google it. There'll be several themes. Sometimes a particular element will be specified, other times it's quite open. Usually kicks off in June. Great publicity, if you make the finals. Better still if you win. You can also find a host of comps listed on GIA, Gem Institute of America. Some are limited to people living in certain countries but it's worth a look. If you're too busy creating and selling, maybe Jeannie could have a hunt and find something suitable for you."

"And you think I'd have a chance?"

"Absolutely, Stella. You have real talent. Even Jim thinks so, and he's a hard man to please. He's seen a lot of jewelry in his time. Seen fashions come and go. He tells us about them sometimes, and about some of the classics. He thinks you have a rare talent."

As they pulled in to Jeannie and Matt's drive, James leapt out. He ran around to open Stella's door and walk her to the front door. Warmth hummed between them. James touched her shoulder and she flushed. *She remembers, too.* More than anything, he wanted to draw her into his arms, taste those lips again, feel her small body against his own, but something about her told him she wanted to keep her distance. *Alright then.* The last thing he wanted to do was push her away with his eagerness. But it was a hard ask. Maybe too hard. Why should he play it cool when his whole heart and mind and body were telling him otherwise?

"Stella," his voice was rough. He couldn't help it. This *hurt.* "Why won't you even look at me? What's wrong?"

"We've both got work to do, James. It's been the loveliest weekend, but the holiday's over now."

"For good? Just like that? After all we've …"

"For now. I need some space, James. I came out east to achieve a life for myself. Let me be."

"Let you be." He let out his breath between tight lips, looked away, then back, into her eyes. "I can't believe you're shutting me out like this. There is such a thing in life as enjoying business *and* pleasure."

"I need to prove myself, James. I just need to do this. I need to make Stellar fly, just like you need to save Huntleys. You're too much of a distraction for me, James."

He held her with his gaze, hands awkwardly at his sides. Was she really pushing him away? Completely?

"So I'm just meant to disappear. Pretend you don't exist. Pretend I'm not attracted to you. Pretend you're not the most amazing woman I've ever met. Pretend..."

"Stop it. If you respect me you'll listen to me. I like you, James. I like you too much. Way too much. But I have to focus on my business right now, see what I can achieve professionally. I've wasted a lot of years, James."

"So I'm a waste of time."

"Not at all. Just give me a few months. My licence runs till April."

"And then?"

"I'll see what I've been able to achieve."

"And you expect me to wait around for you."

"I haven't said that."

"You do, though. You know how good we are together. How good we can be. But why can't we have it all? Have our businesses and each other? Help each other. I can show you so much, introduce you to suppliers, people who can do the stringing and the finishing, free you up so all you have to do is keep drawing, keep dreaming, keep creating. We could go to Antwerp together. The diamonds there. I'd love to see what you could design with those materials!"

"I'd like that, James. Truly I would. But don't you think we'd be even better together if our businesses were strong, and they're not yet, are they? There's no one else for me, James. Only you, and Stellar."

"Well, I guess I might talk to you in May, then," he snapped, mystified. Hurt. "You think you can just dismiss me. I'm not sure I want to take that."

He turned to go.

"Wait!"

"'Wait?' 'Don't wait?' Are you sure you know what you want, Stella Rhys? I know what I want, and I've told you so. I want you to join our business. I don't make such offers lightly."

"I know that. And I thank you. But I have competitions to enter, and Christmas is coming. I'll be working harder than ever."

"So will I." He gazed at her again. It was all he could do not to cup her cheek and chin in his hand and draw up those lips to his, and he did, slowly, just brushing his against hers as if to farewell something he could not have, as if he knew it made her crazy for more. *Of him.*

"Alright then." And he turned away from her, strode back to the car, started the engine, backed out and drove away without giving her another glance. He wouldn't let her see how much she'd hurt his pride. If his business had been booming, would she be sending him away like this?

Inside, Stella leaned against the door and closed her eyes, her body raw with need for him. Maybe she'd blown it. Lost him. Pushed him away for ever.

She'd thought of inviting him in, but knew Jeannie would be busy trying to bathe the girls and settle them into bed.

Her skin tingled as James handed over her things, but she'd stepped back, away from him, away from the vortex. James Huntley was dangerous. She could lose herself forever in those blue eyes.

Maybe it's for the best. Being with James felt so right it scared her. *Surely something so good couldn't be trusted.* Was it the Flame in her? Would she become like her mother, never settling for one partner, always on the move? She shuddered and pushed away the possibility.

She studied her phone, then wished she hadn't.

Damian had left a message.

Coming to Sydney soon. We'll meet up.

Chapter 24

How could Stella ignore James completely? There he was, at least twice a day, entering and leaving Huntleys. But now, to her sorrow and regret, he no longer looked her way, nor stopped to chat, nor even slowed down.

Despite her request that he keep his distance, it surprised her how much she missed him; how lonely his indifference made her feel.

Yes, there was still the usual passing parade of shoppers and browsers, some of them regulars now, and the easy camaraderie between the stall holders, but there was no one who took as great an interest in her work as James had done.

At first, Stella had been irritated by James's comments - about her pricing, his suggestions about what item might complement another, how she could source better quality wholesale items from here or there, or higher quality fastenings. She'd always taken his words as criticism. Had he been trying to help her?

Her feet hurt. The humid heat of summer was draining her energy, and ignoring James was making her cross. The moment she saw him each morning, her heart would pound, but she was too busy and too proud to put an end to their standoff. Once or twice he tried to engage her in conversation, but he'd been formal with her, the exchanges guarded, clipped. She hadn't wanted to hurt him, but how could she focus on making Stellar a success with James in her life, distracting her? She needed her business to fly during this busy Christmas period. She had to pay off her debt.

The summer crowds kept her flat out. The days were long and hot. Over at Huntleys, she could see they were working just as hard. In the evenings when she was locking up, she sometimes looked up. There'd be a light in the corner of the top floor. Someone was up there. Once or twice she thought she saw James's familiar silhouette, watching her peering up at him.

James took the wrought iron spiral staircase to the very top of the building. He climbed slowly, studying the ornate curves, remembering the first few times he was allowed up here by himself, finally judged sensible enough to stay out of danger.

While his parents stayed down on the lower floors with the customers or deep inside the safe or office, this was Jim's space, the magician's lair, where solids became molten, glowing like fire and hardening into the unique and beautiful creations people travelled from all over Australia to buy.

Young James was allowed to stand and observe, and never interrupt. To disturb Jim's focus could be to ruin a piece. To venture too close and try to touch could mean a terrible burn. Maybe a fire in the whole shop.

Even as an adult, James fell under the spell of the space. He arrived at the threshold and stood, hit by the old smell of the flux and the glow of the burner, mesmerized by his grandfather's eyes, so focused behind the magnifying visor.

He watched Jim extruding gold threads for claws.

It was late. Did his grandfather ever sleep? Since his grandmother died, Jim worked longer and longer hours, completing repairs in the shop all day, and creating jewelry by night.

James was reluctant to interrupt him. With Stella still top of his mind, day and night, he'd far prefer to go find her, give up on their crazy stalemate, take her to a fancy restaurant and wine and dine and worship her. A thousand plans had swirled around his mind, all ending up with them back in bed together, but he had had to dash them all.

She'd told him to keep away. Practically told him to get his act together. Virtually told him to put her ideas into practice. There'd be no prizes for a reckless, restless dash to her bedside. Not yet, anyway.

But how could he make his mark on the business without his family's consent, without their help? How could he break it to Jim that the processes of a lifetime must change?

No matter. It had to be done, for all their sakes.

It was high time for action, starting with Jim, here in his lair at Huntley's crown.

James approached Jim at his semicircular workbench.

He leaned against it and remembered how much larger it had all appeared when he'd been a child. From this height, he could observe Jim and the long selection of pliers, tweezers and sanding heads. The ornate old drill set up and the array of burners of different sizes were just as fascinating, but the time was over for watching in silence.

Now, Jim fitted a fresh blade, James reflected on just how many times he must have reached for the jigsaw.

Then, as he'd done when James was older and had proved he could be trusted, Jim moved across slightly, making room beside him for James to sit.

It was a long time since they'd been together like this. James remembered how much he'd loved it, loved being included. Jim would always open up to him as he worked, his voice a running commentary on whatever he'd chosen to share.

Jim handed him a blob of wax as he'd done when he was small, and as James warmed it in the palm of his hand and pressed it with his thumb, Jim kept working.

James's visits had ebbed and flowed over the decades. This was the first up here in more than a year, the first since he broke up with Helene.

Jim continued his work without speaking at first, pulling the lengthening thread of gold through smaller and smaller holes in the heavy metal block till it was just the size he needed.

Still James was silent, waiting.

"You think life's always been easy, my boy?" Jim began. "You think Huntleys never had challenges before? You think we never had employees with their fingers in the till, suppliers giving us glass stones when we'd paid for the real things? You think we never paid taxes higher than ever before, taxes we had to pay in advance? You think we always had Sundays off? You think the money just dripped into our bank accounts week after week and we never had to think about it? You think we never found rats in the attic, white ants in the rafters, rust in the elevator cables? You think we never had that winter when everyone was sick at once and we had to pay them all sick leave, and we were all sick, too, but we had to work, and we did? You think I sit up here, a happy old man, and everything came easy? You think we never had a worry in our heads? You think my wife's father wanted us to change his emporium into a jewelry shop? You think my Eleanor never had a thought in her own head? You think she just followed along and did whatever I wanted?"

"Sir," James conceded.

"You think it didn't rip us apart to see our first son die, and the next one, a little girl? A little girl, so perfect. And then we had Jimmy. And he lived. Please God, he lived, that one. You think I sit up here and smile because life's always been easy, that the business created itself day after day, that Eleanor didn't want more children, and more of them. You think I didn't have to watch her, miscarriage after miscarriage, then leave her and go into work here, to keep the business alive. Every day, work to do. Every day, tough decisions to make. Pricing, employees, customer satisfaction, supply, manufacture, pricing, employees, manufacture... Enough.

Couldn't pick it all up again after Jimmy died, after Eleanor died. Could pick up my tools, but not the whole business."

"No, sir."

"Yes, James. You took on this business when you were too young. And our accountant was good. Good accountants. Like gold. But it's not easy. Never been an easy life. You think I haven't been watching? You think I don't notice Will, nowhere to be found, not pulling his weight, not interested at all? You think I don't see Nic tugging at the mooring, wanting to grow in other directions?"

James squashed the wax flat in the palm of one hand, threw it to the other and began to speak.

"I promised dad I'd look after Will and Nic, Jim."

"That was a big promise, James, a good promise, a promise well meant. But looking after them doesn't necessarily mean keeping them in the business."

Jim turned, pushing up his magnifying visor and stared at James.

"I can't even contact Will, Jim. He never returns my calls or emails. He still files his expenses to Scottie. They're from Vegas, casino restaurants, hire cars... Scottie's always kept paying them but he says we're going broke."

Jim picked up the jigsaw, and cut off a section of gold rod, then selected a pair of needle nose pliers without looking and curved it, folding it into the shape of an oval before speaking again.

"If Huntleys goes broke, you certainly can't pay him."

Jim returned to the ring he was making, pedalled on the grinder, then lit up a burner to add one of the claws.

"So you're saying it's okay to stop paying him before we go broke? Cut off my own brother?"

"You want the business, you protect the business. Or you can go broke. Or sell it. Float it on the stock exchange. Business is worth something. Huntleys' name. This building. More than one possibility, my boy."

"We've been living off our assets, Jim. The money from the house is almost gone. You told me you didn't want to see the spreadsheets any more. You told me you just wanted to make beautiful things, and I reckon you've more than earned the chance to do what you want, to not be bothered. But I keep trying to make everyone happy. Not rock the boat. Keep a steady income for everyone, keep everything ticking over, but I wonder why. Will takes, takes and takes. Mother's away. Always away. She has no interest."

Jim stopped the grinder, pushed up his magnifying visor again and looked James in the eye.

"Question is, what's your own interest? What is it *you* feel for Huntleys, James?" Jim rotated away, pulled down the visor, flicked on the flame and heated the piece of gold on the heat proof matting, then picked it up and plunged it into water with a great hiss of steam. It was mesmerising, the flow of his movements and the gold take shape beneath the force of his imagination.

"What do I feel for Huntleys? Lately? Duty. Exhaustion. Exasperation..."

"Me, I know that feeling. Duty. Exhaustion. Exasperation. Yes," said Jim. He put down the pliers and swung on his stool towards James. "But Eleanor? She felt passion. Destiny. You know the story, my boy. I made one ring for Eleanor, and all her friends wanted one too. So I made them. And their friends wanted rings, and here I am, 70 years later and all I can do is make rings! Maybe I still do it for Eleanor. Not everyone can create beauty. Not everyone wants to. Me? That's all I can do."

Jim picked up the oval, placed it on the ring, added some flux and waved the flame at it till the two pieces became one. He plunged it again in water in a hiss of steam.

"And your father? He loved to sell. And he was good at it. Loved people. Expanded the showrooms, brought on more staff, imported pearls. Ah, Huntleys was a destination when you were born. Huntleys was bigger than ever. Your mother enjoyed it well enough, but she's lost her way. Hard on her the way Jimmy was sick for so long before he died. They were a pair, alright, in their day, and now she's … "

"Drifting. You miss him, Jim?"

"'Course I do, just as I miss my Eleanor, but one day blends into the next, and I have my memories. And I'm an old workhorse. This, in here, brings me simple satisfaction. My rings take shape, every one of them different. And I watch you and Nicole. I'm a lucky man to have my grandchildren around me. Fine young people. Don't mistake me. I'm proud of you, James, and proud of Nicole. But I don't want to be a burden to you. You must find your own way. You did the right thing, got Will through school. As well as anyone could, anyway."

He'd picked up the drill, fitted a bit and was peddling away. He drilled three holes on either side of the oval.

"But I've lost him."

"Will doesn't have to be your burden. Maybe he's lost himself. He can't be your responsibility forever. Will's a grown man now. Has to take responsibility for himself. And I certainly don't want to be your burden. Believe me, James you don't have to do anything to please me. You're a man in your own right now, James. You were a good boy. You've always been a fine fellow. Caring for others, caring for Will and watching out for Nicole. You've done a good job. But I worry that you do things because you think I expect you to do them, that you carry on the business the way it was because you think I want it that way. 'Duty.' You said it yourself. But no one wants to see their beloved grandchild suffer. You're free. I set you free. Now you must set yourself free."

"If only it were that simple."

"Why isn't it that simple?" Jim pulled a key out of his trousers, still working on automatic. He surveyed the room out of habit, but there was no one there but the two of them. It was well after hours.

He unlocked a little hidden drawer under his desk and pulled out some folded paper, carefully tipping some tiny diamonds onto the bench in front of him. They picked up the light from his lamp, glittering like sunlight on Sydney Harbour on a windy afternoon.

James loved this part, when the magic of the ring neared completion. He handed over the wad of soft wax.

Now Jim pinched the gemless ring in the hand clamp and placed a diamond in each hole, smoothing enough gold over each edge to hold it safely in place, anchored there until a lifetime of wear thinned the gold and set the gems free once more.

James stared at the glittering facets.

Who would he be without Huntleys? What would he do? Take to gambling, like Will?

It was only then that he knew with a fierce certainty that he wanted Huntleys, with all its challenges. That he cared about the old building and the Huntleys brand almost as much as he cared for his grandfather. Free to make changes, he could make his own mark on the future.

Jim witnessed his change of attitude. James saw it reflected in the set of his grandfather's head, his own determination shining back at him, the fire in his eyes.

He scooped the remaining diamonds into the paper and folded it again, then scanned the room again before unlocking his drawer, slipping the paper back inside and pulling out a tiny, flat case.

"Which one will it be, my boy?"

They leaned over the case, as each gem gleamed and glittered. Loose emeralds, rubies and sapphires.

It was an old game. James studied the size of the oval bed Jim had made for the gem, and guessed which one would fit.

"That one," he said, pointing to a sapphire so blue it was almost black.

"Right every time."

Jim lifted it and placed it in its bed, using pliers to bend each claw into place, and a file to smooth them over.

Again Jim sanded the gold, then used tweezers to dip it into a cleaning fluid. When he removed it and rinsed it in water, he sat it on the bench and blew it dry with an old hair dryer.

From such simple materials, came a ring fit for a queen.

"You've done it again," James marvelled.

"Only thing I can do. You? We've yet to see what you can do, James, my boy."

He smiled at him and handed the ring over to be admired.

Warm and heavy in James's hand, it winked up at him, glowing with a life of its own.

"It's a beauty."

"You like it?"

"I do. I always like your rings, but this one's special."

"Why this one?"

"You set me free with this one, Jim."

"Yes?"

"At about the third diamond."

"That I did."

"Want to know what I'll do?"

"I trust you."

"First, we'll lock this treasure away in the safe. And then I'll make some plans."

"You do that."

Chapter 25

James visited Jim every night that week. Brought up a spare stool and sat with him. Heads bent over the bench, the two of them worked away. Occasionally, James piped up, testing an idea or pointing out something on his laptop.

"It's all happening online now. Take a look at this."

"Hmmph. 'Triumphs.' We can do better than that."

"We can. I've been thinking about using the shape of the building for our website. See this?"

"Ha! Show me again. What's that up there?" Jim's strong index finger, knobbled with age and rough with a lifetime of working with metal and tools, pointed at the screen.

"That's you, Jim. That's you in your workroom."

"What's that?"

"This might sound crazy, but I want you to be in the big gem on the roof. I want people everywhere to be able to click on it and your voice will explain the history of one gem a week. Through podcasts, Huntleys can educate the world."

"Absurd," Jim grumbled, embarrassed. "Make a good product and people will buy it. It's no great secret. Besides, I thought you left those crazy marketing ideas to your sister."

James had no intention of backing down.

"We need to record you. Talking about your work. Talking about gems and jewels. The history of metalwork, the pieces you've repaired, the meaning of the stones, the names of all the shapes of diamonds, that sort of thing. Let's give it a go."

"Ha!"

"Things can't stay the same. We've got to get into this online game. We've got to win it, Jim. We can do it."

"What's that about me talking?"

"You're an expert. Think about it. You know more about jewels than anyone in Sydney. That's an asset."

"Hmmph."

"It doesn't have to be a big deal. Here."

James pulled out his mobile phone. Pressed record.

"Tell me what you're making."

"This one's an engagement ring."

"Why's it that shape? Why don't you just import the bases and put a stone in? Why make it from scratch?"

"Every diamond is unique, just like every person. Basic components might be the same. Every diamond is made of carbon, like every man and woman is flesh and blood, but you've only got to get a few diamonds together to see they're all different, especially the ones at Huntleys."

"Tell me."

"Well, you've got all your different sizes, the carats, of course, but then you've got to remember that every diamond starts out as a tiny pebble, all a different width and depth, and then there's the cutting. All the facets are different, too. And even if the facets are cut by machine, and a lot of them are these days, you've still got your natural stone underneath, and each will shine through a tiny bit differently."

James gestured for Jim to continue.

"And of course you've got your different cuts. You've got your round brilliants, the most popular, but then there are all the others which come

211

in and out of fashion; your ovals, the princess, the cushion, the marquise… They've each got their different histories, the different princesses who made them famous… And then there's the way you set them. That can make all the difference."

Jim looked uncertain, but James was smiling and waving him on.

"Well, the setting's the most important part, and that's why Huntleys prefers to set each stone individually. Just as different stones suit different people, different settings suit them too. I've never talked about this before." Jim sounded doubtful, but James kept nodding.

"To me, they have personalities. Some stones are shy. They need a subtle kind of setting. One that lets them glow. They're not for show offs. They're beautiful, alright, but not in an obvious way. Then of course you've got your stand out diamonds. They're just out there. You see them on the cloth and they're calling out to you 'pick me, pick me' and you can't resist them. I know it might sound fanciful and old fashioned, but I call them my brightest girls in the pack. And they're crying out to be on show. You have to set them right up high. Maximize the light under them."

"And you can do all that?"

"That's exactly what we do. That's all we do at Huntleys. I love it. Quiet ones and show offs, and everything in between. We get those girls and we set each one just right, so then it's just a matter of the customer coming in and finding the right one."

James pressed "stop" on his phone, took his grandfather's gnarly old hand and shook it.

"You're a natural, James Huntley the First. Straight out! Won't even need an edit! Tomorrow night, sapphires."

Stella was so busy the days flew by, and the nights back at Jeannie's were a blur of creating stock.

Jeannie had absolutely adored Huntleys version of her choker which was also a brooch, even though she kept telling Stella she shouldn't be so generous. She'd treasured it, as Stella had expected. It was something exquisite, something she could wear for special nights out with Matt when Stella was babysitting, something for the future - an heirloom. Jeannie loved Stella's design as well as the improvements Huntleys had made to it.

Occasionally Jeannie would try to talk about the quality, about Stella's potential to design highly valuable jewelry.

"Thanks, Jeannie. A bit flat out right now. Hopefully one day!"

Each day, Stella noticed that Huntleys, too, was busier than ever. A couple of weeks before Christmas, they draped purple ribbons from the roof to the ground and right across the second floor, making the whole establishment look like a wrapped gift. It was eye catching and effective. When they teamed it with two large sashes that seem to tie the large doors open, it transformed the entrance.

That night, when Stella mentioned it, Jeannie dragged her over to her computer in the kitchen, and showed her Huntleys' revamped website, featuring the festive purple ribbon and open doors. The animations were entrancing.

"And look at this content, Stell. They're taking pictures of the old jewelry people bring in, and Jim provides a bit of a history. They're storing them in a glass cabinet at the entrance so you can pop in and see them. It's created quite a lot of interest on talk-back radio."

"I wondered what was up. I've noticed so many more people going in there. It brings more people past my stall, too, but maybe that's just this time of year."

Once or twice in the sweltering heat, Stella had seen James head out with his beach towel, out for a run to Bondi. She remembered with a pang that he'd once offered to take her with him.

If he noticed her glancing at him with regret, he didn't let on. He was as distant as the day they first met. Moreso. It hurt her, though she could hardly complain. The idea had been all her own.

Chapter 26

A woman with a portfolio left Huntleys and came straight across to Stella.

"James sent me," she said, smiling, holding out a business card and opening a display case.

Stella's heart jumped at the mention of his name.

"Sydney Stringing Service," the card read.

"I'm Julie. I'm in the old Badgers building in Pitt Street. Fifth floor. Special wholesale prices. Come and see me." Stella glanced inside the portfolio at examples of the work - beautiful cut jet beads strung on a black thread with knots; some amber on knotted thread just the right color; and several strings of pearls of different sizes.

Stella reached for the pearls, so lustrous in the bright summer sunshine, their luminous greens and pinks shining back at her as she turned them in her fingers, design ideas bubbling through her brain.

Julie sensed her interest and smiled. "Plenty of pearl suppliers in our building, too. Come and see us."

She would have loved to chat, but customers were waiting.

"Thank you, Julie. I will."

Julie's visit was an invitation to dream of an easier future, when she might be able to share her good fortune with others, to share her workload, multiply the benefits and minimise the personal labour so she could focus more on design.

It ignited a little spark of hope that the drudgery of these days would lift, that all the hard work would pay off. And it was rewarding to see James putting some of her ideas into action. *James.* For an instant a hot stab of pure desire rushed at her, a memory of his kiss, the way he held her. *No. No. No.* She had far too much work to do. She forced her mind to the beads and chain in front of her. How quickly could she work? More than twenty of these had sold today. She must make more. More.

The other half was business as usual as Stella laboured to make products for the Boxing Day sales, then scoured the internet for suitable expos to show her wares.

"You can't keep working like this, Stell," Jeannie said quietly.

"I can and I will. Three months down. Three to go. That was the plan."

"Aren't you going to go see James? Wish him Merry Christmas?" Jeannie had referred to him a couple of times, obliquely. This was the first time she's been so direct.

"We're not seeing each other."

"Shame."

"Not really. He was a great distraction."

"'Attraction' more like."

"Exactly."

Jeannie sighed. "You can have fun, you know. What about a balanced life? Some work, some play. You're not a machine. You're not a robot, are you? Where's the joy? What's the point?"

"That's for me to decide, isn't it?"

It wasn't often they snapped at each other like this. Maybe it was time to move out, find a place of her own. It wasn't fair on Jeannie and Matt for her to be here but not contributing.

"Look. Maybe it's time I got my own place." Once she'd paid down that credit card debt a bit more, she could probably afford to pay some rent.

"I'd be lonely without you, Stell. It's alright when Matt's here. But I drive myself crazy without him, and without you."

"But I'm hardly ever here."

"Sure you are. This time of year is crazy. Just relax and do what you need to do. I'm here for you."

And she was. And she was wonderful. But she wasn't James, and in the days to come, Stella missed him more than ever, treasuring the memories of their few times together as if they'd happened a lifetime ago in another universe.

Chapter 27

Stella worked even longer hours in the weeks before Christmas, along with all the world in retail. Now was the time to create enough stock to trade right up till the last moment on Christmas Eve, and then sell, sell, sell.

Even better if she could take advantage of the frenzy of the post-Christmas sales. It was exhausting; this treadmill of her own making, yet seeing those queues and the pace of card swipes? What a thrill!

There was no respite. Online sales were also booming. She had to fill backorders as well as keep her stall stocked. Frantic. Exhilarating.

Days passed in a blurr, but one face jolted her out of her automatic smile.

James. Just as she was locking up, he approached, a flat package tied with a large gold ribbon tucked under one arm. She stopped, dropped her arms by her sides, her whole body lighting up as he stood in front of her. Those blue eyes were solemn, yet she detected a quiet joy at seeing her again, at being so close, a joy that matched her own.

Just as she was leaning towards him, her phone buzzed.

She had it out on her counter, just in case Jeannie wanted to make contact, ready for her to snatch up as she was leaving.

A message flashed onto the screen.

In Sydney. Meet up? Miss you.
Damian.

Stella froze. So did James. The message sat there in front of them, its cold blue light insistent.

Awkward.

The moment was poisoned. Stella's hatred for Damian filled her with disgust and she frowned and looked away. Misinterpreting her retreat, James took a step back as if he didn't want to intrude.

He must think I'm seeing Damian, she realized. *Damn Damian!*

James held out the package to her. It looked like a chocolate box, but as she took it, she felt its weight, unusually heavy.

"Merry Christmas, Stella," he said. "Happy New Year." He was sombre, deliberately keeping his distance.

She jolted herself out of her fury for Damian, tried to bring her mind to this moment, to be fully here, with James.

"James! How've you been?"

His eyes grazed her face as if he were deciding whether to answer, and her heart pumped staccato. Surely his own was doing the same. Did his hand tremble a little as he'd brushed her fingers handing the package over? She wanted him to touch her the way he'd touched her that weekend. She wanted to reach across the distance and grab the lapels of his summer suit and pull him closer but it was awkward between them.

How had she sent this man away?

"Huntleys has been really busy," she tried again. "I really like your new website." She looked at the wave at his forehead and then forced her eyes down to his chest. She wouldn't seek his eyes either then, if he wouldn't share his with her. It was too sad.

Again, part of her wanted to leap forwards, lean up and kiss him, claim him, tell him she'd been a fool. But the ornate box was in the way and he was keeping his distance, and just then, her phone pinged its message again.

"I'm going away for a while," he said, eyes dropping to her phone. His voice was level, devoid of emotion.

"Oh?"

"France. The US."

Then he turned abruptly and walked away.

She was still numb. She could neither think nor act quickly enough, holding this big box at the end of a long day.

"Good luck," she called after him, his tall figure so remote. Should she drop everything and run to him? Tell him she'd made a mistake? Tell him she wanted him back in her life, in any capacity, that she missed him and wanted him, all of him, anything of himself he wanted to share? Her heart was pumping and her mouth dry. And now the moment had passed.

She despised herself. Despised her own desperation. It reminded her of the way she used to think about Damian. Desperate to please him. She couldn't allow herself to be that pathetic. Not ever again.

She continued locking up her stall as if she were an automaton, replaying James's visit again and again, trying to work out what his visit had meant, and to talk some sense into herself.

He's said he's going for a while, not forever. That's all. And it wasn't as if she had nothing to do while he was away. There'd be all the crowds to serve during the post Christmas sales. And she'd promised herself that in the quieter weeks at the end of January she would enter some competitions and research some conferences and expos, plan an expo display featuring her best work, see if she could attract some distributors, and maybe even find suppliers to help her with the more repetitive work.

She was clutching his package to her heart. Too bad if they were chocolates. They'd all be melted.

Stella packed it carefully in her roller bag where she'd stashed some gifts for Jeannie and Matt and the girls, then took up her phone and carefully typed in a response to Damian.

Do not ever contact me again.

Then she walked slowly to the bus stop and caught the night bus home, tiptoeing into the house of sleepers.

Chapter 28

Christmas Eve. Edging towards midnight. Stella scrambled some eggs, had a shower and sat cross legged on her single bed in her summer nightgown. She pulled James's gift out of her bag and began to unwrap it. Had he wrapped it himself? Had his fingers touched this sticky tape?

I'm losing it, she told herself. *Like a lovesick teenager*.

Slowly she peeled back the paper. It wasn't at all what she'd imagined it might be. It wasn't a necklace, nor any other item of jewelry.

It was a packet of professional color pencils, the brand among the most coveted in the world, and a new sketchbook of high quality paper. She ran her hand over a page and marvelled at the texture, creamy as skin. She opened the box of pencils, and began to draw.

Already her design mind was playing with concepts. The tail of a lyrebird? Heads of bower birds with sapphire eyes? She was feverish with plans.

Dawn was nudging at the sky and the sketchbook a third full before she stopped. She'd worked without regard for anything but the creations in her mind's eye, a series of jewels based on birds, on lyrebirds, eagles, wrens and seagulls.

The final picture was of the heads of a male and female bowerbird, superimposed, beaks crossed, the domes creating the top of a heart, a deep blue sapphire eye in the centre of each.

Her own eyes red-rimmed and streaming from exhaustion, she finally closed them, curled up and slept, pad and pencils hugged close against her chest.

Christmas Day was hot. Lucy ripped the wrapping off everyone's gifts and toddled around distributing and redistributing them while Stella stopped Sienna from eating the paper. Stella had bought the girls a bright aqua blow-up paddle pool. For Lucy she had added a fluorescent green waterproof sunsuit with a matching hat, and for Sienna, a smaller, fluoro orange set. For most of the morning, Stella held Sienna in her sitting position in the shallow water as she splashed and squealed, while Lucy lay on her tummy in the water pretending she could swim.

Matt, wearing a goofy pair of reindeer antlers, mixed cocktails and added tiny umbrellas stuck in pieces of pineapple while Jeannie brought out a feast of seafood and salads.

Later, as they washed up, they phoned Flame. Jeannie put her phone on speaker.

"Merry Christmas, mum," said Jeannie. "Where are you?"

"Byron Bay, with Grady. Beautiful. Picnic. Near the lighthouse. Dolphins, dears! Merry Christmas."

"How's the mesclun?" Stella asked.

"Hmmm?"

"The lettuce?"

"Hail storm. Last Tuesday. Not good. Most of it was crushed. Have to plant some more, won't we, Grady?"

There was a muffled sound of agreement.

"Or maybe we'll get a few ducklings. High demand for duck eggs. Grady says they love lettuce. Now. Jeannie. How are you? And Stella?"

"We're fine, mum."

"Follow your dreams, girls."

"Yes, mum."

"Whatever your challenges. Isn't that right, Grady? Grady? I might need to go, girls. The dolphins are back."

"Merry Christmas, mum."

"Is she getting loopier, Stell?"

"Maybe we're just getting more conventional."

"'Follow your dreams, eh?' She'd be proud of you, Stell."

"If she had half a clue what I was doing. Maybe."

"She knows. I phone her up sometimes."

"Thanks, Jeannie. I've been neglecting her. So. Ducks, now."

"Quack."

Worn out by their water play and full of Christmas pudding, the girls slept all afternoon. So did Stella, dreaming of James and wondering whether and when she might hear from him again.

That evening, Stella checked her finances. She had to order more silver supplies, but she was steadily making progress on her credit card debt.

In the cooler evening, she was glad to give the girls a walk along the esplanade in their double stroller, giving Jeannie and Matt some time alone together. The glow of the sunset on the horizon completed a perfect day. She wondered how James was faring, how it might have been to have him with her, striding along together, like some of the other couples. Her smile was wistful. How she wished he would come up out of the surf to greet her, eyes dancing with blue. Impossible.

With the Christmas and Boxing Day rush receding, Stella turned her mind again to expo opportunities. She found one coming up in Singapore - Asia's Fashion jewelry and Accessories Fair. Perfect.

One evening, Stella took herself to the beach after work; wandered down to the shore at Bondi and waded in, the cool waves fizzing at her ankles then rolling in to wash away the heat of the day and tumble her body in a great swathe of churning white froth.

It was good to hand her body over to the motion of the surf, to be rolled and buffeted with the power of the waves, bobbed like a tiny cork on the edge of the ocean.

She emerged clean, washed, fresh, renewed and reinvigorated.

That evening, Jeannie met her at the door, all smiles.

"Huntleys has launched a design competition, Stella! You should go for it; seriously. It's a national design competition for all budding jewelers; to design a heart pendant for Valentine's Day! You could win this with your eyes closed, little sister. The winner gets their design made up and there'll be an unveiling. They get a pure gold H brooch, free tuition with Jim, their old goldsmith, for a whole month, and Huntleys will retail their limited edition design on their website for a year!"

"What a great idea!" Stella didn't let on it was her own, shared with James one cosy evening in Bowral after drinking too much red wine, before sinking into a glorious night of love making together, before she banished him. Unfortunately. She kept quiet.

"It is. A brilliant idea. Will you go for it?"

"How do you enter?"

"Just with a sketch and a blurb. It's so right down your alley. You've probably got some heart designs right now that would win. That's clever to have the closing date next week, well before Valentine's Day. Get people thinking of jewelry for gifts. Huntleys are really picking up their act."

A design competition. As if she had time for such things. She must prepare her expo display. And she needed to make more stock. Everything was running low. Keeping on top of demand was far more challenging than she'd imagined it would be. It meant finding more supplies of silver.

She'd put in a big order online, trying to find a better price, but every day that passed without the order arriving, she was regretting her decision. What if her supply never arrived at all? What if someone had stolen it from Jeannie's letter box? It wouldn't be unheard of, junkies thinking about their next fix, ripping open every envelope or parcel they could find, seeking cash or something to sell. How long had it been since she'd placed her order? She checked her credit card statement. The total still made her wince, but she had to believe she was making progress reducing it. $1,040 worth. Seven weeks ago. Those silver supplies should be here by now, no question. She'd have to buy locally after all, spending more than twice that amount. *Damn it. Running her own business was so hard. Harder than she'd ever expected.*

But that evening, she remembered Jeannie's comment about Huntley's competition. Maybe she could win that prize money. *Worth a try.* She grabbed her sketchpad and flipped through it, seeing the bowerbirds she'd drawn after receiving James's Christmas gift.

The design was pretty good. Heart-shaped, it was perfectly appropriate, and practically ready for submission. She took it in to Jeannie and tossed it on her lap.

"That's it! If that doesn't win, then Huntleys have no taste. That is super classy, super Australian and unique. I adore it. I want one."

"Yeah. The design's okay," she laughed. "But it wouldn't be easy to make."

"But that's the beauty of this comp. They'll teach you how to make it. That Jim can make anything, according to their Facebook posts. Have you seen their posts on old treasures people bring in? Jim explains how they were made. It's fascinating. They've been running a whole series of workshops, on the lost wax method, etching, setting gems. Silver and gold. He's got quite a following. It's all the rage among the yummy mummies. Everyone wants to make their own rings, bracelets and brooches."

"Good for them," Stella said. And she meant it. James was steadily turning her ideas into reality. It was impressive. There was a little glow in her chest. She was proud of him. She made her way back into her room, filling in the entry, smiling to herself. There was a box which asked about the contestant.

In as few words as possible, describe yourself or the purpose of your business.

What to write? What was her business? Why did she care about it so much? It wasn't just about what she loved to do; it was about what her business made possible for others, the enjoyment she witnessed in the faces of her customers. It was simple, really. Whether they bought her jewelry for themselves or as gifts, she wanted them to experience joy.

Stellar - so you can shine.

She was grateful for this opportunity to review what she was doing, grateful to James for believing in her, and for giving her the sketching set. Had he known then that the competition was coming up? Maybe. For just a few seconds, she allowed herself to close her eyes and savour the memory of their weekend once more. They'd been so close in the storm, safe in each other's arms. The memory thrilled her, gave her strength. James believed in her talent. She would get over these challenges of not having enough materials and stock, of labouring day and night, of an almost insurmountable credit card debt, of surviving on no wage, thanks to Jeannie and Matt's kindness.

"Follow your dreams," Flame had told her girls every day of their lives. She crossed her fingers as she pressed "send." Stella was already living her dream. She just had to make it pay.

She scrolled through her inbox. It was so hard to keep up at this time of year. Suddenly something official caught her eye, something about Stellar, something she'd missed. It was from the council.

Dear Stellar *stallholder,*

Stellar *must cease trading by* 4 January. *due to trading condition 73 c.*

By order.

General Manager

Surely this was some kind of joke.

She checked it again, focusing on the message, these words from nowhere, in black and white, pulsing on her screen. *Doom.* She scrolled up and down and found an attachment, a long list of trading conditions. There it was, 73 c. The words were officialese, but it all boiled down to exactly what James had explained when she'd raised with him her concern about what Donna had told her she'd heard, the day of their picnic. James had said a stall could only be closed if a permanent trader complained that their goods were too similar to their own, creating unfair competition. Donna had been right!

But surely there'd been some kind of mistake. James had told her that the only store which could do this to her was Huntleys, and he'd said…

Had James lied to her? Surely not.

But it seemed the only possibility.

Stella's world went white. She felt as insubstantial as a tissue, empty. Blank. Until a great wail of panic rose in her, like a tornado.

She studied her screen again. Was there a phone number? Was there any right of appeal? Was it all over?

Worst of all was the suspicion she'd been wrong about James. Surely not. Everything had felt so right with him. Yet there seemed no other explanation. Unless he wanted to force her to come and work for Huntleys by taking away her livelihood. Impossible?

Emotions cascaded through her.

What a fool she'd been to trust James, to fall for his charms!

So. James had betrayed her utterly. Played her so he could steal her jewelry ideas and use her body for sex. Maybe it had all been some kind of game for him after all. If so, this was sabotage. *Traitor!*

She was weary, drained.

If she couldn't even trade tomorrow, what was the point? Rage and weariness and confusion washed over her. She could barely speak.

What was the fine for trading without a permit? Would there even be an inspector in the heat of high summer? Was there a phone number she could ring?

We are here to serve you, said the recorded message, except they weren't. *Council is closed until the twelfth of January. Please visit our website FAQs or ring back later.*

Surely they couldn't close her down with one email. Had there been a letter? Maybe it had gone the way of the silver supplies.

And James. She could just phone him. Anger surged in her. Then bewilderment. Then fury again. White hot rage. She stared at her phone. No. Why would she ring James? He wasn't even in the country. Off on some fancy international trip.

She should just accept that James lived in another world. *Disaster.*

She stepped into the hallway, thinking she could discuss it all with Jeannie, but Jeannie and Matt's light was off for the night.

She turned off her own and slipped into her single bed, reliving every memory of James, every exchange.

She had to admit it. Huntleys had had it in for her since her very first day, and she'd been a fool, utterly blind, falling for every trap they could lay in her path, including James's charm.

She cried now, huge, hard sobs from deep in her gut, muffled by her pillow. What a fool she'd been. Especially about James. She'd felt they'd truly understood one another, unlike Damian. Was every man so untrustworthy?

Maybe she was like Flame after all, doomed with relationships, bound to run from one failed love affair to another, again and again throughout her life. Had she expected too much? If Stellar had to close now, after all her hard work and high hopes, then coming to Sydney had turned into a disaster. Her life in Perth hadn't been perfect, but this was a nightmare.

Chapter 29

James's mother was waiting for him at Nice airport. It was surprisingly busy, but nothing like the crush of Charles de Gaulle.

She was smaller than he remembered, and happier, proudly if nervously introducing him to a tall Frenchman, Émile.

The two men regarded each other with some suspicion. Émile was protective of Cynthia, James noticed, as he sized him up, and more than a little uncomfortable at this unexpected addition to his mother's life.

James hadn't imagined another man in the picture. The last few times he'd seen her had been in Bowral, where she'd been fussing about the condition of the house and its contents. His most vivid memories of her were from the bleakest moments of his father's funeral, and in the years before, when she'd sat loyally at his father's bedside, worried, comforting, patient, grieving.

This Cynthia seemed uncharacteristically happy. She held Émile's arm as they wandered past the new fountains under a pale grey sky. James flipped up his collar against the cold, though he admitted it was as mild as a Sydney winter.

"You should see it in the summer, James, when it's full of children playing in the jets of water," she said. "Look; see the ferris wheel? It's a winter addition."

They headed for the Promenade des Anglais, where Émile and his mother had made a booking for lunch at one of the clubs right on the beach.

They wandered along the avenue of palm trees, and crossed to the beach, so Mediterranean. It was a puzzle to James, this beach. The smooth grey stones clicked and tumbled against each other in the small waves. He could never understand the appeal, not when there were such wide golden beaches in Australia, with their clean sand and the bluest skies in the world, where you could catch a decent wave. For a moment a pang of homesickness rose in him. He regretted not kidnapping Stella from her stall and taking her with him to Bondi Beach. A golden dream.

Feeling like a sulky teenager, he followed Émile and his mother to a table overlooking the beach chairs, all lined up along the stones. They each sipped on a festive, bright orange Aperol Spritz, even though the day was as cold as winter in the south of France.

The clouds lifted as their buckets of moules arrived, and, warmed by the rich soup, James began to thaw. The sun came out, transforming the grey sea to jewel-like azure. Côte d'Azur.

Despite the jetlag, James sat up and listened with greater interest to his mother's news, postponing the conversation they needed to have, the real purpose of his trip.

"We were haggling over a piece of furniture at L'Isle-sur-la-Sorgue," his mother laughed indulgently, patting Émile on the arm. "Émile couldn't understand why l'Australienne would need to have a chandelier."

For once James raised one eyebrow and looked across at the Frenchman with some shared understanding. Émile shrugged in that French way and turned to his mother and smiled, as if to say, "Who could deny this woman anything?"

"Emile needed it for his business, but I wanted it. It's magnificent, James. Wait till you see it. You'll understand."

Again, Émile shrugged indulgently.

"Well, it wasn't fair. He started yacking away in French to the vendor, bla bla bla. I've studied French for years, as you know, and I can certainly get by, more than that, but this was completely incomprehensible. The two of them were at it, a hundred miles an hour, the fastest French you can imagine, and all in slang. The vendor knew me. I've bought quite a few things from him, as it turns out, and all I could understand was the 'l'Australienne' from time to time. Then there was this long silence."

His mother turned to her food, forking out a mussel or two or three like a local and tossing the shells in the bucket, enjoying the suspense she'd created.

"So who got the chandelier?" James asked, mopping up some of the soup with his bread. It really was delicious.

"We did," she said, smiling across at Émile to continue the story.

Émile used both hands, shrugging again, in that "what was I to do" sort of way. His accent was thick, though his English was good.

"There was this beautiful woman. A beautiful chandelier. An antique like this, it is rare, yes, but there may be another. But a beautiful woman…," he smiled at Cynthia with his eyes, as if he truly appreciated her. "She is unique, non? L'Australienne. She is, 'ow you say, *un vrai trésor*, the treasure." It was his turn to eat a mussel or five, dabbing his chin with the thick white napkin from time to time.

"I thought I was so clever," his mother continued. "I'd brought euros; thank you, James, darling." She halted to lay a hand on his forearm. *So charming*, he thought. *So, she appreciates her expenses account. Our big talk is going to be even more difficult now.*

Émile was listening, rapt. Both men nodded at her to continue.

"I just kept pulling out more notes. I was determined. And I got it, and Émile was just standing there watching, and then I realized…"

"She 'ad bought it, but she could not move it. Puis… so…"

"Émile has a wonderful truck. Wait till you see it, James. And he was such a gentleman. He offered to transport my 'find.' And, would you believe it, we were going to almost the same place! You'll see it soon. I can't wait to show you! Oh. Gelato? Marvellous for cleansing the palate."

An attractive young waitress hovered, offering coffee. She was particularly attentive towards James. With Émile and his mother comfortably leaning towards each other at the end of the meal, Émile's hand caressing her arm on the edge of the table, James, jetlagged, felt far from home. He closed his eyes for a moment, and Stella jumped to his mind, her quick, clear eyes, the curve of her brow. *The taste of her lips.*

When he opened his eyes again, the waitress was still there, so eager to please. He surprised himself. In previous years he would have had no hesitation. He would have asked her what time she finished work, asked her to show him around her favourite places in Nice in exchange for a drink, or dinner. But this time? He was here for a greater purpose, with a longer term goal.

James and Émile tussled to pick up the tab.

"Non. This is for me. You are in my country, n'est-ce pas?"

They ambled back to his mother's Peugeot, watching seagulls hunched against a cooler afternoon breeze.

James had planned to stay in Nice, but his mother had insisted he accompany her to her place near Aix en Provence and see a little more of her home away from home. As they began their journey towards the hills, Émile at the wheel, the long flight and large lunch took their toll, lulling James to sleep.

...

It was late afternoon when the hum of the engine stopped, and James lurched awake. Where was he?

Picturesque stone houses with pastel shutters, cobbled streets, ornate street lamps, red chimney pots, pigeons, a fountain. It was a small town, pretty as a jigsaw puzzle. Émile manoeuvred them into a parking spot half on the curb in a narrow back lane, while his mother shook out a large old key.

"Voici, voici! Come and look, James. Come and see my chandelier!"

Émile stood back, letting his mother usher him through a laneway into a courtyard. She shook the key again, then inserted it with a flourish into an ancient ornate pale blue door. The building was old, several stories high, some of the floor tiles the same pattern of white with tiny black corner pieces that Cynthia had chosen for her Bowral house. These originals had the charm of the patina of age. They'd seen generations come and go. Forgiving.

Everything was old in this house. No angle was perfectly square. This was how his mother looked now, a little imperfect, her edges softening, more comfortable in herself.

"We've done so much work, James," she was saying. "You wouldn't recognize it. It had been some kind of boarding house when I found it, and terribly run down, but I just fell in love with it, and you can see, can't you? You can feel it. The bones are so good. I just adore every room, so special, so charming. See the windows? The fireplaces. It's so French. So cosy, yet elegant. I absolutely love this place, and Émile has helped me so much." She stopped and patted Émile on the arm, smiling up at him.

Tall and quiet, Émile nodded a little and gestured for the tour to continue.

Cynthia bustled James through and up an ornate staircase and up again.

"This whole floor is for guests. You have your own bathroom and small kitchen. See? You can be quite independent. There are several rooms as well as the sitting room. Enough for you, Nic and Will to stay, or any of you with…" she looked up at Émile, then said it outright.

"I'm waiting for grandchildren, Émile. I'm ready." His mother stared at James hopefully. She'd learned not to ask about Helene, but she was clearly holding her tongue, desperate to ask if there was someone new in his life, someone special, yet not wanting to offend or upset him so soon after his arrival.

If only she knew the real purpose of his visit. He was dreading raising the subject, intruding into her lifestyle with the crass talk of living beyond one's means. Now was not the time, not while he was jet lagged and she was so keen to show him more of her life.

There was an awkward silence.

Émile had brought James's bag, and they ascended another set of stairs. He placed it in one of the rooms beside a cast iron double bed. This room was on a corner of the house, with sets of french doors, tiny balconies on two sides and a view to the hills. Conversation had stalled.

"Le chandelier," Émile offered, when they were both clearly seeking a way forward.

"Yes, yes. Come down now, James, and let me show you our *best* room…"

At the foot of the stairs, she turned sharply right and through a little doorway into a room full of light, with a large marble fireplace, sets of windows along two sides, and, best of all, an ornate entrance, stepped in from the edge of the building to offer shelter against the elements.

Surprisingly, it was completely empty, except for the chandelier, beautifully positioned in the centre, under a large white ceiling rose.

"Émile hung it for me," she said. "He's very clever. Looks like it's been there forever, doesn't it, James, darling? It belongs. You can see why we both fell in love with it."

James nodded. It was true. It was exceptional. The space was beautiful, and the chandelier crowned it. The question was, what was it all for?

He was bone weary.

He looked at his watch and his mother took the hint.

"Well, then. You'll want to freshen up after your journey. Such a long way, James, my darling. You must have a rest. Émile and I like to have a quiet time in the late afternoon, and reconvene at about 6.30pm or so, then wander along and find a restaurant. You're welcome to join us, or you can make tea and toast in your suite. There are eggs and cheeses in the fridge. If we don't see you by 7pm, we'll see you in the morning."

She rushed up to him and gave him a hug, smelling of lavender. He was so tall now, he felt like the adult, and his mother, the excited child. He was dreading putting a pin in her balloon, being the spoilsport, putting a stop to this lifestyle she so clearly adored.

He hugged her back, still holding his tongue. Then he shook the hand of the doting Émile, deftly avoiding the double or triple kiss with this stranger, before retreating to the peace of his tasteful room.

Showered, he slipped between the linen sheets and slept like the dead.

…

James awoke to birdsong, profoundly content. He stretched, leaped out of bed, strode to the French doors and threw them open, to see three black birds swoop past the chimney pots and then dive, disappearing into a grove of deep green pines.

There was a chill to the air, but already a promise of warmth to the day. No clouds. No wonder the world was in love with this part of France, Provence, with its fields of lavender, and vineyards that had supplied the Roman empire for centuries if not millennia.

The French doors were double glazed and had sealed perfectly, keeping the space warm enough.

The building was clearly centuries old, but it seemed in good condition. Was this where some of their funds had been going? Into maintenance and repairs? Was the mysterious Émile some kind of a builder?

As he went to head downstairs, he found a basket beside the staircase, with a paper bag holding a croissant, and a note and spare key.

"Out. Back for lunch with fresh supplies. Mother."

Supplies of what? He headed down the stairs and found his way to the empty front room. Bread and fruit, or more chandeliers?

Even at this time of day, the beautiful room was flooded with light. It must face south.

As he slipped out onto the crooked street, he wondered what his mother's plans for it might be. Would she just fill it with more expensive old furniture? What would she do when the house was full of antiques? Buy another?

The air was fresh. It was nearly lunchtime and the croissant smelled fantastic, whetting his appetite after the skipped dinner and breakfast. It was perfectly crunchy and soft, slightly sweet and salty, as only the French could make them.

A black cat with golden eyes regarded him, and he stooped to tickle it under the chin and offer it some crumbs as he found his bearings. Uphill to the cathedral, or downhill to the bridge and river, past the bar on the corner?

He was in a long main street, quite narrow, with a couple of cheese shops, three touristy kitchen shops, some menswear outlets and a drapers, a bakery which smelled superb, a newsagent and tobacconist, a creperie, a tea shop, two cafes, one on each side of the street, and at least seven restaurants. Surely there couldn't be enough custom for them all...

From every position down the narrow streets there was another picturesque view of mountains, stone houses, fruit trees awaiting spring, statues. It was a painter's paradise, and he wasn't surprised to pass a shop selling artists' materials and several small galleries.

He saw his mother and Émile in the distance carrying a bulging string bag, before they noticed him. His mother was cradling three sticks of bread, leaning into Émile, laughing, while he had his arm over her shoulder, bottle of wine in one hand.

It struck him he'd never seen her so relaxed, so happy, certainly not in Sydney, nor in Bowral, where nothing in her old-styled but new house had ever totally pleased her.

They spotted him and separated, Émile gesturing with the wine bottle and his mother wiggling the bread. They were like guilty young lovers, shy in public. He knew he should feel happy for them, even though the shock of losing his father never quite went away. He waved back.

He passed a doctor's surgery, a chemist, bookstore, charcuterie and several more cheese shops. Did anyone do anything but eat in this town? It must be quite a centre, though small. If there was a supermarket, it wasn't obvious. There were several church spires, but no traffic lights.

He was marvelling at some of the ornate Juliette balconies and window boxes, some even sporting exceptionally late roses, when he was nearly bowled over by a child coming around the corner on a scooter, a dog scampering behind, ears flapping. Keep left? Keep right? Where were her parents? He remembered again the runaway child back in Sydney and the moment he'd saved Stella. Stella. For a moment he felt alone, too alone, hunching his hands in his coat pockets. But perhaps he would bring Stella here one day, if...

A couple of old people in berets walked past, walking slowly in grey coats. They looked him up and down as he did the same to them. The French cared what they wore.

"You like our village?" Émile asked James as they met up, and he nodded, taking the heavy bag of cheeses as he turned and they headed back together.

"You should see it tomorrow, market day!" said his mother, her face alight. "The square at the back of our place fills up completely! It's unrecognisable, full of stalls and people and movement and sound. You'll absolutely love it!"

Back at the house, out came the big key again and his mother opened the main door with a ceremonial flourish. Warmish sunlight was streaming in through the windows.

"Bring in the little table, would you, Émile? Let's picnic!"

James's mother's idea of a picnic was very civilized. Émile had reappeared in the doorway, carrying an ornate gateleg table with turned legs. Moments later, he returned with first two and then a third spindle backed chair, followed by a blue and white linen tablecloth and a wooden board.

His mother laid out several of the cheeses and a loaf of bread on the board as Émile disappeared again. James paced the room.

"We need to talk, mother," James said.

"Oh?" Her childlike joy in the moment receded, overtaken by the familiar imperiousness he remembered so well.

"It's all very well…" he began.

He was interrupted by Émile's return, this time with a tray, laden with the wine, three crystal glasses, a knife, a bowl of mixed olives, a clump of semi-dried grapes, a perfect pear, still with a leaf or two, and an array of confiture, each jar more golden than the last.

It was like something out of a Dutch still life painting, with the low winter sunlight flowing in through the old-fashioned windows and spilling onto the rich red of this tiled floor. Octagons? Hexagons?

"Later, darling," she said. "Let's not spoil our time together."

"A votre bonne santé," said Émile, congenially, and they toasted, clinking their glasses.

James was reminded of Stella. What had she said of her own mother? "Rich in the things that matter."

Stella. His sudden longing for her was visceral. What was she doing? Was she missing him as well? Or was she with that Damian who kept messaging her? The prospect tortured him. Should he have risked leaving her; going away like this? He must text her. Whatever she'd said about not wanting to hear from him till the end of May, it was too long. Too long for him to wait. Hopefully she felt it too, this need to be together. He wanted her to know that she mattered to him. What time would it be in Sydney? Evening.

He pulled out his phone. He would do it. He stepped back to take in the whole scene, photographing the perfect provincial "picnic" in the centre of the beautiful room, chandelier and all, his mother and Émile poised with their glasses in the air.

He sent it to Stella. No explanation. No actual text. Anonymous. Surely that wasn't breaking the rules.

Chapter 30

James wrenched his mind and body from desire for Stella back into the beautiful room, back to his mother and this stranger.

"So, tell me about yourself," James said to Émile.

"Je suis l'étranger, un vrai vagabond," Émile nodded, squeezing his mother's arm and looking across at her. They toasted each other and drank again. At the edge of their joy, James was alone.

"It's true, James," said his mother, laughing. "He's a stray. I picked him up. He's been very useful."

"A 'stray'?"

"He's not actually French. He's from Belgium. He started travelling south a year or two ago in search of the sun, after he sold his hardware shop. Émile and his family have always been able to make and fix things. He has the most marvellous van full of tools. We'll show you this evening."

"Sud," Émile nodded, helping himself to a chunk of bread, dollop of apricot jam and slab of cheese.

"South," she said. "And he's very clever. Émile can do everything. Plumbing, wires, repairs. He's so handy."

Émile began to tell him of the journey, the people he'd met, especially the English. So many of them needed help to convert the stone barns they'd bought into holiday houses and retirement homes.

239

"It was good. They needed … the advice, the ideas, the work. Moi? I needed … the work. Voilà."

He'd liaised with local builders, joined in for the odd jobs that sometimes became longer jobs. Sometimes he became a caretaker, staying until winter when the need to travel south again became so strong he would pack up his truck and continue the journey further and further from the cold winters every year.

How was it that all their glasses were empty? And all the bread was gone, but for a scattering of crumbs. James broke off another branch of the shrunken grapes, so sweet, with a tiny crunch of bitter seeds inside.

"Lovely, aren't they?" his mother said. "This area used to specialize in dried fruit, and of course, there's all the wine. We'll take him to the wine service station, won't we, Émile? It's a co-op. You bring your own containers and you literally buy the wine out of bowsers, like petrol. There are 20 or so varieties. We haven't even tasted them all. Let's go tomorrow for lunch. We'll book." She yawned.

As the sun dropped lower in the sky, so too did the angle of Émile and James's mother in their chairs, lit up with a golden tinged glow. He wasn't feeling so lively himself.

"Time for siesta, darling. See you back here at 7pm and we'll walk up and find a restaurant. You can choose."

James stifled a sudden burst of anger. Was that all this was? One never-ending feast?

Émile packed up the remnants of their meal, and James helped, carrying the chairs and table back inside the rest of the house. It was as he thought. The ground floor rooms were stuffed full of antique furniture. What could his mother possibly want with it all? Surely she must have exhausted her capacity for collecting every last piece.

…

At 7pm, when they met in the empty room, James was determined to get some answers.

"A work in progress?" he gestured at the space, while his mother adjusted her warm hat and scarf and fished some gloves out of her pocket.

She refused to answer.

"Mais, c'est la vie, n'est-ce pas?" said Émile, with his customary shrug, trying to ease what was becoming awkward. He seemed to have a sixth sense, ready to protect Cynthia from any accusations.

Hippies in their sixties. Again James felt like the only adult.

"Relax, darling. When did you last have a holiday?"

"I didn't come here for a holiday, mother. We have to talk. We can talk with or without Émile, but we have to talk."

"Shhh, darling. Let's not spoil dinner. We see each other so rarely. Is this about money?"

"Yes, it is about money." James stared at Émile, who was clearly going to stand his ground, right next to Cynthia. He had no choice but to plough on. "It's absolutely about money. It's about your never-ending quest for French antique furniture. Don't get me wrong. It's beautiful furniture. But how much can you possibly need? The Bowral house is full. And this one is too. Except for this room."

His mother was silent. Lips pursed. She looked like a child caught doing something wrong, and James worried he was going too far. He deliberately made his voice more gentle.

"Mother, we need to discuss the future. It's a lovely lifestyle you're living, no question. I'm glad to see you so happy. Truly. And Émile here, well. You seem like a great bloke."

"He is," she practically pinched Émile's cheek, who leaned down and kissed her in the semi darkness. Irritated, James maintained control.

"Émile, I wonder if I could have an appointment to speak with my mother. Privately. Would you mind?"

"But not at all. Not at all. Moi? I will cook. We eat 'ere. Was un restaurant, this room. Tonight. Un restaurant. Moi? Le maître di."

"Qu'elle bonne idée!" said his mother, removing her gloves and unwrapping herself slightly, though the room was hardly warm. That was another thing. How did they afford the heating?

"Merci beaucoup," James dredged up from his schoolboy French.

He retrieved the chairs and table they'd used for their "picnic" lunch, and he and his mother sat, facing each other.

"Well?"

"Thank you, mother. Émile. Are you serious about each other? Is he living here? Does he pay rent?"

"Have I ever asked you about your girlfriends, darling?"

"Yes. Actually. All the time, mother. You know that."

"Well, Émile is wonderful. As you see."

"Yes, but is he contributing? Financially, I mean."

"Why is this your business?" The imperiousness was back.

"It is exactly my business. It is exactly our business. This is the whole point, mother. Huntleys is going bankrupt. Do you want that? What with you here in France buying up every antique, and Will in Vegas, supposedly finding better suppliers and outlets but actually throwing away our inheritance and working capital on gambling, Huntleys is on its knees."

She was shocked. Chastened. She was no fool, his mother, though she did like to play. James was relieved she was listening carefully now.

"Things need to change, mother. Or your own supply of cash is going to disappear, and fast."

His mother remained silent. The sky deepened from pale lavender to a rich purple. Other couples strolled past as mother and son sat in the beautiful room in darkness.

"So when I ask about your plans, I really need to know. Do you own this place, or are you renting? What is Émile's contribution? And are you actually creating any value for Huntleys? You're my mother and I love you. I couldn't be more pleased to see you happy. But how can I justify keeping you on the payroll and paying all those expenses? It's not just about me and what I want for you. It's about the Australian Taxation Office and Huntleys' bottom line. I need to show cause to the Australian Securities and Investment Commission that Huntleys should continue to trade. And it's becoming more and more difficult. Much as I'd love to ignore it, for your sake and for mine."

He reached out then across the small table and took his mother's hand. She seemed so small in the darkness. Was that a tear rolling down her cheek? Despite the beautiful clothes and obsession with France, she hadn't had an easy life. Not for the last couple of decades, with Jimmy's illness and death. The last thing James wanted to do was to hurt her.

"And Will?"

"I'm going to see Will after this. The tabloids haven't been kind. Maybe you don't get that news over here. There's been another bust up. He's booked himself into some health spa. I was going over to see him anyway. Flying out first thing Tuesday. Have you heard from him?"

She was silent. Her reply, when it came, was in a monotone.

"Only when he needs more money."

"Is that what you're doing? Sending him your money?"

She nodded in the darkness.

"I'd do the same for you, James. He was my baby."

"Mother! He's 27 years old! Nearly 28. He's no baby. He'll never grow up if you don't let him take responsibility for his own decisions."

"He's promised to give up gambling."

"How many times?"

She was silent again.

"I know, James."

"Yes. Let's talk about this, mother."

"The health spa. It was my idea. It's a clinic. There are counsellors, too. Healthy body, healthy mind. Have a look at the website, James. It has an excellent reputation. There's a gym and healthy food. Takes away from the stigma of the mental health part, you know, dear. So many celebrities go there. It's almost a badge of honour. A club for the rich and famous when they're sad."

James baulked at the "rich" part, but held his tongue. He almost said "infamous and spoilt" but resisted.

"Your idea, mother…" he said, measured. "And it's a good one. But the money's got to stop. You understand that, don't you?"

She nodded, matching his serious tone.

"But it's not all bad, James. It hasn't all gone. I'm not completely stupid. I own this place. I bought it for a song. I was planning to rent out this room, for some sort of shop. That's why we're keeping it empty. It isn't private enough for us to use, not with all these windows. It's been all sorts of things in the past, a dress shop, even a saddlery… Oh, you should see this place in summer when it's absolutely crawling with tourists. They love it. They come for the wine, for the lavender, to paint, to speak French, to eat. It's hugely popular for hipster weddings. Even with Aussies. In summer, I'm no longer the only Australienne. And Émile. Who knows? Maybe he'll stay with me. I hope he will. But maybe he'll keep travelling south. Every day is precious when you get to my age, James. I don't expect you to understand that. But it doesn't cost much to live here. Even the wine is affordable. And I can also rent out the top floor as well as this shop space if I have to. Or maybe I'll sell up and keep travelling with Émile. Maybe I'll come back to Australia. Bring him with me. But you can keep my allowance if you need it, James. Well, most of it. I understand what you're saying. Of course I don't want to send us all bankrupt. I had no idea things were so bad. No. I can see you need the business to be strong. We all need it to be strong. I don't need the allowance. Not all of it. Not really. It's a long time since I earned my keep at Huntleys. I still have some investments from the sale of the old house. You can see. I have enough. We don't need much. Maybe just give me half of what I've been getting? Or even a third of it? That would do. And I promise I'll try to stop sending it to Will. But I do worry about him. So, you're going to see him? Talk to him, James. Maybe you can make him see sense."

James squeezed her hand, and she placed her other one over his. She still wore Jimmy's engagement ring, he noticed, the exquisite row of marquises. His father had not been entirely forgotten.

As the relief at having had The Conversation with his mother flooded through him, James became aware of the rich aroma of beef casserole invading the dark room.

James's memory catapulted to the meal he'd shared with Stella the night of their lovemaking. How he missed her. He replayed their conversation, all her ideas for Huntleys, of jewels for every price bracket. An idea began to form at the back of his mind.

"Now, since we're having frank conversations, James, my darling, how are you?"

"You mean 'where are my grandchildren'?" he laughed.

"Exactly."

"I've met someone."

"Tell me."

"I've never been more serious, mother. That's why I had to come here. She's a jeweler, mother. Immensely talented. She doesn't even realize, I don't think. She's only new to the game, and she's creating in silver, affordable pieces, but she has so much more potential. There's so much we can share with her, teach her. She has all the ideas I've never had. She has a designing mind, like Jim. He likes her. You'll like her. I know you will. Her name is Stella."

Just saying her name in this room, he wanted her beside him. Her absence was an ache. He closed his eyes, summoning her memory, her wild hair and dark eyes, the feel of her skin, that spark between them...

"So why didn't you bring her?"

"I will. I will now. I'll be able to. Now that you can help me get things back on track, and as long as things go well enough with Will. It's only then I'll have something to offer her. I know now. I want to marry her, mother. I've never wanted anything more."

She jumped up and threw her arms up around his neck before running to the door, calling out to Émile.

"Darling! Champagne! Champagne!"

Émile burst in with a large antique silver tray and three lit candles in an ornate silver candelabra. He returned cradling a matching champagne bucket complete with some Moet; three shallow French antique glasses expertly clutched in his spare hand.

If he'd been listening at the door, he was forgiven.

Chapter 31

James was woken by the sound of hammering and the aroma of warm croissants. Once again, a basket of fresh ones was waiting for him at the top of the stairs as he made his way to the other side of the building and peered out.

His mother had been right. The square was being transformed into a riot of bright activity. Someone was ramming pegs into the ground to secure a small marquee, sandwiched between dozens of others. Market Day was a swirl of bright flags, canvas tents of every color, dresses and scarves swinging in the breeze and customers in berets, hoodies, puffer jackets and leather coats, some with backpacks and others with shopping trolleys and baskets like the one holding his croissant.

A truck or two had rolled into town with larger wares. There was the glow of old marble and the shine of brass and polished wood, the strange greeny grey of old linens. He guessed his mother was down there already, and sure enough, there was a note. "Buying more olives and bread. Meet back here at 1 o'clock."

James wandered. A crowd had appeared as if from nowhere. There was barely space to move. He was drawn to an intriguing hair ornament, a jewelled twist of wire for holding a bun in place. He reached for it - a gift for Stella - but had to wait for five other customers to be served first, getting jostled from behind.

Securing his purchase, he wandered on, astounded to discover that the stalls spilled from the square in every direction through the other streets of the town. He couldn't wait to tell Stella, to bring her here.

He came across his mother and Émile by chance, making another purchase. As he waited for them to find the perfect silver soup ladle and some fish knives, sorting through an enormous basket of the things, he found himself peering through piles of bric a brac nearby.

There was costume jewelry and a small case of older stuff, art deco, art nouveau and older, and even some worn out old fob watches, and silver and gold watch chains in various stages of disrepair. They were the sorts of things Jim would love to work with, using his loupe to unravel the mystery of their makers and guess at their provenance before carefully repairing them.

He asked to look, and weighed them in his hands, querying the stallholder about the prices. He pulled out his wallet and made some purchases, strangely excited. He understood the appeal of this kind of shopping. More importantly, the idea at the back of his mind continued to take shape.

He picked up some contributions for their lunch as he strode back, setting up the lunch table and chairs before pacing out the room.

"You're a builder?" he asked Émile, as they sat down to another picnic lunch.

"Oui."

"He can do anything," his mother said, beaming up at Émile.

"And your spare furniture, mother. I've had an idea."

"Tell us!"

"There's no jewelry shop here, is there?"

"No. You have to go to Avignon, really."

"Why not make this the French branch of Huntleys? It would be different to our Bondi Junction branch, maybe pave the way for some of the changes we'd like to make there. You could offer evaluations, repairs, estate jewelry, as well as top of the line contemporary pieces and more affordable ranges. Something for everyone. You say this town is even busier in summer. Everyone wants a memento of their travels. What do you think?"

His mother's eyes darted around the room. She touched her fingertips together, a mannerism he remembered now from childhood. She was thinking. She turned to him, eyes sparkling.

"Oh! It's brilliant, darling!" Now her hands were in the air. "I could pick up suitable estate jewelry at the markets. You'd like that, Émile, darling, wouldn't you? No more lifting heavy furniture!"

Émile nodded. He actually seemed relieved.

"But we'd need to set this up right. We'd need the right sorts of cabinets, built to take advantage of this beautiful space. Or maybe you could source some old jewelers cabinets and repurpose them, or reconfigure some of the furniture. Is this something you might do, Émile?"

Émile was nodding at the proportions of the room as Cynthia took up the idea, her hands already marking out spaces. Both of them jumped up.

"It's perfect, darling! And we could also have a section here selling some smaller items. The silver spoons and candlesticks. Crystal! Nice souvenirs which might appeal to people a bit more widely. And this corner could be dedicated to larger items, a couple of chairs and a small table for example, or a beautiful dresser, the sorts of things Émile does up so nicely. Not everyone can make it on market day. We would make our mark-ups affordable. Gain a reputation. Tourists can't eat and drink all day. They need to wander and find special souvenirs! Huntleys can become a French destination, too!"

"Why not? This would be your branch, if you want it, mother. You remember balancing the books? You taught me, after all. Can I rely on you to make this work? It would be a great advantage for Huntleys. With this branch, we could become international. Global. I could bring out fresh stock from Australia several times a year, and vice versa."

"And I'd get to see my grandchildren!"

"You would." *Could he allow himself to dream that far ahead? Why not?* He hadn't felt so optimistic in years.

"Émile, darling. You've got one of those drafting books, haven't you? What's it called in French? Blueprints. Plans. Sketch our new shop?"

Now James and Émile paced the room together, using their hands to test where the counters might be. The chandelier was sparkling above them, and his mother was beaming at them both.

Chapter 32

"Did you get my emails, James?" Nicole sounded mildly annoyed on the phone. It was an improvement on her usual level of anger. He'd expected far worse. He felt like he'd been travelling for weeks, though he'd only been away a few days.

He'd needed the full stopover in LA to catch up with all her correspondence, each email more frantic than the last. Her most recent had three exclamation marks after "deadline." He couldn't understand why she was so passionate about this competition. Sure, it was important to think about the next big event now that Christmas was over, but Valentine's Day was nearly six weeks away.

"So what did you think?"

"The bird head hearts. No other design is anywhere near as good." James had managed to find a gate with only two other passengers waiting, and they were both asleep, heads on backpacks. He talked into the huge glass window, staring out at flat concrete as far as he could see, with aeroplanes parked here and there, one or two slowly moving.

"I was afraid you'd say that," Nicole said.

"So what's the problem? A win's a win. Don't you agree it's the best design."

"It is, yes, but …

"But? Out with it. Come on, Nic."

"It's Stella's."

A burst of pride spread inside him. He remembered now. She'd been drawing birds at Fitzroy Falls when they'd been there together, in the visitors' centre. She was gifted, alright. *Stella.* Suddenly he needed to see her, to congratulate her himself. She'd barely believed him when he'd told her how talented she was. This win would give her confidence, prove to her that her talent was incontestable.

"It's going to look really awkward, James. After all that aggro social media between us?"

"A win's a win, Nicole. At least no one can say the competition was rigged. In fact, maybe Slavonicus can spin it into a story. 'Former enemy gains top prize,' or something. I don't see a huge problem."

"Yeah. You wouldn't. You're keen on her, aren't you?"

"Jesus, Nicole. You all but told me we needed her in our business. How was that ever going to look? 'Huntleys swallows competition?' Come on. You're good at this stuff. Can't you make it a 'win, win'?"

"You know Ruben."

"So? Cop it. You can handle it. Take a bit of heat. It's all good publicity isn't it?"

"Easy for you to say, on the other side of the world. Actually, James. There's something else I need to tell you."

"Come on, then. Quick. My Vegas flight's boarding."

"Oh... Look... Don't worry about it now, okay? It's complicated. Ring me from Vegas, will you? How's mother?"

Odd. What was Nicole hiding? Something wasn't right.

"Mother's surprisingly okay. I'm excited, Nicole. There's Émile. I have to tell you all about that. But wait for this... We're going to open a French branch of Huntleys..."

"No! That's brilliant! I like that! I like that a lot. Huntleys going international... That's brilliant, James! Vote one Scottie and I go to France to organise the opening publicity!"

"'Scottie and you?' Are you two seeing each other? Wow. I have been away a long time. Jesus. For real? Be kind, Nicole. Don't mess with Scottie."

"Not messing with Scottie. Not in any bad way, I assure you…"

"Good to hear. He's our accountant for starters, not to mention my best friend…"

"I know. To think I barely noticed Scottie. And then once I did, I saw it. I saw what you see. A lot more actually."

"Yeah, okay. I don't need to know the details, Nic. I'm pleased for you. Always thought you two'd be good together. That's such good news."

"Yes. It is."

"Now. The design comp. Remind me. What does she win?"

"Lessons with Jim. A couple of K. The chance to make her design in gold…"

"And a bit of humble pie for us on social media. You can handle it fine, Nicole. Shows we're 'big hearted.' How's that! Can you run with a pun like that? 'Big-hearted Huntleys buries the hatchet for best heart design.' What do you think?"

"Maybe… There's still a problem. Call me when you get to Vegas."

Chapter 33

Stella was torn. Still reeling from being forced to close her stall, and unable to find out more or negotiate while the council was still closed for the festive season, she'd received some unexpected good news - she'd been listed as a finalist in the Huntleys Valentine's Day competition.

Jeannie was over the moon and was insisting she attend their prize event and collect her credential.

"We need this photo for social, Stell. You deserve to shine. You can't run away from this. At least go get your award. You've invested so much in Stellar. Don't be too hasty about refusing to go. I know you're upset, but I'm still sure there'll be an explanation, a way forward."

Jeannie had at least convinced her to wait till the council reopened the following week and then explore her options. Every time the horror of the possibility James had betrayed her rose again in her, she pushed it down and channelled her energies into preparing for the international design show, but fronting up to all the Huntleys at a public event? That would be difficult. Suspecting them. Furious. Too hard.

"But even if it was Huntleys, you owe it to yourself to be sensible, Stell," Jeannie argued. "So, your stall only lasted three months instead of six, but what a brilliant three months! Besides. When the council gets back I'm sure you can lodge an appeal. You can't let this stop progress. You've still got all your online sales."

Jeannie didn't get it. The way her heart was broken. That dead feeling inside. Even the girls understood. Instead of running up to her to be hugged, Lucy would creep towards her with a sad face. Tears kept seeping out of her eyes. It was like her whole body was grieving. It was. She felt like her heart had been ripped out. It had.

But Jeannie was right. She should at least show up and put a brave face on it. Maybe she could get to the bottom of what had happened, find out whether it truly had been Huntleys that had closed her down.

Jeannie was such a saint. So kind. She kept trying to distract her from the immediate setback, to help her see the bigger picture.

"And then when you get to Singapore, people will be able to see you're already an award-winning designer. You need to think about your image, Stell."

"I haven't won yet, Jeannie. I'm just a finalist, remember."

"But you're the best, Stell! You've got to be. Why else did everything you made sell so well? Why are your online items still going like hotcakes? People recognize beauty when they see it."

Stella still wondered if she should simply apply for another office job, in Sydney. She'd been great in her previous role. At least she'd have a proper income again.

"Over my dead body, Stella," Jeannie had said. "Not after all you've achieved."

"But I can't earn enough money any more without the stall. I can't pay my debt."

"Think about what *you* need, Stella. It's not all about money."

Stella closed her eyes. A vision came to her unbidden, of James's arms around her. She'd trusted he believed in her skill, that he respected her. She still wanted it to be true, even if the evidence said otherwise - that email from the council. Her body would never forget the way he'd cherished her that weekend when they were alone together in the storm. Damian had never touched her like that. She shivered with longing. For

James. For her creative life. For the world James might have offered her if only she could have trusted him.

She shook her head and opened her eyes.

"All that's impossible now, Jeannie. James isn't who I'd hoped he was."

"We don't know that yet, Stell. You're just tired. You've never had a thick skin. It's a shock. Okay. I get that. But you've actually got lots of options. Why don't you give James a chance? You've been full of joy out here with us, living your dream. Life's not supposed to be easy, you know. 'Never give up.' That's what Flame would say.'"

"Flame gives up all the time, Jeannie! How long do you honestly think the duck eggs are going to last? Or Grady?"

"You've got a point, Stell. But maybe that's why she never wants *us* to give up. And Flame never entered a competition in her life. And she certainly was never shortlisted. I'm so damned proud of you, little sister!"

Stella frowned and shrugged.

"I'm just tired, Jeannie. This whole thing has been hard. So much harder than I'd hoped it would be - the debt, my silver supplies disappearing off the face of the earth, all the stock I have to keep building up, the accident, the theft. I do still want jewelry to be my career. I just don't know what to make of this."

"Give it some time."

Stella nodded, but she was still so flat when the big evening arrived that she couldn't bring herself to face Huntleys. Not if they really wanted to close her down.

"You have to go for me, Jeannie. Stand in. I'll stay and mind the girls. I tried. I washed my hair. But I just can't do this. And I don't need to. You can do it for me. Please, Jeannie. You be strong for me. I trust you."

"Tell you what. I'll go. But only if you come, too. Matt'll be home soon. He caught an earlier plane. So I'll go early and put in an appearance. You put the girls to bed, and then follow, as soon as Matt's home. Just go and see what you've got in your wardrobe. You'll cheer up."

Jeannie was right. Stella came back with one black stiletto and one red one.

"That's the Stella I know!" The sisters laughed and hugged.

"It's so long since I've been out like this," Jeannie said as she stepped out her front door towards the waiting Uber. "Feels like the school formal. OMG, Stella. Clever you. This is a big deal, sister."

...

It was lovely being at home with the girls, nestling them into bed with their soft toys.

After six books, and two of them read through at least twice, Lucy was so tired she fell asleep still propped against Stella's arm. Stella lifted her heavy little slumbering body and laid it gently in her cot with a few safe toys at the end so she could play with them if she woke early.

Sienna stirred, and Stella stood above her, rocking her gently till her breaths became snores. How glad she was to have left her old life, whatever the challenges she now faced.

She heard Matt's key in the front door. He wheeled his bag into the bedroom and washed his hands, running himself a glass of water.

"Go on. Get dressed. Jeannie made me promise I'd see you out that door."

"Did she tell you Huntleys tried to close me down? At least we think it's them. Can't work out how else I got that notice from council. Thanks so much for taking over. Jeannie looks fabulous. She's really excited. I'm so glad she can get a bit of value out of this. She deserves it. She's been running all my online sales, social media. She's amazing."

"She is. And so are you. She told me you'd try to get out of it, but the way I see it, you should march right in there and hold your head up. You're not the one who's done anything wrong. If it is Huntleys trying to close you down, they're the ones who should be ashamed, not you. You're the star, Stella. Gotta stand up to bullies. Do what's right."

Stella smiled. Matt. He was right. She looked at her watch, excitement surging through her.

"Go!" He pointed back down the corridor.

She rushed through the shower, pulled on a little black dress and some heels and grabbed the scarf she'd worn to their picnic. Why not? If she was feeling awkward about this, let James Huntley feel it too! As a finishing touch she fixed large hoops to her ears, one of her new designs with a zig zag at the front to catch the light. She hauled her shoulders back and forced herself to smile at her image in the mirror. Lipstick. Better. Yes. She could do this.

The front of Huntleys was all lit up, with banners at the entrance and a security guard who checked her name and opened the door.

Would James be there in his best grey suit? Her heartbeat ramped up as she waited for the old elevator.

Ruben was just outside the VIP room, recording.

"Well, it's an exciting night in Oxford Street Mall ahead of the inaugural Huntleys Valentine's Day jewelry design awards. Pretty soon we're going to meet five talented designers who've been shortlisted for the prize, a whopping $5,000 and a chance to attend a workshop with the founder of this iconic Sydney jewelry establishment, none other than Jim Huntley himself. See you a bit later, inside, when we meet the finalists." Ruben winked at her.

How Stella hoped to win! The money would be great, but the lesson with Jim would be better still. Attending lessons would be awkward if James was around, but she knew how to be professional. Surely Jim wouldn't have tried to close her down. Jim was a gentleman. As she slipped in, behind the crowd, she saw him near a dais, uncomfortable in a new shirt and tie. He kept pushing his gnarled old finger into the top of his stiff white collar, adjusting it. His eyes lit up to welcome Ruben, then her. James's eyes. Stella felt a blush and chastised herself. It wasn't James, and if it was, wasn't he the enemy? But there was something about the twinkle in those eyes she loved. Jim was a charmer like his grandson, alright.

There was a cluster of VIPs and finalists. She scanned the room, heart jumping. No James. Now disappointment stabbed at her.

She headed towards Jeannie, whose red hair was blazing in the spotlights, her hot pink figure-hugging outfit perfect for the occasion. Jeannie was positively beaming, having a great night out.

There was Nicole in purple, at an ornate gold music stand, with a kind of Huntleys flag hanging from it, the H H J, worked in gold lettering, looking at her run sheet.

A waiter was filling champagne flutes on a sideboard. Nicole gestured to a tall man who came and stood beside her, and to Jim, who came to her other side. A camera flashed a few times, and Nicole began to speak.

"I'm delighted to welcome you all here to Huntleys this evening for the presentation of Huntleys inaugural Valentine's Day jewelry Design Awards. Huntleys has been a fixture on the Sydney jewelry scene for six decades, and we are thrilled to be in a position to crown our reputation for quality and excellence by sponsoring this competition. Huntleys attracted more than 500 entries from all over Australia, and I would like to take this moment to thank Ruben Slavonicus for helping us publicize this opportunity. We've been blown away by the level of talent out there, and would like to thank each and every one of our competitors. Choosing a winner has been exceptionally difficult, and I would encourage all of our entrants and all of our finalists to continue designing jewelry. We plan to run this competition next year and to make it an annual opportunity to showcase the work of a young designer and contribute to their jewelry making skills. And now, I would like to honour my grandfather, Jim Huntley, without whom Huntleys would not exist. Can we take this moment to recognise Jim's achievements over many years? I can honestly say that Valentine's Day in Sydney would not be the same without this great jeweler, and there are many couples out there of all ages who would 'heartily' agree with me."

As everyone applauded, the waiter circulated, topping up glasses.

"We will shortly come to that time in the evening when we name our five finalists - a 'heart stopping' moment. I'll ask you to hold your applause until all five finalists have come to the front of the room. And to announce their names, I'd like to introduce Luke Scott of Scott and Sons accountants who have worked closely with Huntleys for three generations. Luke Scott, ladies and gentlemen."

"Good evening, ladies and gentlemen," he said, clearing his throat. He looked like he'd be far more comfortable behind a desk with a balance sheet, but with his purple tie, he seemed proud to be up there beside Nicole. Nicole was different. More confident. More relaxed.

"It's my great honour to be involved in this awards ceremony and to make this surprise announcement. I will take this opportunity to let you know that with this honour comes a donation to the Children's Heart Unit at Westmead Children's Hospital of $10,000, made jointly by Huntleys and by Scott and Sons. We are absolutely honoured to be sharing the love this evening. Can I call forward LucyAnne Tang from the Children's Hospital, please, to receive this heartfelt donation?"

LucyAnne stepped forward amid an eruption of cheers and applause and camera flashes, and accepted the cheque. Ruben's tweets were hashtagging the Children's Hospital as well now.

"Thank you, Scottie. I now call to the front of the room our five finalists, Jerome Montgomery, Eloise Chin, Stella Rhys, Sergio Russo and Nina Phillips. I'm sure you'll all join me in congratulating these talented designers," Nicole continued as the room erupted in applause.

Jeannie gave Stella a small push, and she stepped up, head high. She'd never liked the limelight, but she'd do this. Cameras flashed in their eyes.

"And now, Jim will open the envelope and reveal the winning design and the name of the winner!"

Jim smiled and opened the envelope, drawing out the winning design and holding it up for the guests. Lined up with the others, Stella couldn't see it, but Jeannie's eyes lit up and she pulled down her fist with a triumphant "yes." Jim turned the page towards the finalists. Yes, indeed. There were Stella's bower birds with sapphire eyes! Her own heart design!

"Congratulations to Stella Rhys, of Stellar," Jim read out, his old voice raspy.

Stella stepped forward to shake Jim's hand and accept her prize, heart hammering in her ears. Jim's smile and handshake were warm. She could hardly wait to take up his lessons.

Jeannie was beaming, trying to clap while videoing the action and preventing herself jumping up and down with excitement.

"There'll be plenty of time for public shaming, if it really is them," Jeannie'd said before leaving the house, helping her strategize. Stella was glad now they'd decided to play it cool. Jeannie was right. It was best to get the prize in the bag first, and then to work out their next moves, if indeed Huntleys were the culprits.

It was hard to keep a level head. It wasn't Jeannie who couldn't get James Huntley out of her head, out of her heart, out of her dreams...

A congratulations message popped onto her phone, and she checked it. Maybe it was from James! He must have yet another new phone.

Congrats, Stella. Champagne? I'm in Sydney tomorrow. Dinner? Will pick you up at 5. Damian.

Dinner and sex, more like. No strings attached, as usual. No commitment.

Fuck off, Damian.

She blocked the number. Put him out of her head. Stood tall and smiled at Ruben who was coming over to interview her.

Chapter 34

Vegas airport was a misery, a mix of the grey-faced walking dead who'd drunk too much, gambled all night and lost, heading out, and the irrepressible optimists on the way in, who couldn't get to the machines fast enough and were sure James would get there first.

How he detested the place! The sooner he saw Will and went home, the better.

A wide woman with a wig and too much matching luggage was blocking his way, fiddling with her mobile phone.

"Excuse me, madam," he squeezed past. She was wearing sunglasses. Maybe she simply couldn't see anyone else.

A miserable looking woman trying to feed a crying child in a stroller was waiting patiently while her husband had another desperate punt at an airport poker machine. The thing was flashing gold treasure symbols and making sounds of victory, while her husband punched the side of it and put out his hand for more money from her. James wanted to tell her to go, get on a plane without him, head for the hills. Who needed a husband with a gambling problem? He hoped against hope that Will's treatment would be effective, that his mother's insistence that Will attend the clinic had come in time to stop any serious gambling habit from developing.

Outside the airport, it was flat and dry, with gambling logos flashing like fishing lures in the beige desert. It was a world away from the gentle southern hills of France, green and rolling.

His mother hadn't done so badly, he reasoned, especially now that she had another mission. He'd left Émile and Cynthia sorting through some of the ground floor furniture and making more plans for the front room. Émile promised them both the shop would open by April, in time for the Easter crowds and a busy summer.

He wasn't surprised Will wasn't there to meet him. Since when did Will think of anyone but himself? He wasn't hopeful anything could be retrieved here, but he had to give Will a chance. He was his brother after all.

The Uber driver was also hidden behind big sunglasses, with a large G on them. He was wearing a number of gold rings and didn't talk at all. The music was loud and pumping and giving James a headache.

As they swooped in past the strip, James was astonished to see not one, not two, but no less than three Elvis chapels of love. He'd forgotten Vegas was also a wedding destination. As they stopped at traffic lights, he noted up to seven shops selling wedding dresses. An idea began to form.

He hadn't known what to say to Will, beyond asking him to clean up his act. Now there might be another opportunity. Something concrete. Something Will could turn his competitive mind towards, beyond the big win.

He wanted to give him another chance, even if it was the last one. He owed him that.

They arrived at the clinic.

This place looked as fake as the rest of Vegas, with two ornate plastic hedges framing the front door. Was nothing authentic here?

There was too much marble for the place to be taken seriously, surely.

The receptionist's false eyelashes looked like insects and lips pumped up like sausages. James tried not to judge. At least she was trying.

She showed him into a large room with a fountain in the middle and french faux production furniture perfectly spaced around it. It could be a film set.

Will entered in a check shirt and jeans, flicking his bleached blond fringe out of his eyes with a toss of his head and fixing him with that impish smile of his childhood; the "hey, bro, you'll forgive me again, won't you?" smile.

James was never sure how he'd find his brother. He'd seen it all before - lies, charm, anger, defensiveness.

Today he seemed surprisingly mild. Maybe they had him on some kind of sedative. Or could this place actually be making a difference? James barely dared to hope.

"Yo, bro!"

"Bro!"

They did that awkward kind of male embrace, a handshake and a quick thump on the back.

"So? Good news? Bad news?"

"Up to you," said James.

"What's that supposed to mean?"

James had tried to work this out on the flight. How to spell it out so it was crystal clear.

"Is there a garden, Will, some place else we can go to talk?" The splashing fountain and ornate decor was just too Hollywood. He needed to get Will's full attention.

"You're in luck, bro. Getting sprung from here for my afternoon outing in about 20 minutes. I've been good. I get three hours today."

"Oh?"

"Keep away from gambling and I get to do other things."

"So what're you going to do?"

"Head for the hills."

It was the same phrase he'd used in the airport for the poor woman married to a gambler. Was this some kind of weird dream? Anything could happen in Vegas.

"You got your running gear?"

"Sure." James never travelled without it. It was the way he relaxed, but it was new for Will. Hopefully it was a good sign he's working on a better lifestyle.

"Always made fun of you with your cross country running, bro. What a 'sport'! No 'balls.' Ha! Well. Turns out you were onto something. Come on. Leave your bag in my room. Runners on. Take a jacket. Gets a bit breezy up there. Dr Bakker'll be here soon."

"Dr Bakker?"

"One of the therapists. You'll see. She's cool." If Will was enjoying holding off on divulging some secret, being the only one in the know, then James was happy to go along with it. He'd made a pledge to himself to stay three days. Make it clear to Will the gambling must stop, or he'd be cut off from Huntleys' payroll for good.

As they waited in the foyer, doing some stretches, a tall, slim woman with long blond hair in a high ponytail turned up in a kind of lab coat with a name badge. Her smile at Will was warm yet professional. She glanced from Will to James and back again, taking in their running gear.

"My brother James, Dr Bakker. The responsible one. The good one," said Will.

"Now, now. Positive self talk, please, Will. Wanna try that again?" she said quietly and calmly as she extended her hand to James. It was a cool handshake. Strong. Controlled. This woman was no fool.

"Just joking. Great to see James. Truly. All the way from Australia, via France. Been a couple of years since we've seen each other, I reckon. Jamie's a runner, too, Dr Bakker. Okay if he comes with us?"

"Sure."

Dr Bakker entered something on a tablet, got Will to swish his signature onto it with one finger and left it with the receptionist.

"Back at 7, Mindy," she said. As Mindy fluttered her heavily mascaraed eyelashes at both men, it felt a bit like the old days, but James wasn't interested. His mind was full of Stella and his haste to see her again.

They exited another door, which led through a long corridor to a parking area where Dr Bakker unlocked one of the white suburbans.

When she took off her coat to get into the driver's seat, James sucked in a breath. She was in shorts, her legs long and tanned. Surprising. Looked like Dr Bakker was an athlete. No wonder Will was showing some interest.

"How long you staying, James?" Dr Bakker asked.

"Few days. Just arrived. Where are we going?"

"Northwest. Mount Charleston. Spring Mountain Range. Toiyabe National Forest. Maybe you've heard of it? We've been across a few times, Will and I. I've got a new trail I want to show him today. You okay with a few miles? There are loops, so we can cut back, and rest stops if you want to wait us out. I promised Will this new one. We're up to 17 miles now."

"Okay with me."

"You won't mind if we have our consultation now, will you? Will has already told me he doesn't mind if you listen in. It was completely his idea you come along. Drive takes about a half hour. Some regulation questions, then we're free to enjoy ourselves."

"Fine. Fine with me. I'm jet lagged, anyway. Taking a doze."

After a long stretch of outer suburbia, the beige desert slipped by beside them as they headed for the mountain range and its dusting of snow. Dr Bakker's questions and Will's answers were muffled by the sound of the engine and the road. She was examining him about what "just joking" really meant. James was intrigued, but he couldn't really hear their exchange, and his eyelids were heavy.

James woke as the car began to climb. They were in foothills, with the green of pine trees a welcome change from the glare.

The engine came to a halt and Dr Bakker unlocked the vehicle's doors. She handed out cool water bottles and some energy bars and offered sunscreen.

"Gotta look after ourselves," she said, her eyes wise. It occurred to James this Dr Bakker might have heard of him already, and he wondered what part he might play in his brother's complex psychiatric makeup. He'd always tried to be fair, though it was easier to expect the worst of Will, especially in recent years.

While it was a pleasant surprise to find Will amenable and inclusive for once, and this unconventional doctor was the last thing he would have expected, the jury was still out on Will as far as he was concerned. None of this was going to change the message he had for him. It just might influence the way he said it, and when.

The sun was bright and still hot overhead, even for winter; the air dry and a bit hazy.

He stepped over to an information board to do his warm ups and check the map. It was a cross country runners' paradise, with trails of all lengths, and a wide variety of vistas.

After days of travelling and too much cheese and wine with his mother and Émile, James was raring to go and was pleased to see the same anticipation reflected in Dr Bakker and Will's faces.

"Right," she said. "This is not a competition. We're pacing ourselves. This is for fun. This is a kind of reward for Will for keeping away from gambling, and a great alternative. It's been how long now, Will?"

"Three weeks. Longest stretch ever."

"And how are you feeling?"

They'd started to jog, away from the parking area and along a trail, startling a bird or two, who swooped out over the distance beside them, up into higher peaks.

"Feeling great. Never felt so good. Forgot what it was like to be out in the open air like this. Sky running. I'm a sky runner, James. Not all easy, but look at this!"

The heat of the valley dropped away as they ran in easy companionship.

"You do a lot of this?" James asked Dr Bakker.

"Yeah. I've always loved it. It's becoming more and more popular."

"Unusual treatment regime."

"Oh. It's up to our clients. Will's a natural. Not everyone's so athletic in the first place, but it looks like running runs in your family, so to speak."

"Will's the star with anything sporty," James said. Will punched him on the arm, though he was clearly pleased to hear his older brother finally concede he was actually better at something. "It's true. I ran because I had to do something. Our school insisted we do some sport, and running was my choice. Will was the one who always got the ribbons and the medals. Our dad was so proud."

"We've been talking about rewards, intrinsic and extrinsic."

"Dopamine," Will explained. "Addictive. Poker machine manufacturers know that. Turns out there are better ways to get high. Literally."

From here, the view was spectacular.

They took a rest stop and enjoyed a cool drink at a clearing. Will pointed back at the cluster of towers in the flat desert.

"So tiny. Big temptation up close. Not so bad up here. Cooler air. Cooler head."

"Will's doing so well," Dr Bakker said. "He's a natural runner, but he's also been working hard."

Will basked in the praise.

James resisted the temptation to mention Will had been running from responsibility all his life. It was in everyone's interests that Will recovered and got his life on track.

"What's that?" James pointed to a body of water.

"Hah!" said Will, the local expert now. "Hoover Dam." He stared meaningfully at Dr Bakker, and smiled.

"Hoover Dam?"

"Big Depression project. Colorado River. Can't believe you never heard about the Colorado River. See that, right near it? Boulder City. That's where the project was centred. It's got a good exhibition. What do you say,

Lisa? Can I get leave to show James Boulder City? Meet you there tomorrow, maybe?"

Dr Bakker was silent, regarding the two brothers. What was going on here, James wondered. Maybe she worried James would lead Will astray.

"You could join us, Lisa," Will said. "Say. Why don't you? It's your day off, isn't it? You know the place better than I do. Let's treat James to some of those proper American pancakes. Join us? 10am?"

"Okay."

Will was thrilled, and James was happy enough. He'd envisaged days of hospital corridors, not sightseeing. He still needed to work out how to talk about the future with Will; wondered if Dr Bakker could give him a prognosis for Will or at least a bit of professional perspective.

He seized the chance to speak with her when they started up again and Will sprinted ahead, still needing to win, needing to prove himself. Some things never changed.

"My brother," James began. "I don't know how much you can tell me, but presumably this is some kind of treatment he's on with you."

"He's responding so well."

"I can see that. Seems happy. Seems stable. How long has he been at the clinic? How much longer does he have to go?"

"That's up to Will. He's been with us nearly the full three weeks. Out of trouble. No drugs, no drink, no gambling. We help, but he's the one who has to do the work, and he's doing it. He's complying. He's a mild case. It's good he's come to us so soon. Prognosis is good in cases like this."

"And this running thing. Do you do this with everyone?"

"Oh no! This is *my* hobby. Will expressed a real interest in it, so we've been able to weave it into his treatment plan. It's important to have something to replace the addictions, you understand, to find a healthy alternative. Some of our clients play music, learn to dance, take up cooking … anything that has a positive benefit, and ideally something that involves others in their lives. It's about reconnecting, how we spend our time and finding the things that reward us. Will can keep up the running after he leaves us, of course. It's a great group of people. There are comps. He'd do very well if he chose to continue. I have no doubt. And there's something about the fresh air, and the exercise. This is what human bodies are meant to do. For people with a lot of adrenalin, it brings a kind of calm."

"I discovered that in school," James said. "That's why I've kept it up. Not the same distances of course. There's never enough time. But yeah. It's kind of grounding. Literally."

"And it's so free from all the pressures and stresses. Traffic, money. Running's a great, healthy escape."

"Agreed." James's phone dinged. "Okay. Right now, I need to escape from the escape. You two are certainly fitter than I am. How about I sit out the next loop while you two keep running. I have emails to catch up on, a few calls I need to make."

"Of course." And she sprinted away from him, pony tail swinging back and forth, shining in the sun. She seemed younger without the doctors' coat. Hadn't Will called her "Lisa"? Was Will onto his next conquest? Or maybe Dr Lisa Bakker was onto hers. James was confused. Surely dating your therapist would be right on the edge of wrong. Exactly where Will liked life best. James shook his head.

Chapter 35

The real reason James was taking a breather was that he wanted to try to catch Stella by phone. He couldn't stop thinking about her. Was she thinking of him? Would she reconsider his offer of her joining the business? It felt like weeks since he'd seen her. Christmas had come and gone.

In the car on the way back from Bowral, she'd asked him to give her some space, not to crowd her. But how much space was enough? She'd accepted his Christmas gift, but given no response to his photograph from France.

Surely she must be thinking of him sometimes, however busy she was. They'd been so good together that stormy weekend. He knew it sounded like a cliche, but he was incredibly optimistic about their future together. She was perfect for his business, perfect in bed. More than that. He cared about her, cared for her in a way he'd never cared about Helene. Helene had been a habit, a conventional kind of expectation, and ultimately, a great disappointment to him - no doubt she'd felt the same way about him. But Stella? He couldn't get her out of his head. She brought out the best in him. How he wished she were there, beside him. He wanted to run his fingers through her dark hair, to curl it behind her ear, to lift her chin and seek out those lips, to hold her close and closer.

He knew then, with the winter sun weak above him and the fresh air of Arizona in his lungs, he must tell Stella. What did he have to lose from coming on too strong? He had to know if she was feeling the same way, and if she *was*...

James found a rock at the far end of the lookout, forcing himself to drink some water and admire the view again before pulling out his phone. The scenery was striking, so green and vertical, the spiky mountains dusted with snow, and in the distance, the desert was flat and brown and barren. It was a land of contrasts.

He could see why Will might enjoy living here. The landscape was surprising; presenting no end of challenges. But for James, it was far too far from the sea to ever feel like home. He missed Sydney, with its friendly bays and golden beaches, the red roofs and the fig trees, the scale of the place - just right.

He was ready again for the rhythm of his business, to sit and study the books, to make some big decisions, allocate resources to the French branch, explore some options for Will.

But most of all he missed Stella. It hit him in the heart.

A chipmunk scampered up beside him, hoping he'd share some food. He took another long swig of water just as his phone "pinged" again.

A message from Nicole and some unknown callers, maybe suppliers, a gazillion unread emails and some stuff on their Facebook page about the design competition. The competition! The comp that Stella had won!

Several more messages came in on his phone in quick succession. The awards ceremony. He peered at the pictures. There she was! Stella! His heart lurched. He must congratulate her. Surely she wouldn't mind. Or would she? She'd been adamant he didn't hassle her. What would be best would be to get this trip over and done with and go home to her. How he wished he'd been there. What time was it in Sydney? Mid morning?

Could he simply phone her? Could he risk it? *What is there to lose?* Maybe everything. Maybe he was a gambler, too, no different to Will.

He punched in her number.

"James?"

He couldn't decipher her tone of voice, and there was an annoying delay on the call, and a kind of echo. Awkward. Maybe phoning her was a bad idea. But it was his only way to reach her, and he couldn't put it off any longer. Didn't want to put it off.

"Stella? Congratulations. I saw on Facebook… The competition. Your design. You won!"

"Yes."

Why so clipped? Wasn't she happy to have won? Was it wrong to be phoning her when she'd asked him to give her space?

"Stella? Anything wrong?"

"James…"

She sounded upset, her voice tight.

"What is it, Stella? Talk to me. Please. I'm in Arizona. Is there some problem? What's going on?"

"You really don't know?"

"Stella?"

"I got notification from the council. They've closed down my stall."

"No. But. How…? Oh no."

"You told me only Huntleys could do this, and you said you wouldn't, you hadn't. And I believed you, James."

"Stella! Oh no. You think I … God, no. Stella, listen to me. It's possible that Nicole might have ... This has to be reversed. I have to talk to Nicole. Let me talk to Nicole. Let me fix this. Stella. You think I'm a liar, but Stella. I'd never do anything to hurt you. I couldn't. Stella. Please. Can you hear me? Can you hear me okay? Sit tight. I'll be there. Just a few more days, then I'm coming home. I need to see you. I'm going to reach Nicole and find out what's going on. This is terrible. This must be terrible for you. Can I ask you this? Can I ask for you to wait for me? I need you to trust me. I… I love you Stella."

"Goodbye, James."

Silence. Alone and still in the forest, at the edge of the ravine, he slowly sat, cradling his phone like something infinitely fragile, replaying the conversation word for word. He felt sick. Horrified. Angry. Sad. Maybe it was too late to salvage anything, but he was going to try. *Hell, yes.*

Chapter 36

James stood and punched in a call to Nicole.

"James! Hey. How's Will? How's it going? The design awards went brilliantly. You should stay away more often, bro."

"Cut the crap, Nicole. What's this I hear about you trying to shut down Stellar? Why would you do such a thing, particularly without discussing it with me? Apart from the fact it's morally wrong to stop someone else from making an honest living, do you have any idea how stupid this makes Huntleys look?"

"Hey slow down. It's fine. It's all fine. Stella was there. She might have been a bit tight-lipped, but she accepted the award alright. Ruben gave us great coverage..."

"Stella is not alright. I just spoke with her. How would *you* feel? Nicole, I can't believe we're having this conversation. What got into you?"

"Hang on. I did it ages ago. The day she turned up and ruined our Antoinette event. She stole our limelight big time. I was furious. I marched right into the council and did it straight away. And then I forgot about it, alright? Council took months to act on it, and we've had all those other things to deal with, the flooding in the south corner, and then all the new initiatives, the website, Christmas, the comp. It's been bloody busy, and that's a good thing, thank you very much. Have you got a thing for this Stella?"

"Nicole. Listen to me. That order is a big mistake, and you need to fix it. Fast. Now. Go to the council and revoke it. Immediately. Is council even open again after the break? I'll submit a letter explaining you didn't have the authority to make that request in the first place. And as for my relationship with Stella, or lack of one, it's none of your business. The sooner we solve this the better, for all of us. We're just lucky Ruben hasn't got wind of it. Can you see how stupid this makes Huntleys look? How small minded?"

"Alright, alright. I've got the message. I'm onto it, alright?"

James wanted to get on the next plane home, but he had to focus on Will, see this thing out, do his best to help settle Will while he was here, achieve what he'd set out to do. He emailed a letter to the council's general manager himself before heading out for his breakfast, copying Stella. He'd done all he could do for now. He'd make these few hours with Will count before he boarded the plane for Sydney again.

Will and James had just ordered coffee when Lisa walked in, wearing jeans and a casual top, her shiny blond hair up in a ponytail.

For the second time, James was suspicious. Was there something going on between Will and Lisa beyond their professional relationship? Will sprang up and pulled out her chair.

It was a showy gesture. Will always had a presence. But there was more to it, a studied concentration, a genuine level of care for another human he'd never seen in his younger brother. Not for the first time, he wondered if Will could be becoming addicted to his therapist. *Complicated.*

"Lisa, how are you?" Will was asking.

"Calf muscles a bit sore today, actually. And ready for pancakes!"

Will was radiating happiness, studying Lisa as if she was the real menu. Maybe she was. Surely not. Surely they both knew that any real kind of relationship would be unethical.

James noted Lisa's ring finger. Nothing. Unusual. Maybe a trace of where a ring might once have been.

"Nice little town, Boulder City," James ventured.

"Isn't it? I love it here. It's the kind of place you can keep your feet on the ground," Lisa said, looking at Will as she said the last words. Will was smiling like he knew something. Yep. James could be right. Their bodies were turned to each other under the table. There was barely a pancake's width between them, with static flying back and forth to span the distance. There was definitely something going on between them.

"And the best breakfast in America," said Lisa. "Have you two ordered yet?"

"What would you recommend?"

"Can't go wrong."

It was a hearty breakfast, and they all ate their fill, talking about how they'd spend the day.

"Coming with us to the dam, Lisa?" Will asked.

"Might sit that one out. Leave you two brothers with some time alone. Besides, I need to do my laundry and shopping for the week."

James paid the bill and they parted outside on the pavement.

James shook hands with Lisa and she, too, was instantly more formal.

"You're doing a great job with Will, Dr Bakker. I need to thank you for your care."

Her smile was warm and genuine.

"He's a good man, your brother," she nodded. "We all need to find our feet sometime."

...

The dam was magnificent. Acres of pale concrete. The brothers soaked up the history, learning of the wild Colorado river's flood-prone nature before the dam was built in the 1930s, the optimism the federal project sparked during the great depression, the vice-free planning for Boulder City, the city of workers.

"They still don't allow gambling here."

"No way? No gambling?"

"Nup. Only one other town in the whole of the US is gambling-free," Will said.

"Close enough to Vegas if you want to be tempted, I guess."

"Yeah. And far enough away if you don't."

"Nice little town, Boulder City."

"Sure is. So many other places I could show you from here. You can go in almost any direction and find nature reserves. Backpackers, skiers, rock climbers. There's this whole world of adventure. Sky running's just the tip of the iceberg. Lisa's shown me just a few of the runs, but I'm betting there's a lifetime's worth of exploring to do just from this one place."

"Yeah? I can see that. And Lisa."

"Yeah. Lisa." Will turned and gave James the full smile, the kind he remembered from one Christmas before their father became ill, when his younger brother received a shiny new bike, a pure kind of joy without artifice.

"So what's the plan, Will? You coming back to Sydney?"

"Nah. Staying here, I reckon. Get out of therapy. Next week. Set up here. Boulder City. I'm taking the training seriously. Lisa thinks I've got potential. Maybe I can get a sponsor. If I can keep clean..."

"Sounds good. Lisa's seriously cool, Will. Now we have to talk. This is serious stuff. This is why I've come to see you. You have to know that the business is in trouble. So I've got to ask. How are you planning to support yourself?"

"What do you mean, 'support myself'?"

Not for the first time, James wondered about the wisdom of raising this with Will, when he was clearly vulnerable in some way, still receiving therapy. It was a cold, hard reality though. It couldn't be sugar coated. There simply wasn't another choice.

"Let me spell this out. Gravy train's gotta stop, Will. Huntleys can't afford it anymore. No more expenses. No more allowances. Mother's given up two thirds of hers, for the sake of the business. And you need to do the same. Otherwise there's simply no more money. At all. We're nearly bankrupt as it is. We go over that edge and there'll be no support. At all. Not for you, not for me, not for Jim or Nicole or mother. So. I need to ask you. You need to ask yourself. What are you going to do to support yourself?"

Will stopped. Stared at the ground. Of course it would come as a shock to him and for a moment, James regretted his words. Would this harsh reality set Will back in his recovery, send him off the rails again and back into the gambling parlours? James was worried. Maybe he should have consulted Lisa about this, about the best way to raise the subject. Too late now.

At times like this, James missed his father, felt the loss of him again, that great gaping hole in their family he'd done his best to fill. He knew he hadn't always been up to the task. He pushed away the thought and squared his shoulders. Self pity never solved a thing. Nor did hiding from the truth. He couldn't shelter Will from reality any more. They'd all grown up now. Will must take responsibility for his own future.

Will ought to know the value of money by now. Living on the streets wouldn't have been much fun. Still, he was taking this more calmly than James had expected. No fireworks. No tantrums. Amazing. Maybe he was finally growing up.

"Win some prizes? Get some sponsorship? That's short term. I know this might surprise you, but I've been talking about this stuff with Lisa. Longer term, I'm betting there's a retail opportunity right here in Boulder. Combination adventure and camping gear. Maybe a little bit of jewelry."

"Seriously?"

"Seriously. I couldn't see it till I saw the other side of Vegas. There are plenty of hipsters get to Vegas and get turned off by all the hype. Lots of 'em end up doing day trips out here looking for something more familiar, something more wholesome."

They walked past a vegan restaurant. It was doing well.

"Boulder is hipster, and it's so close to California, loads of 'em have money. Techies. Could be just the place for some of Jim's rings. Could be needing one myself..."

"Ha! Good luck to you, Will! So! No more playboy?"

"That was always a beat up, James. My big mistake was to date that *Tele* journalist and then drop her. She's never let me forget it. Went to the gossip columnists every time I went near anyone with any kind of social media following. Lisa's helped me understand that's not normal. It was the journalist's problem, not mine. Well, maybe I could have dumped her more kindly. We were just kids. How was I supposed to know she'd get all hurt and bitter? Well, she's more than got even with all that playboy publicity. But I can make it work in my favour now. Take it carefully, like you plan a run. I've got some serious planning to do. Never planned a thing in my life before I met Lisa. She's helped me grow up, James. I'm getting my act together."

James was amazed. Maybe that was just it. Will had been slow to mature. Well. Even James had had some growing up to do, beyond stepping up to take on Huntleys. To decide to actually "own" Huntleys. Not just pay tribute to the past, and carry on things the way they'd always been done, but to "own it," as Stella inspired him to do, and as Jim invited him to do.

"Makes a lot of sense. I've been having to do my own planning."

"What? I thought big brother always knew best. Born knowing everything, bloody James Huntley the Third."

They punched each other on the arm, laughing.

"Look. You come up with a plan, Will, a proper business plan, and we'll see what we can do. I told you mother's opening a Huntleys in the south of France? You open a branch here, and we could be truly global. Wouldn't have to be huge. Start small. But you'd need to make it work. We couldn't afford to prop you up. Set it all out properly on some spreadsheets. Do some predictions. Set some goals. You'll need to convince Jim as well, and Nicole, and Scottie. And then you'll have to stick with it, to really make it work. I won't be bailing you out. All that's stopping now, you understand? But it looks like you're chasing something worthwhile here, Will. Make your own luck. Stick with it, Will. Make that shop of yours a winner."

James was no fool. Will had made promising noises before, then gone back to his old wasteful ways. He'd need to see real plans and real progress before he'd part with any serious money, and he told Will exactly that. But he'd never been more hopeful.

The brothers clapped each other on the shoulders then shook hands.

James frowned. Should he mention Lisa, and probe Will on his intentions? Surely Will would already know that relationships with health professionals were unethical and illegal in the US, just as they were in Australia.

Will was beaming, and James bit his tongue. Why suggest something that might be just in his own imagination?

James's mind was now on going home. Home to Stella.

Chapter 37

On the return flight, James peered out at the thin layer of clouds. Through the occasional hole in them, the sea shone like aged pewter. James considered Will's plans. It made sense, Will staying in the US, if he could get a visa. Will needed somewhere big enough to challenge him. Somewhere he could build his own life of adventure, pace himself, taking it one step at a time.

The big question was the same as always - whether he could be trusted. The evidence said no. But maybe with the help of someone sensible like Lisa, Will could keep one foot on the ground, and run his own race.

James couldn't wait to tell Stella. The plane couldn't fly quickly enough. He urged it forwards as it droned on over the grey ocean, spanning the continents, hour after hour after hour. Stella. Just imagining her had him smiling, at 37,000 feet, but he couldn't return to her fast enough, to apologize in person for Nicole's mistake. He hoped she could forgive them.

Sydney. Humid. Even at this early hour, when the city was just waking up. Stifling after the cool and dry Nevada desert. It hit James the minute he exited the airport.

He could head for Bondi Beach. As soon as possible. Maybe even take Stella with him.

He took an Uber home, showered, dressed for the beach, grabbed his towel and headed out the door, jogging to the mall, past the fragrant frangipani and box hedges with their tiny white flowers, smiling at the thought of surprising Stella.

But when he reached the mall, he couldn't believe his eyes.

Stella's stall was missing. Gone.

He panicked. Maybe all he and Nicole had done to reverse the council's order hadn't been enough.

Fritz's stall was there, and the others, but it was as if Stellar never existed.

He pulled out his phone and called her.

It went to voicemail.

"You've reached Stella Rhys, Stellar. Please leave a message."

"Stella! James here. James Huntley. I'm back. Back in Sydney. Where are you?"

The moment he left the message he doubted himself. Who was James Huntley to keep tabs on Stella Rhys? He sounded like some kind of jealous stalker. She didn't have to answer to him. It wasn't like she owed him anything. But why hadn't she told him she was leaving? It was only a few days since they'd spoken. This complete absence made no sense.

On top of the long flight, he was crushingly disappointed. He'd been counting on Stella to be here, as she'd been for so many days and weeks and months before he'd left for France. He'd looked forward to their reunion. Could barely wait.

And now? Nothing.

He felt emptier than the mall at this quiet hour. Slapped. Shocked. Betrayed. It reminded him of the feeling when his father died, but at least there'd been some warning back then. The lingering illness had helped to prepare them all.

He checked his phone again. It was still too early to phone Nicole or Jeannie. Fritz wasn't even there yet, nor Donna or Clint.

James turned and ran full pelt for the beach, flung his towel on the sand and swam out, out, out, beyond the breakers, till his shoulders ached and all he could do was float on his back and stare at the blue, blue sky, catching his breath in great heaving gulps.

Gradually his heart and lungs settled. "All right," he told himself. "It'll be alright."

He became aware again of his body, floating in the cool, salty blue between the headlands, the sun climbing, hotter and brighter above. He studied the sets and selected a wave, catching it back to shore.

It wasn't as if there was nothing else to think about. There were plenty of preparations to be made for the French branch, and he'd need to stay in touch with Will, closely. Check he was still heading in the right direction. Maybe even plan a return visit before too much time was up.

And he'd been away from Huntleys for more than a week. He must take stock of all the changes Nicole might have made; check Jim was still happy with the pace of change and all the podcasts he'd been recording.

He returned to the apartment. Dressed for business. Made an appointment with Scottie. He had to get his head around the latest numbers. See if Christmas had made a difference. But first he had to phone Nicole.

He barely gave her time to answer.

"What happened with the council, Nic?"

"Well hello to you, too, James. Welcome back and all that. Settle, petal. I went and saw them. They only reopened yesterday. They've lifted her closure. It was a bit of a hassle. They're on skeleton staff; didn't want to deal with it, but I stayed there and asked for the manager till they did something and it's all okay now."

"Then why isn't Stella there today?"

"I don't know, alright?"

"Did you apologize?"

"You're the one who seems to know her best, James."

"You've got her details, Nicole. She's our inaugural competition winner, for God's sake!"

"No answer. But I left her a message. And I emailed her."

"You can't do this again, Nicole, acting on the business's behalf without consulting me."

"Calm down. I rarely consult you, James. I have to make marketing decisions on my own all the time to do my job. It's called 'professional trust.'"

"Yeah. Well you blew it this time."

"I did. And I've admitted it. And I've fixed it. My bad. Can we leave it, please? How's mother? How's Will? What's this about opening a French branch? Crazy idea. I love it."

"Yeah. Well, there's plenty of work to do to make it a successful one. I'll tell you and Jim more when I've seen Scottie."

"Say hi from me."

"You two an item now?"

"Ask him." She sounded happy. He could practically see her smiling. He was the one who sounded grumpy for once. As he hung up, he knew why. He tried again.

You've reached Stella Rhys. Stellar. Leave a message.

"Stella. It's James. I have something to tell you. I have lots of things to tell you, starting with an official apology from Huntleys for lodging that application. I understand that's now been reversed, and that Nicole has apologized. But how can we make that up to you? Could you ring me back, please?" Official. Had he sounded too official? It was an official matter, but his relationship with Stella was personal, too. At least he hoped it still was.

"James!"

"Scottie!"

If James had shadows under his eyes, Scottie had never looked better. There was a fresh photo on the desk, of Scottie in a tux with a purple bow tie and Nic looking radiant in purple. James seized it and raised his eyes at his friend.

"Yeah, mate. Dream come true for me. She's a stunner, your sister. Absolute stunner. That's at the awards ceremony. Did she tell you about it?"

"A bit. Great move to make that donation. I assume we could afford it?"

"Yeah. All good. Just. Here, I've got the balance sheet. Take a look at this."

They studied the numbers, and then some of Scottie's graphs.

Visitor numbers were definitely up on the same time last year, and return web visits were through the roof. Turnover was stronger than ever, though that was always the hope around Christmas time. For the first time in years, Huntley's wasn't just level pegging. The graphs were turning.

"Should go away more often, mate."

"Evidently. Nic said the same thing."

"Nah. But Nic's brought in lots of those changes you wanted. And Christmas is always a good season for you. But yeah. Better than ever this last quarter, and with Valentine's Day around the corner, things are definitely trending up. Nic's been working like crazy on the website. Don't know if you've seen it but there are lots of followers for Jim's blog. Been in the shop yet?"

"No, mate. Just flew in a few hours ago. Wanted to get the lowdown first." He went silent, remembering the dullness of the mall without Stella's stall. How flat it made him feel.

"So, how'd you go?" Scottie filled the silence.

"What? Oh. The trip. Yeah. Good. Nic tell you? Big news, actually. What do you think of us opening a French branch? Hear me out. Half the work's already done. Mother's found the perfect place. We'll have to take a closer look at the numbers of course."

"Sounds pretty interesting," Scottie frowned. "And Will?"

"A bit early to say yet, but I'm hopeful. He's at a clinic. Seems like he might be okay."

Scottie raised his eyebrows and frowned again. He'd grown up watching Will's antics.

"Well, whatever works, I guess."

"Yeah. You bet."

"Is that the right word?"

"Bad joke."

Scottie's eyes snapped to his own.

"You feeling okay, James?"

James shrugged. Maybe he'd picked up some kind of bug on the flight.

"Take it easy."

"Yeah. Thanks. You too, mate."

"Mate."

Chapter 38

There was a new vibe in Huntleys. James felt it the moment he entered. There were more customers, and the staff were busy helping them, happier, heads up. Alive. Lorna noticed him and gave a huge smile of welcome.

So why wasn't he happy? Wasn't this what he'd been working for, ever since Jim asked him about his feelings for the business? Sure, he'd tried to step into his father's shoes when he'd inherited it, but it wasn't until these last few weeks, fired up by Stella's ideas, that he'd been truly excited by its potential, determined to improve it, make it better than ever, in new ways.

He'd discovered Jim was glad to modernize and share his skills and knowledge. After sharing Stella's ideas with Nicole, he'd given her the freedom to adopt them, and had actively supported her online efforts to grow brand awareness and value, empowering her to run the Valentine's Day awards in his absence.

But for what, damn it?

When he found himself glancing down at the mall for the sixth time that morning to where Stella's stall used to be, he pulled out his phone. He wanted her back there. Or right beside him in the business. Hell. He wanted her right beside him in his life. He wanted to marry her. It had become a certainty, an incontrovertible truth. He must tell her. He must find her.

It went to voicemail again. "You've reached Stella Rhys of Stellar…"

"No I haven't," he told the spreadsheet in front of him, wishing he could see instead her wavy hair and special smile, and those bright eyes.

"Leave a message."

...

At 11 o'clock, the quietest time of day, Stella entered the mall. She wore a cream suit with pale blue piping, and matching shoes, her hair twisted into a chic bun pinned with a mother of pearl comb. She clutched a slim, cream laptop bag.

She walked carefully in her high heels. She'd had to get used to them again.

A few older men were chatting at a coffee shop, some office workers smoking outside their building, and nothing much else except a few pigeons pecking at the paving and strutting about for each other.

She went up to Fritz's stall and smiled at him.

It took a minute for him to recognise her all dressed up, and when he did, his smile was wide. He raised his eyebrows at her appearance.

"Jetsetter. She returns!"

"Fritz! Did you miss me?

"Of course."

Stella extracted a small gift from her handbag.

"What's this? Tiger Balm?"

"For those long days, Fritz. Works a dream on tired backs, so I'm told."

"You young one. Thank you!"

Donna waved, and Stella rushed across to give her a hug, thrusting a small silk purse into her hand.

"I owe you these, Donna. Thanks for everything."

"Darling! Not real ones? Gorgeous! I'll never take them off." Donna dropped her coathangers and put on the pearl earrings, admiring herself in one of her mirrors. "Thank you. Can't offer you an outfit today, obviously. Where'd you find that suit? Shmick! By the way, congratulations! I heard you won that Huntley's competition!"

The mall felt like home, and the stallholders, like friends.

It was wonderful to be back, this perfect day.

When she stepped into the foyer of Huntleys and smelled again the faint whiff of furniture polish, she was enchanted.

Things were different. There were more customers for a start, and the foyer lighting was better, showcasing enticing displays of jewels from different eras. There was a definite buzz.

She scanned the ground floor. There were several men, but not the one she was looking for. She was surprisingly disappointed. In her mind's eye, he would have been there to greet her. Maybe she should have phoned in advance.

The whole floor had been rearranged, with the distinctive older cases set back towards the walls, and several complementary new ones in the centre. Had James engaged a consultant? She panicked for a moment, imagining him with a smart young advisor. Maybe she should have kept in touch better. But she'd been so busy, flat out negotiating with a myriad of company representatives, maximizing the amount she could get for her designs, signing contracts. This was the earliest she could have returned in the way she wished, in a position of strength. Confident. Ready.

She jumped when she heard his voice.

"Stella?" Smooth. Her stomach jolted. She turned, slowly.

There he was, extending his hand, charming as always, his eyes taking in her new sophistication, telling her he liked what he saw. She could tell by the way he caught his breath.

She couldn't help but admire how perfectly his suit fitted him. It was the pale grey one, the one she'd first seen him in. She reached for him. The jolt of electricity was visceral. Yes. It was still there. James could never be just a business associate. Everything she remembered about his effect on her was real. Time was stopping, excitement bubbling inside her. She shivered with anticipation.

"Welcome. Can I help you?" he asked, as if she were any other customer, though his eyes betrayed his deeper interest, his thirst for her. Good. He felt it too.

As his eyes drifted to her face, her lips, her throat, she could feel herself blushing.

"I'm looking for several things," she said.

"Oh? I hope we can help you."

"There's something serious I'd like to discuss."

"Let's go upstairs."

He summoned the elevator.

When the doors closed on just the two of them, he reached out to gently hold the tops of her arms, to caress her shoulder blades with his thumbs, then run his hands to her elbows, and to her waist, and pull her close. She shivered. *Delicious.*

"You got my messages," he said into the top of her hair. "I've missed you." It was glorious, the buzz of his voice, the warmth of his embrace. "Do you want to tell me? Tell me everything. Where were you? I'm so glad you're here. I have something to tell you."

Slowly, as the elevator rose, he moved one forefinger under her chin, tipped her face to his and brought his lips to hers, gently, softly, as she leaned into him. It was like coming home, the wonder of it stirring inside and rushing to every part of her.

This man. This one.

She was glad they hadn't yet replaced the elevator with something more rapid. There was time to pull away and stare deeply into his eyes, to see her own desire for him reflected, liquid. Delicious.

He led her to his office and closed the door, reaching for her again, for a deeper kiss, but she pulled away.

"This is important, James."

"I agree. Nothing's more important."

"No. Seriously. Wait. I want ..."

"What? Anything."

"No. We need to do this right."

"We are. Tell me this isn't right."

"Please."

James let her go. Moved around to the other side of his desk. Sat down. Gave her his full attention.

"Tell me. Tell me, Stella."

"I want to join Huntleys."

He narrowed his eyes.

"Tell me again."

"I've come straight from Singapore. I've sold several suites of designs. And I've come to collect my prize, to take that free workshop with Jim."

"Yes. Good." He swallowed. Leaned forward. Reached for her hands across the desk. That buzz again. "I have another offer I'd like you to consider, Stella."

"What's that?"

"Will you marry me?" He looked into her eyes as he held her hands tight. "It came to me while I was away. I've wanted to marry you since you first stood your ground out there in the mall. You're magnificent. So talented, so beautiful, so brilliant. You're the only jewel I've ever wanted, Stella Rhys, and I love you. I want to be with you day and night. Marry me."

"You're making this up. You're just saying it. If you're trying to tell me you had this planned, then where's the ring, James?"

"Actually. The ring is the least of our problems," he laughed. "Come on. Let's go see. Right now. You can have your pick, Stella Rhys. Or talk to Jim. Design your own. Make your own. Come with me. We'll look at every one of them. You can't say 'no' to me, Stella."

He put his arm around her waist and led her out the door and into the store. There was another new cabinet. She drew a breath. Time stopped. She stared at the cabinet. Walked around it as if in a trance.

The engagement rings were exquisite, each unique, but there was only one that called out to her.

She was in a dream. "That one," she said.

He pulled out a key from his breast pocket.

"Allow me," he said, unlocking the cabinet. From beneath it, he pulled out another swathe of black velvet, lying it gently on the counter top as he'd done countless times before.

Gently, he lifted out the dancing blue piece and placed it on the velvet in front of her, as if all the world revolved around it. It did. Her world.

He waited, his hands behind his back as she stared at it there between them, mesmerized.

"This is very beautiful," she said, picking it up and twisting it backwards and forwards in the light, watching it shoot sharp sparks from every facet.

"This one," he smiled. "I hoped you'd choose this one. I made it with Jim, just after you'd come to Bowral with me, and shared all those ideas. This is a special ring; my favourite. It marks the change in our fortunes; the moment I committed to the future of Huntleys as brilliant as you imagined it could be, the moment I committed to you."

"But it's you who's made those ideas come true, James. So many of them. You've brought them to life. It's amazing what you've achieved in such a short time."

"I had some incentive. I wanted something vibrant to offer you; not just an inheritance, withering away, but something brilliant. And we have more plans now. I have so much to share with you. We're going global."

The ring sat, glinting, on the velvet between them.

Stella picked it up.

"This is exquisite, James."

"Let me slip it on? See if it fits?"

So many memories ran through her mind. All the men in her mother's life who'd let her down; her years of disappointment with Damian.

Building Stellar had been about so much more than just building a business, more than making her dreams real, more than making a living from what she loved. It had been about learning to trust again. And that trust had been tested.

And now. Could she really allow herself to be loved? To trust James Huntley the Third?

Yes.

As James slipped the ring on her finger, heavy and warm, she didn't want him to take away his hand. She placed hers across his and they interlaced their fingers, eyes catching.

"James, I have to tell you this. For me, it was never about Huntleys and Stellar. It was only ever about you and me. And now I know. I know I can live without you. Most importantly, though, I know I don't *want* to live without you."

The ring fit.

James went down on one knee again, this time in the middle of the shop, in full view of colleagues and customers. Jim watched from the back of the floor, his visor pulled up, blue eyes ablaze.

"Will you marry me, Stella Rhys?"

"I will, James Huntley."

As James leaped to his feet, he crushed Stella to his ribs, lifted her off her feet and spun her around, the lit cabinets blurring into a smudge of light and color as they laughed.

As he set her down, Stella grabbed both his hands and held them, palm to palm, lacing her fingers into his again and holding on tight. The ring was warm and solid between them, flashing its own fire, a tiny reflection of the light in his eyes, that blue, joyous now, proud and glad, hungry for her, poised for their future.

"Let's go to the beach, James."

And they dashed down the stairs, and out into the bright mall, out into the future.

If you liked *House of Diamonds* you might enjoy

House of Hearts

House of Hearts is Volume 2 in the *House of Jewels* series.

What does it take to be lucky in love? Opposites attract in *House of Hearts*, set on the edge of Las Vegas.

Gambling addiction therapist Dr Lisa Bakker never breaks rules, but her bad boy client Will Huntley, good-looking youngest heir to an Australian jewelry business, breaks them all.

The one rule neither can ignore is the two-year dating ban between clients and therapists. Will calls Lisa his "Queen of Hearts" but her hard-won career hangs in the balance. *What will it take to win her hand?*

House of Spades

***House of Spades* is Volume 3 in the *House of Jewels* series.**

Can love call again later in life? He calls her a trespasser. She calls him a hermit and thief.

Free spirit and serial single Flame Rhys has sworn off love, but try convincing her reclusive neighbor Ross Archer.

Fiery redhead Flame accidentally rekindles the widower's passion for life, for his land and a wife.

But is there more to Flame than meets the eye, as Ross's daughters suspect?

House of Clubs

House of Spades is Volume 4 in the _House of Jewels_ series.

Who holds the key to her heart? When stylish Australian widow Cynthia Huntley moves to France and begins to renovate a centuries-old property, she and handsome handyman Émile tussle over a "perfect" chandelier.

Cynthia lets the mysterious yet gallant Émile into her house, but will she let him into her heart?

What is Émile fleeing? And what is worth seeking in life?

As winter closes in, will Cynthia abandon her French adventure? Or can she and Émile claim love again later in life—together?

Full House

House of Spades is Volume 5 in the *House of Jewels* series.

What can you do when you've friend-zoned the one you love? Nicole Huntley froze out family friend Scottie back when they were teenagers.

Now she's the Huntleys' jewelry retail marketing manager, and he's their financial advisor.

Just as they seize a fresh chance for happiness together, "conflict of interest" threatens to shatter her family, destroy their retail empire — and to break her heart.

Get ready for the showdown in *Full House*, Amber Jakeman's latest international heartwarmer in the Huntley *House of Jewels* saga.

About the Author

Partial to sunsets, picnics and poetry, feel-good fiction writer Amber Jakeman was a journalist, ghost writer and editor before succumbing to her addiction to uplifting endings.

With readers in more than fifty countries, Amber writes from her tiny apartment on the edge of Sydney Harbour, creating historical and contemporary fiction with an international flavor, including romance, on the sweeter side.

When not writing, Amber enjoys time with family and friends, sailing with her husband, travel, walking and savoring other writers' creations.

Amber Jakeman acknowledges Australia's first storytellers, our First Nations People, and offers respect to their descendants.

Visit www.amberjakeman.com to find out how to order other novels by Amber Jakeman, and sign up for occasional email updates.

Amber's contemporary love tales — on the sweeter side — may be read in any order.

Amber Jakeman's *House of Jewels* series features the romantic fortunes of the extended Huntley family.
The books may be read in any order.
House of Diamonds
House of Hearts
House of Clubs
House of Spades
Full House

Don't miss out!

Visit www.amberjakeman.com to find out how to order other novels by Amber Jakeman. Sign up to receive occasional email updates.

About the Publisher

Lorikeet Press publishes feel-good fiction for readers of all ages. If you enjoy books with uplifting endings, you're in the right place.

Visit www.lorikeetpress.com for more information.

www.ingramcontent.com/pod-product-compliance
Lightning Source LLC
Chambersburg PA
CBHW020336120726
47904CB00002B/425